EYE *of* FIRE

N. M. CHAMBERS

KINGS MOUNTAIN PRESS

California U.S.A.

Cover Design by Rose Daniels Design

FIRST EDITION

ISBN: 978-1-7341238-1-4

For my father
R. E. M.
who gave me everything

Do not be afraid; our fate
Cannot be taken from us; it is a gift.

Dante Alighieri, *Inferno*

Prologue

"It's time, my brother. We must flee this place."

His comrade walked over to the steep rock wall and started the climb up to the secret entrance. Mid-way he paused, and looked back with worry in his eyes.

"You have it?" his aide asked anxiously, even though he was sure of the answer.

"Yes, in my satchel."

"Then let's leave and let her be damned. They were wrong. It's only a woman, and she is of little consequence."

"Yes, I know," he replied, but he could not stop staring at the heap on the floor. "Get the horses ready. I will meet you and the others outside in a moment."

His aide pulled himself into the small hole that was barely big enough for him to slide through. "Hurry, my brother," he said before disappearing into the darkness.

Left alone, he wiped his blade off on his pants. It had already dried—he could not get the metal completely clean. He walked closer. Next to the pile of silk clothing was a mass of hair flowing from the back of her head. Wavy dark-brown, beautiful and blood-soaked.

He wedged one foot under the shoulder and flipped her over with one push of his boot. Her arms spread across the ground like angel's wings. Her bodice was ripped open from the battle, revealing breasts so perfect it seemed almost a waste that his knife had torn the spirit from her body. As he stared down at his victim's lifeless form he realized, with pride, that she was perhaps the most beautiful kill he had ever slain. Even with her eyes closed and the breath snuffed out of her, she was radiant with ferocity.

He pushed away any inkling of sympathy by letting out a sharp, triumphant laugh. He crouched down to get a better look at his mark. *You thought you were so clever. But not this time. Luck always runs out.*

Her eyelashes, still wet, stirred with a fraction of movement. He leaned in closer. *Impossible.*

Her eyelids parted with a jolt. Not wide, but she stared straight into his eyes as if magnetized to them. Her irises glowed in a fiery, pulsating orange. He wanted to look away, but his eyes were frozen open, locked with hers. He fell backward onto the ground in an effort to get away from her. But he could not close his eyes or look away however much he struggled to regain control. The blood orange light from her eyes blasted through his mind. He screamed, unable to push back against the agonizing heat piercing through his head.

He fell onto his back, his eyes suddenly freed from the penetrating grip. He rubbed his eyes, still seeing flashes of orange. When he sat up, her eyes were closed, her face and body just as lifeless as before.

He quickly got up to his feet and felt around his satchel to confirm it still held his prize. Whatever he had just imagined, two things remained. It was still his. And she was still dead. He kicked a pile of dirt into her face before turning around never to return.

Chapter 1

"Aaaa-uu-eeemm."

"Aaaa-uu-eeemm."

Serena, sitting in full-lotus pose, tried to savor her last few moments of calm and inner peace before the yoga class ended. She drew in another deep breath and joined in with the other students for one final refrain of the sacred Hindu chant.

"Aaaa-uu-eeemmmm."

One eye popped open to peek up at the clock on the wall. She couldn't help it. 4:15 p.m. *Damn it.* The class was running late. Inner peace started to give way to anxiety. She was going to be late picking up Drew.

The teacher, a fresh-faced redhead in her mid-twenties who went by the name of Moon Blossom, sat calmly on a meditation cushion in front of the class. "Please bring both your hands together at your heart," she said warmly. Serena opened her eyes and brought her hands together, anticipating that class would be ending at any moment.

"And so let us end our class today by extending ourselves out to the world with our closing intention," Moon Blossom said before she began to recite, "May all beings everywhere be happy and free, and may the thoughts, words, and actions of my own life contribute in some way to that happiness and freedom for all." She closed her prayer and bowed with a soulful "Namaste."

Serena felt a strange twinge of guilt and inadequacy. She knew she was supposed to be feeling selfless and inspired about life, but even after a full hour of class, all she could think about was the fact that she turned another year older today. She looked up at the clock again. 4:17 p.m. *Shit.* All around her, the men and women in the class bowed along with Moon Blossom, but Serena slowly edged herself off her mat and began rolling it up.

When people began coming out of their forward folds, Serena hopped up and quickly finished her rolling. She would have to hustle if she was going to make it to Drew's school by four-thirty and then pick up Asher from Intro to Guitar by five. She hurriedly grabbed her two bags from the back cubbies, trying to balance the unwieldy load as she also fished for her car keys in her handbag. Waving a quick thank you to the teacher, Serena scooted out the back door, losing a little peace and serenity with every step.

Pressing hard on the "unlock" button of her

remote, she hurried toward her mini-SUV, which was parked on the street in front of one of her favorite clothing boutiques. As she started the ignition, she looked longingly at the cute, hippy-chic items displayed for maximum impact in the shop windows. Last week she went in "just to browse" and found a pair of perfect jeans—for the unaffordable price of $220. She laughed inwardly at the memory of the Guess jeans she was so proud of back in high school—they cost 70 bucks. Serena shook her head, yanking her mind back to the task at hand. She put the car in drive and pulled out into rush-hour traffic.

As she made her way across the town of Redwood Hills toward Drew's elementary school, she heard her phone vibrating from somewhere deep within her purse, which lay half-open on the passenger seat. She leaned over and rooted around blindly for it, finally feeling the tell-tale hard plastic and metal block on the fourth ring. She looked down at the Caller I.D.—it was Mallory. She pushed the button for speakerphone.

"Haaappy Birthday!!!!" Mallory crooned.

Serena backed the phone away from her face—even with the buffer of speakerphone, Mallory's voice came blasting through at about a thousand decibels.

"So you say," Serena grumbled. She lifted her head to view herself in the rearview mirror. She scrunched up her face and assessed the skin around her eyes. She could definitely spot the beginning of crow's feet.

"Oh, I'm sorry, do I have the wrong day? Is it the Day of the Dead instead? No, that's not right...now I remember! It's Incredibly-Sexy-Super-Mom-With-My-Whole-Life-Ahead-Of-Me-But-I'm-Too-Stupid-To-Realize-It-Because-I'm-Still-Wallowing-In-Self-Pity Day. How on earth I could I forget?"

"Thanks," Serena conceded. "You're right, Mal."

"Didn't you *just* get out of yoga?"

"Yes..."

"And aren't you the one who's always telling me about how yoga and meditation have taught you all about living in the present and letting go of the past and all that 'power-of-now' crap?"

"Point taken, Mal. It *is* all about living in the present and letting go of the past. And in the present, there are crow's feet emerging on my face and cellulite growing on my ass. On top of which, I'm going to be late picking up Drew."

"I'll let you go. But please be aware that tonight I'm bringing a chocolate cake that's about ten thousand calories per slice."

"Sounds perfect. The boys will be thrilled. See you around seven."

"'Kay, ciao, birthday girl."

Serena checked the clock as she turned into the driveway of Drew's school. 4:29 pm. She'd made it with a minute to spare, which meant that she could take a moment to freshen up bit.

She pulled down the visor, opened the mirror, and made a more global assessment of her appearance. She pulled the elastic from her ponytail and ran her fingers through her long, brown hair. She grabbed a lip gloss from the cup holder and applied a fresh coat. As she noticed the crow's feet again, she remembered what Drew had asked that morning. "Mommy, are you turning *twenty* today?" She knew that from his seven-year-old perspective, twenty was ancient, but still, the memory made her smile.

SERENA WALKED briskly down the open-air hallways of Redwood Hills Elementary School. At this late afternoon hour, the school was peaceful, especially when compared to the pandemonium that had ensued in this exact space just two hours earlier when school let out. She could recollect— just barely—what it was like to be her son's age, weighed down only by the burdens of homework and clarinet practice. Her reverie was interrupted when two little girls came around the corner, so engrossed in their whispered, giggly conversation that they almost ran into Serena. She remembered that aspect of childhood, too. Serena hid an amused smile as she passed the girls, reminded of how important it was to fit in and not feel alone.

She heard Salli Yakamoto's voice before she

reached the Art Room. The after-school class wasn't quite finished then. Serena slowed her steps and tried to walk quietly. Keeping the rest of her body hidden from view, she leaned her head into the doorway to spy on her little artist.

The Art Room was a sunny oasis of creativity and imagination, filled from floor to ceiling with vibrant paintings, photographs, zany sculptures, and other projects spanning every type of media imaginable. Colors, textures, and shapes seemed to spring to life from every available wall and surface. Serena loved this room more than any other at the school—being in it made her feel as if she had walked into a life-size kaleidoscope perpetually filled with unlimited possibilities of change and wonder.

"Remember to sign your name at the bottom of your piece before placing it on the drying rack. If you would like to take your painting home today instead of waiting until after spring break, you'll have to be very careful not to let it touch anything on the way home." Ms. Yakamoto strolled around the circle of easels, admiring her students' work.

Serena spotted Drew's dark mop of hair sticking out from the side of one of the easels facing the door. She watched him working, concentrating hard on putting the finishing touches on his canvas. Ms. Yakamoto looked up at Serena's head peeking in the doorway and smiled at her, acknowledging her arrival. Serena returned her greeting with a conspiratorial wink.

The teacher walked behind Drew. "Wow! Drew, that's turning out great. I think there's someone here who might want to see it," she said.

Drew turned his attention to the doorway, his green eyes wide open. His serious expression melted into an ear-to-ear grin. He had paint splashed across both cheeks.

"Mom! Come see my painting. It's for you!"

She pointed to herself, dramatically mouthing the words, "*For me?*" and walked over to her son's easel. When she reached his side, she tousled his overgrown brown locks before turning her full attention to his painting. It was a Willy-Wonka-esque picture of a rainbow-hued birthday cake with what looked like a hundred candles on top. A small blue boy with a big red smile danced amidst the flames. She put her hand up to her mouth as tears sprang to her eyes and her heart began to hurt.

"Do you like it?" he asked, looking up at his mother with genuine concern.

"I more than like it," she said, pausing to clear her choked-up throat. "I love it. It's absolutely fantastic, Drew. Thank you for making me such a beautiful painting." She looked down into her son's eyes, beaming with pride and uncomplicated happiness.

Drew turned toward Ms. Yakamoto. "It's my Mommy's birthday today!" Then he turned back to his painting and pointed at the dancing blue boy. "That's me dancing because I want to dance and celebrate with her. The flames don't hurt me because I've got special powers."

"That's wonderful, Drew," Ms. Yakamoto said. "I bet you and your brother are going to give your mom such a special birthday celebration." She shot Serena that knowing expression shared only between women that means something like, *Happy birthday, girl...bet you could use a stiff margarita.*

"Come on, buddy. Let's pack up your beautiful painting and go get your brother." She began untying the back of Drew's smock. Three minutes later, Serena and Drew were loaded down with backpack and lunch box, dripping painting in hand. In the meantime, four other parents had arrived and the classroom was buzzing with activity.

"Don't forget to say bye and thank you to Ms. Yakamoto, Drew," Serena said, pulling on the hood of his sweatshirt to slow down his departure.

"Thank you, Ms. Yakamoto. See you after spring break!"

"Bye, Drew. Have a great spring break, and Serena, I hope you have a wonderful birthday."

"Thanks, Salli," said Serena with a sly smile, and gave her one last *Don't Tell Anyone* wink before stepping out the classroom door.

When they were buckled in, Serena rolled down both her and Drew's windows as she pulled out of the school parking lot. It was mid-March and the winter rains that had soaked Redwood Hills for the last six weeks had finally started to dry up. After only two days of warmer temperatures, tree and flower buds had burst open all over town as if to state for the record it was time for a change. The moist, earthy scent that had saturated the air for weeks had given way to a fresh herbal aroma that could have been packaged as a candle and sold as "Spring." Serena checked the temperature on her dashboard—74 degrees. *Hallelujah*.

"Mom?"

"Yes, Bug?" She looked at her son in the rearview mirror.

"How big is an asteroid?"

She smiled, recalling that Asher had been the same at this age. A hundred questions a day on every imaginable subject. The most endearing part about it was that he actually believed she knew all the answers.

"Well, let me see. Asteroids come in all different sizes, just like planets do. But asteroids are smaller than planets."

"Smaller than the moon?"

"Yes, smaller than the moon." *I think that's right*, she thought. *I've got to remember to check that on the Internet later.*

Drew paused, considering her answer. "Are there places with lots of asteroids, like that part in *Star Wars* when Han Solo has to fly through the asteroid field?"

Serena furrowed her brow as she dug through her memories of grade-school science. "Actually, I think there are. You know how Mars and Jupiter are next to each other?"

He nodded, eager for more information.

"Well, I'm pretty sure there's an asteroid belt right in between those two planets." She was just a little bit proud of herself for pulling out this bit of information.

"Is an asteroid belt like an asteroid field?"

"Yes, except it's a big circle of asteroids that that goes all the way around the sun in a big ring. That's why they call it a 'belt'—because it looks like a belt." She glanced back at her son to see if he was still following.

"How many asteroids are in the belt?"

Serena gave a dramatic pause for effect. "*MILLion*s."

"Millions? For real?" She could tell that he didn't want to get his hopes up, just in case she was kidding.

"Yup, for real."

"That's really cool."

It actually is *cool.* Drew's seven-year-old curiosity had a way of reminding her how cool the world really was. Most of the time, struggling to keep her head above water, she simply forgot.

SERENA PULLED UP behind several other cars

in the pick-up lane in front of Oak Ridge Middle
School. She put her RAV4 into park and looked
back at Drew. As much as he looked like his father,
she had to admit that the shape of his eyes and the
color of his hair were almost identical to her own.

"There's Asher!" Drew shouted, excited to
have spotted his big brother.

She turned back toward the front
windshield and could see Asher's tall, skinny frame
exiting the front double doors. Unlike his little
brother, who had a stout build and a cherubic face,
Asher had always been lean and angular. He was
twelve, and remembering the small, scrawny baby
she'd first held more than a decade ago gave her an
ache. Even though it had been only fifty degrees
that morning, he'd claimed it was "too hot for
pants" and wore shorts paired with a sweatshirt and
a wool beanie. Watching the other students stream
out of the building, it seemed like all the kids in his
school were stubbornly determined to prove that it
was never too cold for shorts in northern California.

He was walking toward the car with Maggie,
his friend since kindergarten. This year, the two of
them had decided to take the after-school
beginning guitar class. He'd told Serena that he
and Maggie wanted to start a band. She loved that
for a twelve-year-old, anything seemed possible.
Even becoming a rock star.

"Asher!" Drew yelled after his brother out
the window.

"Drew, dear, don't yell for your brother. He'll come over in a minute."

"Can I go say 'Hi' to Maggie?" Drew asked eagerly.

Serena's instincts told her to hold him back. "Well, let's wait and see if they come over and say hi. Okay?"

"Oookay." Drew's lower lip protruded in the barest suggestion of a pout.

Despite their age difference, Asher and Drew had always been close. But Serena had begun to notice a distinct change in Asher's attitude since he'd started middle school. The last time she'd asked Asher to take Drew along on a bike ride with friends, he'd asked, "Mom, do I have to take him *everywhere* with me?" He'd also explained, with all the kindness he could muster, that it was totally okay for her to wait for him in the car at pick-up instead of meeting him at the school doors. So, she waited for Asher to initiate contact, and she made Drew wait, too.

Serena noticed movement in her rearview mirror. The gleaming grill of a spanking-brand-new black Ranger Rover pulled up behind her, a woman in her early forties with expertly processed blond shoulder-length hair and oversized Gucci sunglasses behind the wheel. Kirsten Lowell, Maggie's mother. Serena watched as Kirsten talked into her Bluetooth earpiece, which she wore 24/7. *She should buy another one for the other side of her head and wear them as matching pair of earrings.* Still, Serena felt an unwanted pang of envy as she admired Kirsten's luxury SUV. Suddenly, she really wished it hadn't been three months since her last car wash.

Serena hoped to escape the other woman's attention, but no such luck. She suppressed a groan as Kirsten got out of her car.

"Here comes Maggie's Mom," she warned Drew.

"Ugggh, Mom," Drew moaned. "She talks *sooo* much."

"Shh," Serena scolded, preparing for Kirsten's onslaught. She rolled down her window.

Kirsten appeared at the driver's side window, one hand hovering beside her Bluetooth, ready to end the call.

"I just got to school to pick up Maggie and I just ran into an ol' girlfriend so I've got to go, sugar. Don't worry, you know my style, I get the deal done, so don't y'all fret about it. Ciao, honey."

Serena had to give Kirsten Lowell credit. Even though she'd lived in Northern California for at least ten years, her Georgia accent had not diminished one bit. And she'd managed to parlay that Southern belle persona into a career as one of the most prominent real estate agents in the area. Somehow, Kirsten's loud, brassy caricature of Southern Dixie gentility came off as exotic, giving her a certain 'je ne sais quoi' that Californians

17

couldn't manage to understand—or say no to. The kicker for Serena was that Kirsten's husband was a gallery owner from England, and his posh British accent was equal in strength to hers. Being with both of them at the same time was like watching some bizarre mash-up of *Gone With The Wind* and *Monty Python*. But even they seemed to make their marriage work.

Serena gave Drew a sympathetic look that said, *Don't worry, we won't stay long,* before getting out of the car so she could exchange hugs with Kirsten, who did not believe in greetings without physical contact.

"Well, hiya, darlin'! It's been forever since I've run into you! How are y'all doing?"

"We're good. How are you? Business still keeping you busy, I see?"

Kirsten released Serena from her mama-bear hug. "Oh lord, honey, you know me, I'm always a-buzzin'. Can't stand still for two seconds. They say the market's goin' down, but hell, I'm from Atlanta. Nothin' and nobody keeps me down, sugar."

You'd think that she was actually there during Reconstruction.

Kirsten's blue eyes, which were normally blinking with over-caffeinated cheer, became focused and calm as she shifted to a more serious tone.

"But how are *you*, honey?" Kirsten glanced

from Drew to Asher with obvious concern before lowering her voice. "How're you and the kids holdin' up after the *dee*-vorce?"

Serena felt her throat constrict and her chest tighten. It had been nine months since the divorce had become final, but she still couldn't help but feel pained and awkward when someone asked about it, particularly when the person doing the asking was the parent of one of her boys' friends. Redwood Hills seemed to be one of the few places left in California where divorce wasn't the norm. She still felt like a failure.

"Well," said Serena, her voice quivering a bit, "It's a big adjustment, but we are all getting along pretty well. Just doing the best we can under the circumstances, you know? And the kids have been real troopers." *Did I just call the kids "troopers?" I am such an ass.* She hoped Drew hadn't heard her inside the car.

"Well, I gotta tell ya, honey. You look like you're holding up just fine. Clearly, you ain't numbing the pain with our good friends Ben and Jerry."

Serena laughed, thinking she was glad there weren't any hidden cameras in her new little house on Treetop Lane, because she had damned sure stood at the counter with the freezer door still open, shoveling her favorite flavor, Rocky Road, down the hatch.

"Nope, nope, no Ben and Jerry's for me,"

Serena said sheepishly.

"Well, you look amazing," Kirsten said. "And you're still loving that cute little house with the red door, I hope?"

"Absolutely," Serena said, this time with 100% honesty. "Again, I can't thank you enough for your help, Kirsten. It truly is the perfect spot for us."

"Oh, my pleasure! My pleasure, sugar. It really is a darlin' little place."

Serena was sure that Kirsten didn't usually broker tiny three-bedroom houses with bathrooms that still had their original fifties tile, but she had stepped in and helped her when she really needed it.

Kirsten's face lit up just then, almost like a literal light bulb had gone off. "Hey, you still into all that spiritualized stuff like yoga and meditating?"

Serena almost laughed out loud. You really could never tell what was going to come out of this woman's mouth next. "Um, I am, I am. Just went to a really lovely yoga class this afternoon, actually. It's been one of the things that has kept me, you know, grounded this past year." *That, plus chardonnay and the occasional dose of Xanax.*

"That's beautiful, darlin'," said Kirsten. "Listen, a client of mine was telling me about this psychic-reader woman. She's supposed to be absolutely fantastic! She does these readings that can give you all sorts of clues about your past and future. Maybe *you* oughta go. I mean—maybe she could help you find your next big thang, you know?" Kirsten gave Serena an exaggerated wink.

"Huh," Serena said. She wasn't exactly sure how to take the fact that Kirsten thought she needed a 'next big thang,' but she tried to shrug it off. Kirsten's intentions were good—and she always seemed to genuinely care about Serena's well-being.

"Thanks, Kirsten. Sounds like it could be... interesting. I'll definitely think about it." To her surprise, for the first time during their conversation she felt relaxed and sincere.

"AAAAAsshhheerr, let's go!!!"

Serena jumped at the sound of Drew's voice roaring out of the car. She could tell he was at the ragged edge of his patience.

"Drew!!" Serena turned around and gave him her sternest look of reprimand. "I'm sorry, Kirsten. We better go."

Kirsten looked down at her watch. "Oh my goodness, look at the time, we need to skedaddle, too." She called out to her daughter, who was huddled in conversation with Asher. "Mag! Let's go, sugarbean."

To Serena's surprise, Asher strode right up to the car and gave her a hug without a hint of hesitation.

"Happy birthday, Mom."

Her heart swelled. Asher gave Serena a

grin, knowing that she would be startled by his gesture, especially in front of his friends.

"Thanks Ash-sweetheart."

"Birthday? Well, I had no idea, darlin'!" Kirsten beamed. "Well, then all the more reason to think about calling that person we talked about. I'll email you all the info. No time like the present, as they say." She winked again.

"Let's go, Mom," said Maggie, sounding as exasperated as only a tween girl can. "And happy birthday, Mrs. Phillips—I mean Ms. Rayborn." She flashed an apologetic look at Asher.

"Thanks so much, Maggie," Serena said quickly to dispel any awkwardness. "Have a great spring break."

"You, too!" Kirsten and Maggie shouted back in unison.

As she eased the car away from the curb toward home, with both boys inside, she felt a sense of peace as resonant as the feeling at the end of the yoga class. For a moment, she felt they really were doing all right—a little family of three.

Five minutes later, however, as they pulled into the driveway of 8 Treetop Lane, the sense of calmness and tranquility was obliterated. Serena had barely pulled to a stop when Asher and Drew opened the doors and jumped out, as if escaping from a burning building.

"Can I open the door, Mom?" Drew was already straddling the front door, right hand outstretched, waiting for Serena to throw him the keys.

"Sure, bug."

Serena tossed the keys to Drew and then began the process of shutting their doors, which they'd left open, as usual.

"Believe it or not, boys, the doors don't shut themselves," Serena called after Drew and Asher, who were jostling past one another trying to be the first one to make it into the house.

"Does everything have to be a race with you two?"

"Yes!" The boys yelled back simultaneously as the door burst open. Drew and Asher tumbled over one another into the foyer, backpacks and papers flying, the keys still hanging in the door lock.

Serena took the stretch up the brick pathway more slowly. Every time she walked from the driveway up to the quirky little yellow house, she felt a little bit more at home than the time before. Serena had expected the boys to be as devastated as she was by the process of splitting up their home and downsizing. To her surprise, Drew and Asher seemed to truly like the house, even though it was about one-quarter the size of their former family home and didn't have a pool like their father's. Drew said he liked it because it was cozy like a "big hobbit house." Asher said he liked it because "it was a lot quieter," which was his diplomatic way of saying that regardless of the size restrictions, he was happy that the constant arguing between his mother and father had finally stopped.

Serena knew that calling their new home a "hobbit house" had been a compliment in Drew's eyes, but as she approached the front door, the phrase still stung. She couldn't help but feel ashamed by the downgrade. To her, their new home, just like her career path, represented a fall backward, not a move forward. Before she had Asher and Drew, she had aspired to get her Masters and become an art historian. She swallowed hard thinking about her derailment, her lack of direction. In the wake of her divorce, after years of being out of the work force, the best she'd been able to find was a position as a research assistant at the University. And she'd been lucky to get that, at her age. It had taken every penny of her divorce settlement to buy this little "hobbit house." And at her salary, she'd never be able to afford anything more. She worried that her kids would eventually see her the way she saw herself. *I'm a loser. The unraveling of my marriage has exposed me for who I really am: a failure who can't manage to succeed at anything, whether it's my marriage or my career aspirations.*

"Mom?" yelled Drew for her from inside the house. "Can we have pizza tonight?" Drew's bubbly request pulled her out of the train of dejected thoughts that seemed to run through her head constantly these days.

"Sure, bug!" she yelled back, hoping her cheery tone would push back against the despair she felt welling up inside her. As she grabbed the doorknob, she looked at the tarnished brass number 8 on the bright red door and recalled how she knew it was the right house for them. The "8" had spoken out to her as more than just a street number. In her mind, she had always flipped the digit onto its side, and with this transposition it became the symbol for infinity, a marker for a future of limitless possibilities. She pulled the keys out of the lock and stepped inside, gently closing her hopeful red door behind her.

SERENA RUSHED around the living room after they'd cooked and eaten two frozen pizzas, cleaning up Asher and Drew's board games and shoving them into a cabinet. It was almost seven o'clock somehow, and Mallory had texted she'd be there any minute.

"Ash, help me tidy up a bit." Together, they gathered up the books, toys, and random junk strewn about the sofas and floor. Then they dumped everything in a laundry basket that Serena stuffed into a closet.

Giving the living room a final survey and deeming it acceptable-for-a-friend, she went into the kitchen to make sure Asher and Drew had put their dinner plates away.

The doorbell let out its melodic chime right as she was closing the dishwasher. The boys clambered for the door, both practically pushing each other into the wall on the way.

"Asher, Drew, easy!" she called out. She wiped her hands on the dishtowel and came around the corner to see Mallory and the boys coming toward her with radiant smiles.

Mallory came into the living room carrying a big bakery box. Drew was holding a package wrapped in shiny, hot pink paper with a huge yellow bow on top. "Happy Birthday, Serrreeenaa," sang Mallory, emphasizing every syllable. Serena noticed her friend's auburn bob was topped with a bubble-gum-colored party hat.

Serena burst into laughter. "You sure it's *my* birthday, party-girl?"

"Oh don't worry, I brought a special one just for you, too," Mallory said with a satisfied gleam.

"Great... Can't wait."

"Look what Mallory brought for you, Mom! Cake, and something else—something from all of us." Drew was still bouncing.

"From *all* of you?" Serena quirked an eyebrow at Mallory. She and the boys nodded their heads and smiled in agreement.

"Well, then," said Serena, still a little taken by surprise, "I can't wait to see what it is. But first things first... birthday cake!"

"Yeah!" Drew turned on his heel and

scrambled toward the dining room. Asher followed at a slightly more sedate pace.

"Thanks so much, Mal. Let me take that."

"And trust you with a whole chocolate cake? Never."

Serena followed Mallory to the dining room table and Serena lowered her voice to a whisper.

"So," she said, eyeing the shiny pink gift Asher was setting on the table. "What's this all about?"

Mallory shook her head. "Nope. Sorry, birthday girl, I've been sworn to secrecy. You'll just have to wait until you open it." She paused to lower her voice to be sure the boys couldn't hear her. "But all I have to say is don't blame me—Asher and Drew picked it out."

"Hmmm, sounds intriguing."

Mallory reached down into her purse and pulled out a plastic silver crown encrusted with purple, pink, and green faux-jewels. She shoved it on top of Serena's head before she could object.

"There you go, birthday princess. That's much better."

"And so where's my Prince Charming?" asked Serena, placing her hand next to her cheek and batting her eyelashes like a damsel in distress.

"They were out of those at the dollar store."

"Figures."

"Hurry up, Mom! Open the cake!" Drew was practically bursting out of his skin.

Serena placed the box on the table and untied the string. As she pulled the top open, the swirling aroma of whipped cream and fresh strawberries enveloped her face.

"I thought it was chocolate? Where's your cake?"

"It's *your* cake, Mom," said Asher, "And we know you like strawberry better and that you get chocolate cake mostly for us."

"You do?" Somehow, it was hard to believe that Asher and Drew had noticed something that she barely recognized herself these days. As a mother, her days and nights were spent deciphering her kids' likes and dislikes, which seemed to change on a weekly basis. Putting her own preferences last had become second nature to her at this point. Getting this cake meant that her kids had not only appreciated that it was her favorite, but had also sacrificed having chocolate cake for her sake.

"What a wonderful surprise. This means so much to me." Serena looked gratefully at Mallory and the boys. "And you guys are such sneaks."

"Yup. We fooled ya," said Asher, clearly satisfied with the success of their ruse.

"Mom, let's do the candles. I'm hungry," Drew said, his eyes longingly fixated on the cake.

"Hungry?" Serena asked. "We just ate!"

"I mean hungry for cake. That's different than hungry for dinner."

"I agree," said Mallory, reaching again into

her purse. "I'll put the candles on the cake. Asher, why don't you go ahead and turn down the lights?"

He got up and went over to the dimmer switch on the dining room wall.

Mallory stuck four red and white striped candles in the center of the cake and started to light them with a match.

Drew looked from Serena to Mallory hesitantly and said, "But Mallory, you only put four candles on the cake and I thought you said Mom was thirty—"

"I know how old she is, dear," said Mallory, gently interrupting. "But these candles are for her birthday wishes, not for her age. Each of us gets to blow out one of the candles and make a wish for your mother. That's way more important than having the candles match how old she is, don'tcha think?"

Drew's eyes grew wide as he considered the potential magic involved, and he nodded his head up and down. "It sure is. Come on, Ash. Let's pick our candles."

Asher dimmed the lights and returned to his seat. The four of them leaned in toward the cake, each positioning themselves in front of a candle.

"Okay, after we sing "Happy Birthday," we each have to make a wish for your Mom and blow out our candle." Mallory looked at each of the boys as if this were deadly serious business.

Asher, Drew, and Mallory took a breath

together and began to sing, making a real effort to harmonize their voices. After the last refrain, everyone paused, making sure to solidify their chosen wish into their minds. Serena waited for her own wish to reveal itself in her brain, but nothing seemed to come. Instead, a random smattering of images from the day's events streamed through her head. She saw Moon Blossom bowing. *May the thoughts, words, and actions of my own life contribute in some way to that happiness and freedom for all.* Kirsten Lowell winking at her. *Maybe she could help you find your next big thang, you know?* She saw Drew's painting of the dancing blue boy surrounded by candles. She saw the asteroids that flowed between Mars and Jupiter. *Millions*, she'd told Drew. Finally, she saw her own front door. The number 8 falling on its side, the symbol of infinity rising out of a sea of deep red. Serena closed her eyes and drew in one more deep breath as if she were about to dive into the deep end of a pool. She blew out her candle.

Her eyes still shut, a brilliant flash of orange and red light exploded into her vision. She suddenly felt like she was surrounded by heat, enveloped by a circle of fire. Her heart started beating so violently that she could hear the *thump-thump-thump* pounding in her ears. *What's happening?* Just when she thought her cells might explode from the heat, a deep chill started to spread from inside her body, as if all the blood was draining out of her. She saw a clear, luminous object begin to glow from within the center of the orange and red flashes.

Hurry up and open your eyes. But before she had a chance, everything went dark.

Chapter 2

"Mom?! Maaaaoooom!"

"Serena—open your eyes. C'mon, please open your eyes."

Serena got an involuntary burst of air into her lungs. The inhale that was pushed into her was so forceful that her throat caught on her exhale. She coughed and coughed as she tried to breath normally again. Her eyes fluttered open. She could make out Mallory's auburn hair and petite frame hovering over her on one side, and Drew and Asher on the other, holding her hand and pulling on her arm. She scanned the ceiling and tried to make out where she was. She caught sight of the brass chandelier that hung above the dining room table. The lights were turned on brightly. She felt the texture of the rough wool rug that they'd bought at IKEA below her. Serena's breath finally became regulated enough for her to speak.

"What happened?" Serena asked slowly.

"That's what we'd like to know!" said Mallory, her voice sounding a bit more relieved.

"Come on, let's get you off the floor and lay you down on the couch."

Serena felt multiple hands begin to pull her off the floor.

"I'm okay," she said, "I really am. I can get up by myself." Serena got up carefully and walked over to one of the couches in the living room.

"That was really scary, Mom," said Drew, his face flushed and filled with worry.

"Yeah," said Asher, his voice trembling even though he was trying to remain calm in front of his little brother.

"I'm sorry, guys. I have no idea what happened. Maybe I didn't drink enough water today. But I swear I feel fine now." She really did feel okay—in fact, better than okay. She felt almost... energized.

"I'll get you a glass of water," said Mallory, jumping off the couch and heading toward the kitchen. Mallory came back moments later and handed Serena a cup. Mallory, Asher, and Drew watched Serena silently as she sipped, like she was a ticking time-bomb.

"Stop staring at me, guys! I'm fine now. Nothing a piece of cake won't cure. Mal, would you go and cut it? Let's not ruin a perfect birthday party!"

"Okay," said Mallory reluctantly. "As long as you're sure."

She gave Serena's hand a squeeze and went into the dining room to cut the cake. Serena could tell that Mallory did not want to frighten Asher and Drew any more than they were already.

"And how about we open my present now?" Serena knew the question was guaranteed to move her kids on to the next thing.

"Yes, Mom! Open your present!" Drew's worry seemed to instantly dissipate into thin air. He jumped up from the couch and resumed his usual happy-go-lucky bounce.

Asher got up from the couch to preempt his mother from moving. "I'll get it. You just wait here, Mom." He put his hand on Serena's shoulder, still concerned.

Asher brought the pink box over and set it on the couch next to Serena.

"Okay, here goes." Serena ripped open the package, working slowly to try to keep the present a surprise for as long as possible. She tore the paper off from one side to reveal the words:

GenXGamer System
Prepare to Enter a New Dimension

"My God, you guys!" Serena looked to the left to find Mallory standing next to her with two plates of cake balanced in each hand.

"Hope you like it, Mom," she said.

"It's so expensive!" Serena said, giving Mallory a recriminating look. "I told you we couldn't afford it... and you already have one at your Dad's."

"Yeah, Mom, but we don't want to just play it with Dad," Asher said. "We want you to play it with us, too."

This hit home hard. Far more difficult than her financial demotion, the divorce from Tom had left Serena insecure about how to connect with her sons on her own. Fun things like camping, skiing, soccer, and video games were always more within Tom's area of expertise, and without him, Serena felt a bit stripped and grasping for ways to stay close to her growing boys. She looked at Asher and was once again reminded of how quickly he would grow into adolescence and how vital it was that she take advantage of any and every opportunity to spend time with him while she still had the chance. The fact that her boys wanted to include her so badly made her want to cry.

She looked at the three pairs of eyes waiting for her final pronouncement; Drew's green eyes and Asher's and Mallory's brown ones.

"Come here." Serena pulled one kid into each arm and hugged them both. "I love it. And, Mallory, thank you. It really is incredible, and I know it's not cheap."

"Don't mention it. Plus, these guys were pretty convincing," Mallory said.

"Well, let's hurry and set it up so you can teach me how to play some of your games," Serena said, turning to the boys who were already ripping open the box.

"Well, you can count me out," groaned Mallory. "The last game I played was Ms. Pacman in like 1985. But seeing that I also invested substantially in this 'ultimate gaming system,' I guess I'll stick around and watch you guys. Got any champagne for the occasion, Serena?"

While Asher and Drew got busy hooking up the GXG to the television, Serena went to the kitchen, leaving Mallory on the couch. She was examining one of the controllers as if it were a completely foreign object.

"Geez. These things are crazy high-tech now," said Mallory with amazement. "Look at all the buttons. Hey, Serena, do you remember the Atari controller with the one stick and one button? What a difference—this thing looks like it could navigate the space shuttle."

"Hey, don't hate on Atari—I still love those games," Serena said, returning with two glasses of champagne from a bottle that had been in the sitting in the back of her refrigerator for as long as she could remember. She also went back and cut each of them a slice of cake, which she let the boys eat on the floor.

"Okay, I'm almost done. Drew, hand me that black power cord," Asher said.

Drew, sitting on his knees like Robin ready to assist Batman, scrambled over to the cord and handed it to his big brother.

"Great," said Asher, "We're ready. So, Mom, it comes with two games in the starter pack. We can play *Speed Horizon* or *The Rings of Prophesy*. Which one do you want to try first?"

"I have no idea," said Serena. "What are they about?"

"Well, *Speed Horizon* is a kick-a.... um, I mean kick-butt driving game where you can do races all over the world through the streets of real cities, like New York, London, Amsterdam... And the streets are copied exactly from the real cities."

"Wow. Okay, what about the other one?" asked Serena. *"The Rings of Prophesy?"*

"That's also really good, but it's a totally different kind of game. You have to go through all of these different levels, searching for a different ring on each one. Once you find the ring, you give it to a seer who gives you a hint about how to find the hidden treasure on the final level. And of course you have to fight all these gnarly bad dudes you run into along the way. It's pretty awesome."

"Hey Serena, why don't you play the *Prophesy Rings* one?" asked Mallory, who could always to be counted on for a firm opinion.

"The Rings *of Prophesy,"* corrected Asher and Drew together.

"Oh, excusez-moi. *Zee Rings of Prophesy,"*

said Mallory, using a fake French accent. "I'm up for anything that involves searching for potential treasure."

"That one does sound fun," said Serena, "and I could use a little adventure. Asher, go ahead and start the game."

Asher loaded the game disc into the GXG. "We'll just need to create your character, Mom, and then you'll be ready to start ring hunting."

"What do you mean 'create my character'?" Serena was puzzled.

Drew giggled. "Mommy, you are so funny. You really don't know anything about this stuff, do you?"

"Okay, okay," said Serena. "Give me a break and just explain."

"You get to personalize your character. You choose what they look like, what clothes they wear, what weapons they prefer to use—stuff like that," said Asher.

"Cool." This time it was Mallory and Serena who spoke in unison.

"Okay," said Asher pointing to the TV screen. "First, pick your style of hair and color. You've got like twenty to choose from."

"Oooh oooh oooh—pick that one!" shouted Mallory.

Serena, Asher and Drew all turned and looked at Mallory like she had a screw loose.

"What? I love Mohawks."

FIFTEEN MINUTES later, Serena had named her character "MOM" and was racing through the dungeon level of *The Rings of Prophesy* in search of the first ring. Asher and Drew shouted and cheered as Serena used her weapon of choice, the bow and arrow, against the Beasts of Delorium and the Seraph Mummies. They high-fived her every time she succeeded in defeating one of the evil creatures that stood in her way.

"Wow. I can't believe how life-like they can make something look that doesn't even exist in real life!" exclaimed Mallory.

"I know. Look at the gauze on that Seraph Mummy. It looks real enough to touch," said Serena, just before slaying the ghoul with a deadly arrow. The mummy screamed in agony and crumpled to the ground in a heap of dust.

"You're pretty good at this, Mom," said Asher.

"Think I've found my calling? Should I quit my job as a research assistant at the University and become a mummy-slaying ring-raider instead?"

"Look out, Mom!" yelled Drew, who was lying on his stomach on the carpet in front of the television with his chin propped up in both hands.

At that moment, one of the Beasts of Delorium came up from behind Serena and hit her with his massive spiked club. The hit was so hard that Serena's character was thrown across the room, and she ricocheted against a wall and fell to the ground.

"Ouch. That's gotta hurt," said Drew.

The beast that had attacked roared with laughter and bellowed, "You have been defeated. Arrrrgghhh! You fool—you will never reach the ring, and your destiny is mine!" Serena's character flickered and slowly faded away until she disappeared completely. The words "Game Over" appeared in the middle of screen, flames springing from each letter, announcing that she had indeed crashed and burned.

"Bummer," said Drew. "But you did pretty good for your first time, Mom. Can I play next?"

"Actually, bug, we better start to wrap it up. You guys need to get to bed soon. It's getting late." Serena waited for the moaning to start.

"Aaawwww. But Ash and I only had a chance to play once, Mom," complained Drew. "Plllleeeeaasse, just one more game?"

"Sorry, Drew-bug. Your Dad will be here first thing in the morning to come and pick you guys up, so we all better get to bed. We'll have plenty of time to play more when you come back."

Drew pooched out his bottom lip into his signature pout.

"Please don't fight with me about it, Drew," said Serena. "You wouldn't want to give me a hard time on my birthday, now would you?"

Asher gave his little brother a look of

disapproval.

"Ooookaay." Drew wriggled forward on his belly, his finger poised to push the power-off button on the GXG. "But promise we'll play again as soon as we get back from Dad's next weekend?" Drew was reluctant to move any further without some guarantees.

"Promise, bug. Now why don't you guys say goodnight to Mallory and go get ready for bed. I'll be in soon to make sure you're both tucked in."

Serena pressed the button to turn off the GXG and the television, and Drew and Asher shuffled over to Mallory, who was sitting cross-legged on the couch. "'Night, Mallory," said Asher and Drew, one echoing the other, each giving her an indirect sideways boy-hug.

"Race ya, Ash!" yelled Drew, releasing Mallory and taking off into a sprint across the living room towards the hallway leading to the bedrooms.

Ignoring his brother's challenge, Asher held on to Mallory for a moment longer and said, "Thanks a lot for helping to make everything so great, Mallory. Me and Drew really appreciate it." Asher glanced over to the GXG and then to Serena.

"My pleasure, buddy," said Mallory, gently ruffling the top of Asher's sandy-brown hair.

"Ash! We're supposed to be raaaacing!" yelled Drew from the other side of the house. They could hear him scrambling impatiently up and down the hallway.

Asher rolled his eyes and shrugged his shoulders as if to say, *It's a tough job, but someone's got to do it.* A second later he bounded across room to give his brother a run for his money.

"So… Tom's got the boys for Spring Break?" Mallory got up from her seat and headed towards the kitchen.

"Yup," said Serena, "and it's just as well, since I have a ton of research due to Dr. LeMott by the end of this week."

"Is he *ever* going to finish that thing? My God, Serena, it seems like you've done enough research for him to have written *ten* books by now."

"I know, I know. But, sometimes historical investigation into ancient monuments and cities can lead you in all sorts of different directions that can't be anticipated at first."

"Blah blah blah. Give me a break," Mallory said, returning with another glass of champagne. "He's had you working on this stuff for two years, now, and he's managed to have his research grant extended twice so he could keep you on. Professor Dorkus Erectus has a crush on you and that's all there is to it, Chiquita."

Serena knew that Mallory was probably right, but she still felt compelled to defend him. Dr. Julius LeMott may have had a little crush on her, but he was one of the most sincere and decent men Serena had ever met. A year or two shy of sixty, he had spent most of his adult life as a bookwormish scholar within the confines of Bennett University, teaching and writing about the obscure characteristics of ancient civilizations long forgotten by most of the world. Serena could not help but have a soft spot for her awkward, timid employer who had provided a sheltered haven of purpose for her during the darkest days of her divorce.

"Even if that were true, Mal, he's a harmless old teddy bear. Besides, a lot of the research I do for him is pretty interesting."

Mallory settled back into the couch and handed her a glass. "Man, you really need to get out more."

"Shut up."

Mallory shook her head and let out a sigh of frustration. "I'm serious, Serena. It's like you are punishing yourself for the divorce with a sentence of self-imposed house arrest. What happened wasn't your fault."

"I used to believe that, but now..." Serena sat back and pulled her feet up onto the couch. "I look back and I think... maybe it *was* me. It wasn't Tom's fault that I didn't achieve anything great."

"Helllooo? Asher and Drew?"

Serena nodded and rolled her eyes. "Yes, of course I have Asher and Drew, bless their hearts. They are amazing. But you know what I mean. They were born that way. Them being amazing doesn't make me... maybe not living up to my potential made me... too insecure and needy."

"Are you freakin' kidding me?" Mallory sat up at full attention. "Serena he couldn't even be bothered to be there for the—"

"Shh," said Serena, motioning her head toward the hallway leading to the boys' rooms. "I know Mal... you don't have to remind me. Especially not today," said Serena, giving a weak smile and pointing up to her plastic crown.

Mallory glanced back at the hallway. "Sorry," she said, lowering her voice. "You're right. We shouldn't be rehashing that stuff today of all days. But remember, Serena, there's a big world out there waiting for you. Don't let what happen with Tom make you forget that."

"Yeah, a big, bad, scary world," said Serena, staring down into her glass.

Mallory frowned. "Are you thinking about... your mother?"

"Yeah," said Serena, barely above a whisper. "As of today, I've lived longer than she did." She gulped down the rest of her champagne.

Serena heard the boys calling from the bedroom that they were ready for her to come say goodnight.

"All right, I'm going to take off and let you guys get some sleep. But before I go," Mallory began, raising her glass, "Here's to you, and here's to your birthday, and getting you out into that big, bad, scary world. No guts, no glory, baby."

Serena smirked at her as she raised her glass in return, and then they both set their emptied flutes on the coffee table. "Thank you for tonight, Mal," she said giving her a huge hug.

After Mallory was gone, she hurried into Drew and Asher's rooms to give them a goodnight kiss, and then came back into the living room to tidy everything up. She wrinkled her nose as her eyes landed on the glowing orange light of the GXG system.

Could have sworn I turned that thing off, she thought, walking over to the console to press the button again. This time, the orange glow faded to black.

Chapter 3

Serena heard the teapot on the stove begin to whistle loudly. She always predicted that she would be done getting dressed by the time the kettle started screaming, but inevitably she found herself jumping around in a panic, still struggling to figure out what underwear she was going to wear.

"Moooom!" hollered Drew from the kitchen. "The water's boiling!"

"I know, I hear it! I'll be right there!" She started digging through her sock drawer in search of a matching pair. *Hah! Found one. So what if they have Christmas trees on them?*

Serena slid into the kitchen in her holiday socks and removed the kettle just as it was sounding like it might explode under the pressure of the steam. Drew and Asher were sitting at their small kitchen table digging into bowls of cereal full to the brim with milk.

Serena shook her head and poured the hot water into a mug, her Morning Harmony Buzz tea bag waiting inside. "Guys, how many times have I asked you not to fill up your bowls so high? You have enough milk in there for the entire box. It's such a waste."

"It won't be a waste, Mom," Asher said. "Check this out."

Asher picked up his bowl of brown cereal-flavored milk and proceeded to gulp the whole thing down.

"Gross," said Drew, wrinkling his nose.

"Totally," said Serena.

The doorbell rang.

"It's Dad!" Drew sprang up from his seat and started running towards the foyer.

"Wait, young man. I'll get the door," said Serena. "You two need to put your dishes into the dishwasher, like we talked about last week."

Serena walked toward the door, a frog beginning to grow in her throat. She paused for a moment in front of the mirror in the foyer to see how much of a wreck she was. She secretly wished that she'd had time just to put on a little mascara. She gave an exasperated sigh. *Why do you even care?* She ran her hand through her hair, took a big breath, and opened the door.

"Hey," said Tom, standing in a comfortable, relaxed posture at the door. He wore a polo shirt, bright red golf pants, and a sporty white cap advertising the brand 'Titleist' in bold cursive lettering. Serena spotted a leather golf glove peeking out from one of his back pockets.

"Hey," said Serena, wondering how it was possible that he had already been to the driving range this morning while she'd barely had time to brush her teeth. She hated to admit it, but every time Tom showed up to pick up the boys, deep down she hoped that the universe would cut her some slack and that she'd see the beginnings of grey hair, or better yet, a permanent potbelly. But no, once again, there Tom stood looking every bit the successful executive, polished and exuding confidence. Obviously, being divorced from her suited him just fine.

"The kids are ready," she said finally, ending the awkward pause.

Asher and Drew came running up from behind her, one on each side.

"Hi, Dad!" they each exclaimed excitedly.

"Hey, guys," said Tom, breaking into a broad smile. "How are my Jedi Knights? Ready to go?"

"Yeah!" shouted Drew. He was practically bouncing off the walls.

Serena smiled. She couldn't blame the boys for being enthusiastic after a week of not seeing their dad. "Okay, guys, I put your backpacks right here by the door already. Hurry up and put on your jackets and sneakers so you guys can get going and not keep your Dad waiting." The boys hurried back behind her again to get suited up and collect their gear.

"Any special plans for spring break?" Serena asked. She attempted to sound casual and not like she was trying to pry. Even though they shared custody of their boys, sometimes she felt like a "NONE OF YOUR BUSINESS" sign hung between them, making it tricky to ask even the simplest of questions.

"I took the whole week off, so I thought I'd take the kids camping in Yosemite for a few days," said Tom. "Then I suppose we'll just hang out at home for the rest of the week. It's finally getting sunny again, so I hope we'll get to break out the bikes."

Serena felt her heart sink a little at the thought of all of them going to Yosemite without her. She still hadn't gotten used to the fact that their family vacation memories would be made separately from now on. In the future, Serena could imagine the boys having two photo albums— one entitled "Memories with Mom" and the other "Memories with Dad."

"Sounds great," said Serena cheerily, attempting to infuse some positivity into her thoughts through her words.

"We're ready to go, Mom," said Asher. He and Drew were once again standing at her side, this time in their jackets and loaded down with their backpacks.

"Give me a hug, you two." Serena got down on her knees to get into better squeezing position.

"Love you," she said, taking one in each arm. She gave them each a pat on the back. "Okay, get going and have fun." Drew and Asher scampered through the door and down the path towards Tom's car. Halfway there, Asher stopped and turned to look back.

"Don't forget to practice, Mom, so we can play when we get back!" he shouted back with a smile.

"Will do!" Serena shouted back, grateful for Asher's assurance that they *would* be coming back. Serena looked back up at Tom and stood up. For a split second, she could have sworn that she caught a look of sorrow in his eye.

"Play what?" he asked, shifting quickly.

"Oh. The GXG System. A gift from Mallory. The boys are thrilled to have one here as well, now."

"I'll bet. I have to drag them off that thing at my house. By the way, happy birthday."

"Thanks," said Serena, feeling both relieved and slightly embarrassed that he remembered.

"So, I guess I'll just give you a call when we get back from Yosemite so you can talk to the boys." Tom shifted uncomfortably. *Tom and Asher look so similar when they are nervous*, thought Serena.

"That would be great," she said.

"See ya next week, then."

"See ya next week."

Here they were once again, trading their smiles of seemingly happy resignation. It seemed to Serena that she and Tom gave each other the same smile at the end of every custody exchange. That guarded sort of smile that always seemed to say, *It is what it is, so I guess we'll just make the best of it.* Tom turned around and headed down the path toward his BMW. Asher and Drew were already piled in the back seat and torturing each other inside. Serena turned to close the door, feeling, as she always did, emotionally drained by the interaction.

"Hey, one more thing," said Tom, turning back on his heel.

"Yes?" Serena was just about to close the door.

"Nice socks."

Serena looked down at her gaudy Christmas-tree-checkered socks and felt her face begin to flush. She looked up and saw Tom looking directly at her reaction with his charismatic grin. It was his real smile, the smile she'd fallen in love with years ago.

Without saying a word, she shot him an equally genuine smile back and slowly shut the door. Once it was closed, she turned her back to the door and exhaled. She felt as if she'd been holding her breath since she opened it. She leaned back against the door and slowly slid down it until she was seated on the floor in the foyer. *Mom, I'm glad you aren't alive to see what a mess I've become.* Finally alone, she covered her eyes with her hands and started to cry.

SERENA'S BODY shuddered and her eyes sprang open, startled by a sound that she could not identify at first. She was still sitting on the floor, hunched over, her head buried between her bent knees and folded arms. She wondered exactly how long she had been crying down there. She jumped again at the sound of a sharp rapping coming from above and behind her. Someone was knocking at the door.

Serena pushed herself into an upright position and used one of her sleeves to dry off her face. She then tried to straighten her clothes and smooth her hair so she would at least look halfway decent. She looked down at a small wet spot of accumulated tears and quickly wiped it away with one of her Christmas-clad feet. *I must look like something out of a horror movie.* She leaned forward and looked through the peephole of the door, wondering whom it could possibly be.

She stepped back, bewildered. It was the last person she expected to see, especially so soon. It was Kirsten Lowell again, Gucci sunglasses and all. Serena took a deep breath and tried to prepare herself for the act of smiling before she opened the door.

"Well, hi! What a pleasant surprise!" said Serena, trying to step her tone up to Kirsten's normal level of enthusiasm.

"Hi yourself, darlin'! I hope I'm not interrupting anything. I just wanted to drop by because..." Kirsten was just about to give Serena her double-dutch hug n' kiss when she stopped talking to take a more careful look at Serena. She lifted her sunglasses up to the top of her head and slowly scanned Serena from top to bottom, her eyes finally landing on her inappropriate holiday socks.

"Oh darlin'... are you okay? You been crying?"

"Oh no, I was just..." Serena stalled mid-sentence, unable to think of one plausible lie. "Well... to tell you the truth, I guess I was just a little sad to see the boys go. They just left a little while ago to spend the week with Tom."

"Well, of course, sugar. I can't even imagine what you're going through. This situation has got to make you sadder than blue." Kirsten's face was filled with condolence.

"Yes, well," said Serena, "sometimes things like this can be a bit tough." Serena tried to hold on to some shreds of her dignity by standing a bit taller.

"Which is why I knew that I just had to come over to give you a little ol' birthday present," said Kirsten, her expression suddenly animated with excitement. Kirsten reached down into her fire-engine-red Louis Vuitton bag, pulled out a silver envelope and held it out for Serena to take.

"Surprise, darlin'."

Serena took the envelope into her hand and stared at it blankly, once again caught off-guard. "Kirsten... I don't know what to say. Thank you. You really didn't have to—"

"Oh stop thanking me honey and just open it! No sense beatin' 'round the bush when there's a present to be had. We could get struck by lightning just standin' here."

Serena looked beyond Kirsten's silhouette at the perfectly sunny day. She really couldn't help but wonder what the hell Kirsten was talking about sometimes. However, she shut up as instructed and ripped open the envelope. She pulled out a dark blue rectangular card, which read in bold, sparkly silver print:

This Gift Certificate Entitles the Bearer

Serena Rayborn
To One Session of

Journey Magnification
With Devania
Mystic, Sage, & Spiritual Reader

Serena looked back up at Kirsten even more stupefied, not quite knowing what to make of her gift.

"It's from that spiritual reader I was telling you about yesterday!" said Kirsten, clapping her hands with delight. "After seeing you yesterday, something just told me that I had to get you in to see this woman. My client Suzanne Anderson told me she's absolutely fabulous. Happy birthday, darlin'."

"Thank you so much, Kirsten. What a lovely surprise. I can't wait to go." As hard as it was for her to believe, Serena meant what she said. She looked back down at the card and reread it. "By the way, what *is* Journey Magnification?"

"Oh, hell if I know! I thought you'd know more about that since you're the hippie chickie. But this is the one Suzanne recommended and she knows her stuff. She was in Bali for *four whole months*. Need I say more?"

Serena smiled. She found the fact that Kirsten considered her to be a hippie and that spending four months in Bali stood as the ultimate cosmic credential to be both amusing and endearing. "Please, Kirsten, won't you come in and have some tea or coffee?"

"Oh, no honey, but thanks. I'm on my way to a nail appointment. Look, my hands are just a wreck." Kirsten held out her right hand with the grace of a flamingo. Serena looked down at what appeared to be five perfectly manicured and polished red nails. "I just came to give you that lil' ol' present to cheer you up. Feeling better?"

"Actually, yes, much better."

"Good. Now you make that appointment right away and I want a full report from you next time I see you," said Kirsten, already on her way back to her Range Rover. "Ciao, darlin'. And remember, us gals gotta stick together."

BACK IN HER bedroom, Serena pulled off her Christmas socks and tossed them into the hamper. She changed her clothes, brushed her teeth for the second time that morning, and pulled her hair back into a ponytail. She looked at her digital alarm clock on the dresser. Saturday, 10:30 am. There was a meditation class at the Center for Spiritual Being at 12:30 that would be the perfect way to restore a little balance and calm, and then she'd told Mallory she would call her for lunch afterwards.

She walked through the rooms of the house. Chaotic, loud, and full of life when Drew and Asher were around, the house felt strangely empty during the weeks that the kids were with Tom. With all their pictures, toys, books and clothes left behind, it felt eerily quiet, like a carnival that had been shut down. During the first couple days after the boys left, Serena was always forced to go through a period of transition and let-down. She had to adjust to her second life, a life in which she was thrown out of her maternal rhythm, felt acutely alone at times, and missed her boys so much that she counted the hours until they came back.

With over an hour before she had to leave for class, Serena plopped down on the couch and looked around at the disarray of the living room. She knew there were about a hundred chores that she should probably start. There was laundry to wash, bills to pay, bathrooms to be cleaned. But the thought of tackling such drudgery while the boys were surely having a grand Saturday with Tom left her feeling totally unmotivated.

Serena thought instead about what she might be doing if the boys were still there with her. The answer was so obvious that she laughed out loud. As she picked up one of the GXG controllers, she thought about how proud Asher would be. She slid off the couch and crawled forward to push the GXG's power button. As she approached it, though, she paused, index finger still extended in mid-air. The orange power indicator light was already on, glowing brightly. Serena wrinkled her brow. *Again?* Unsure about what to do next, Serena went ahead and pushed the button anyway. The power light stayed lit. *Hmmm*, thought Serena. She hit the button once more. The light seemed to glow with even more intensity. Serena reached up with her left hand, turned on the television, sat back, and waited.

Serena remembered from the night before that a starting screen would load up and she would have to pick her character. Asher and Drew had saved her "MOM" avatar so that she could use it again and again. Serena waited for the initial screen to appear while the GXG hummed, its internal mechanisms coming to life.

She looked down at the controller and struggled to remember what Asher and Drew had explained to her about how all the buttons worked. Just as she was about to lay the controller down so she could find the instruction book to refresh her memory, she heard a woman's voice.

"Prepare to enter your new dimension."

Serena looked up at the screen. She did not recognize it from the night before. The entire screen was a picture filled with flames, a kind of fire that she had never seen. Instead of the usual colors of orange and yellow, these flames flickered before her in dark, shadowy shades of midnight blue, deep burgundy, and emerald green. *That's odd*, thought Serena. *I could have sworn that yesterday the game opened with a screen that said, "*Welcome to The Rings of Prophesy.*"* She waited, but nothing except the inky-hued flames continued to flicker before her.

She looked back down at the controller that she held in her hand. The "Start" button, which was white and shaped like a star, was blinking in fiery red. She heard the same ethereal voice whisper again, "Press start to begin." This time, the words sounded like they were being spoken directly into her ear, hovering somewhere next to her head.

Serena jerked around and looked over her shoulder, startled and confused. She looked back up at the screen. *That voice must have come from the television. But it sounded so close.*

She lifted her thumb and pushed down hard on the Start button. The screen flashed bright white and a thunderous sound boomed throughout the room. Serena looked around the room and wondered what could have happened to suddenly give the game surround-sound. When she looked back to the television, the screen had faded into a black so dark that it seemed to actually have depth, like a deep well. Words slowly became visible on the screen, faint at first, and then brighter and brighter, as if they were being burned through parchment:

Your character has been chosen.

The words were written in a script she had only seen in old documents like the ones she used in her work with Dr. LeMott—the kind of cursive that reminded her of the Declaration of Independence.

'Your character has been chosen'? I haven't even had a chance to pick yet. But before Serena could begin to question further, the letters faded away as quickly as they had appeared, leaving behind only the darkness of the black screen. For a moment, Serena wondered if what she had just

witnessed was real or imagined.

Seconds later, the words "Level 1" appeared on the screen, written in plain white text. Serena gave a sigh of relief at the sight of something familiar from the night before. Another few seconds later, a creepy dungeon-like room materialized on the screen with blazing torches and various medieval-looking doors. Serena gave another sigh, grateful to recognize this room as the place where she had been attacked by one of the Beasts of Delorium while playing with Asher and Drew. Her feelings of familiarity vanished, however, when she caught sight of the character standing at the bottom of the screen. Except for being a woman, this character looked nothing like the cute and punkish "MOM" they had created the night before. Startlingly realistic, she stood there in the middle of the room looking directly out, facing Serena.

The first thing that struck Serena was her hair. She had thick, dark hair that cascaded almost down to her hips. Serena squinted her eyes to get a better look. Within the layers of her hair there was some other texture that she couldn't quite make out. When Serena finally identified it, she spoke out loud in confirmation: "Braids." The character had long braids interspersed throughout her virtual mane of hair.

Serena leaned in a little closer to take in the details of her clothing. The character wore a purple and red warrior outfit that could only be described as both outlandishly butch and feminine at the same time. Her dark purple boots rose all the way up to mid-thigh. Above this, she wore a ruby-red skirt that appeared to be made of a kind of chain-mail fabric. Her mini-skirt was pleated in front, but extended down dramatically in the back into a long, layered train. Her torso was covered in a dark brown bustier-style top that had the texture of leather. Long gloves the same color as her boots came up to the tops of her arms. Her complexion was a rich shade of tan, somewhere between honey and tawny, and her large, cat-like eyes, even at such a miniature size, were a brilliant green. Serena crawled forward until she was inches from the screen. On the top her head, the new character wore a crown adorned with purple, pink, and green sparkling gemstones. Serena closed her eyes for a moment to process, and then jumped to her feet and ran to the kitchen.

The birthday crown that Mallory had given her the night before was still sitting out on the kitchen counter. She grabbed it, ran back to the television, and sat down close to the screen. She held up her tacky dollar-store crown and tried to compare it to the one worn by the woman. *Hmmm, they look similar, but I still can't be totally sure...* She thought for a moment and then snapped her fingers, remembering that Asher had shown her a button that changed the view in the game, allowing the player to zoom in and out. She turned around and grabbed the controller behind her. *I think it was this one...* She pressed the button on the lower right-hand side of the controller. The picture immediately zoomed in so Serena was viewing the character's head and torso at close range. Serena moved back—the character's head was now close to the size of her own.

She held up the crown again. The crown on the character was made of shining silver and was intricately adorned with square, iris-purple-colored stones, alternating with hot pink triangle-shaped ones. The gemstones were so mesmerizingly vivid that Serena extended her hand out to touch them as if they were real. In the center of the crown there lay a large, gleaming emerald in the shape of an octagon. Serena looked at the birthday crown that still lay in her hand. Sure, it was made of cheap plastic and colored rhinestones, but in every other way it was identical to the one worn by the mysterious virtual woman. There was no doubt about it.

Serena slowly sat back against the couch to think. *I'm sure there's a perfectly good explanation. Maybe this design is really common or something. There are probably templates for these sort of things... like buying dress patterns.... except for crowns and tiaras instead? Or how about this? The one that Mallory gave you is probably from China or something where they rip off this kind of stuff all the time. They probably copied this design directly from the video game... but how did this character get into the video game in the first place?*

She rubbed her temples with her fingers. Serena looked up at the screen once again and gave a slight gasp. She hadn't noticed before, but there was something written in the space where the player's name was displayed. She leaned forward to read it. Serena whispered it out loud, as if to be sure she was seeing it correctly.

"ZAHRA."

Zahra? Who the hell was Zahra? But before Serena had a chance to try to figure it out, the woman on the screen, who had been standing as still as a statue before, *blinked.*

Is that normal? Surely, thought Serena, that kind of detail was just another clever part of the game's programming. Now close-up, the character continued to stare back at Serena, absolutely motionless, as if the blink had never happened.

Serena braced her hands behind her on the couch and started to pull herself up. She felt the need to walk around or do something to keep her wits about her. Serena got about halfway up to the couch when the virtual woman *spoke.*

"Are you ready to begin, Serena?" Zahra was smiling.

Serena's knees buckled and she collapsed

back down to the ground.

"Holy shit. Wh-what did you say?" asked Serena, covering her mouth with her hands as soon as the words escaped. *Am I really trying to talk to a video game?*

The woman did not answer. She just continued to stare back with the same inscrutable smile.

Serena shook her head. The memory of passing out the night before came back to her, and she started to distrust her own perceptions. *I think what I need is some fresh air, not video games*, she thought, leaning forward and pressing hard on the power button.

"No." Zahra's voice echoed throughout the room. "It's time to begin, Serena."

Serena scooted back from the TV, her heart hammering in her chest. *She knows my name?* The woman was not smiling any more. Her mouth was set in a hard, determined line. She blinked again, her eyes glowing a ferocious green.

Serena felt suddenly annoyed with the game's clever programming. *What the hell is happening?* Perhaps the boys had changed something in the settings in order to play a trick on her.

"Okay, *Zahra*," said Serena, grabbing the GXG controller. "Fine. I'm ready. Sure, if you say so, let's begin." Serena felt reckless, like she was playing fast and loose with someone who was trying to play her for a fool.

She pressed the lower right-hand button again to zoom out and view the entire room with Zahra standing in the center. Serena started reorienting herself with the controls by moving Zahra around the cavernous stone room. She remembered more than she thought she would, and it seemed to come more naturally this time around. In contrast to her hyper character from the night before, Zahra's movements were graceful and almost stealthy. Everything about her seemed to be in motion at all times. Zahra's hair and dress billowed around her with a gently cascading energy. She moved with the strength and intensity of a tiger, but at the same time flowed through her environment like a diaphanous fairy.

"Cool." Serena realized that she felt free to speak out loud now because she no longer felt like she was alone.

Serena guided Zahra into the next room and panic hit her immediately. She stood face-to-face with three Beasts of Delorium, savage, troll-like creatures that exhaled fire. Serena realized that the one thing she had neglected to figure out was what kind of weapon Zahra used. Last night, Serena had chosen the bow and arrow as her character's weapon, but Zahra carried nothing to defend herself. The Beasts of Delorium moved closer and Serena had no choice but to try to fight them off. One of the beasts was close enough to Zahra for her to try to strike. Serena hit one of the attack buttons, hoping that Zahra could do something to fend off her enemies. In a flash, Zahra reached behind her back and pulled out something, slashing the beast down to the ground and leaving him bloody and wailing.

"What the?" Serena leaned in closer to try and see what on earth Zahra had pulled out to slay the beast so swiftly.

"You've got to be kidding me," said Serena, chuckling with amusement. "A *whip*? Exactly what kind of girl do you think I am?"

Serena moved Zahra toward the two remaining creatures that were about to strike. She pressed the attack button again. Zahra spun around with ferocious speed and the long silver whip swirled around her like a ribbon of lighting, ripping into the beasts before they could even get close to her. After the two beasts had fallen, Zahra stood motionless, but the shiny whip continued to slink around slowly with a snake-like life of its own. It was as if Zahra commanded the power of a live wire in her hand.

"Wow." Serena sat as motionless as Zahra, breathing hard with eyes wide open. For a moment, she was able to forget how bizarre this all was. She felt strangely entranced and exhilarated. Her heart was beating fast. She had to admit, she was having fun.

"Shall we continue?" Serena heard the

whispery voice again that seemed to emanate from above her shoulder.

Serena nodded affirmatively, for the moment able to accept that she had no idea to whom she was responding. She sat up taller and held the GXG controller solidly in her hand. She and Zahra were going into battle. And for the first time in a long time, Serena had the feeling she could win.

SERENA'S THUMBS hurt and she could not believe she was still alive. As she made her way through more than twenty different chambers in *The Rings of Prophesy*, Zahra had fought at least a hundred Beasts of Delorium and Seraph Mummies. She was now being chased through the treacherous Passage of Solitude by the Weir Ravens, flesh-eating, bird-like creatures that made Hitchcock's version look like baby chicks. Serena had become so engrossed and skilled at this point that she felt barely separate from Zahra, knowing her movements as well as she knew her own. Serena had completely lost track of time and hadn't dared to pause the game for fear that that she would jinx Zahra's winning streak.

"We must be close to finding the ring. Come on, Zahra," said Serena as she somersaulted through the air with her silvery whip spinning around her like an electric ferris wheel. The flying Weir Ravens shattered and fell to the ground in a spray of icy hail as Zahra defended herself against their attack. Zahra raced down the passage, jumping over lava-filled puddles and breaking through barricades of Numoa—walls made out of a strange gooey substance that began to freeze your body if you moved too slowly. With one final flip, Zahra destroyed the last two Weir Ravens in sight and crashed through a huge barricade of Numoa.

When she landed, she found herself face-to-face with a Beast of Delorium of gigantic proportions—he was ten times her size and held a massive spiked club. She and the enormous beast were standing alone on a floating disk made of crumbling rock that was surrounded by a sea of dark, shadowy flames. There was no room for error on this final terrain. If the Beast hit her, there was nowhere to go. She would fall into the pit of fire and die.

The Beast lifted the club over its head, ready to strike with all of its might. It let out a ferocious roar that seemed to fill up every corner of the room. Desperate to survive, Serena hit the attack button and then hit every other button on the controller at the same time. Zahra fell back and lay completely lifeless on the ground.

"What?! Oh no," said Serena. "Zahra, please don't."

Just as the Beast's club was about to smash down onto her body, Zahra sent a powerful kick across his legs, felling him onto his side. Her whip flashed around him in a blazing circle of light, severing his head off. The Beast's head, followed by his body, tumbled over the edge of the floating rock and into the hellfire below.

The screen went completely blank and silent. Serena did not know what to make of it. *What happened? Was Zahra still somewhere in there?* Serena sat and waited, listening to only the sound of her shallow breath and her heart beating like a kettle drum. She stared into the screen, still gripping the controller, not quite knowing what to do.

Serena heard the sound of a match being struck and igniting. She looked around her living room for the source, but no one was there—she was still alone. Looking back to the screen, she caught sight of a small flicker of light emerging from the darkness on the right-hand side. The flame of a candle started to glow, and within seconds, a small, austere chamber became illuminated with amber light. Zahra, her stance strong and triumphant, stood on the left side of the room facing the right, where a person cloaked in a rough-hewn, brown robe sat hunched over at a small wooden table with the lit candle on top. Serena could barely make out the features of the mysterious, hooded character.

"Have you brought me the ring?" The crackly voice of an old woman rose out of the chamber.

But we didn't find a ring, thought Serena.

Just then, she noticed that Zahra was no longer holding her whip in her hand. She was holding a small, square wooden box instead. Serena hopped up to her knees and maneuvered Zahra toward the wooden table and pressed the button on the controller that dropped objects. The box landed in front of the old woman. The woman, her face still hidden underneath the brown hood, pulled the box toward her and opened it. Serena sighed in frustration—she still could not see the box's contents.

"Excellent," said the woman, her voice as dry as tinder. "Then it is time for you to come see me."

What the hell? I thought Asher told me I was supposed to get a hint to find the final treasure or something. Go and see you? "Who *are* you?" Serena finally spoke aloud as she tried to sort through the questions in her head.

"I am Devania. And it is time for you to come see me, Zahra."

Serena dropped the controller on the floor and rose shakily after being crouched on the floor for so long. She took careful steps over to the side-table in the entranceway and picked up the card that Kirsten had given her.

"One session of Journey Magnification... with... Devania."

Serena traced the haunting, silvery words with her index finger. The hand that held the card started to tremble. Serena tried to think slowly about what it could all mean. But how could she reason through events that were clearly unreasonable? Serena's heart was pounding so hard at this point that it felt like it might break through her ribcage. She put her hand on top of her chest, closed her eyes, and tried to concentrate.

Okay... okay... okay. You can figure this out. You are not crazy. Everything has an explanation. Hell if I know what could possibly be, but there must be one. Just think. But Serena knew she was way over her quota for logical coincidences at this point, and that scared her.

A high-pitched, melodious ring pierced the dead silence of the foyer, startling Serena so much that she jumped back and stumbled over one of Drew's errant sneakers. A low-tone vibration accompanied the loud and persistent jingle. Serena searched the area for the culprit and found it—her cell phone was ringing on top of the wooden table right next to her. She scooped it up and answered it with more relief that she could believe.

"Mal? Mal, you there?"

"Oh, so you do remember my name. Not that I would know because you were supposed to call me for lunch, remember?"

"I know, I know. I'm sorry. Mal, I have to talk to you about some stuff that's happened since last night." Serena was panting from the adrenaline rush.

"Okay, no problem, slow down. Are you okay? You sound like you're on speed or something."

"I'm sorry. I know I sound weird. I'm okay—I mean I'm not okay, but I'm not on speed or drugs or anything like that, although I wish that was what was happening because what is happening is so much more crazy that being on drugs would be."

"Okay, I'm officially worried about you, Serena, especially after your passing-out episode last night. You sound like... like I don't know what. You need to eat. Let me pick you up and I'll take you to lunch so we can talk about it after we get some food in your system."

"Okay, okay. But then right after I have to go see someone right away."

"Who?"

"Devania."

"D-who? Who the hell is Devania?"

"She's the mystic who's going to do my Journey Magnification reading."

"What in the world is... Journey Magnifi— never mind. I'm on my way over. Just sit tight, okay?" Serena could hear the genuine concern in Mallory's voice coupled with the sound of her grabbing her car keys in the background.

"Okay," said Serena, finally able to take in a full breath.

"And no meditating, chanting, or burning

incense before I get there. I want to make sure you stay in this..." Mallory paused and tried to find the right word.

"Dimension?" asked Serena, reading Mallory's mind.

"Yeah, Chiquita, try to stay in this dimension 'til I get there."

"I hate to say it, Mal. But I think you're too late."

Chapter 4

"Are you *sure* this is the right place?" Mallory removed her sunglasses and leaned forward in the driver's seat to try to get a better view around Serena through the passenger side window.

Serena re-read the small print at the bottom of the blue card that she had been holding in her lap since Mallory had picked her up. They had just driven thirty miles up Highway 101, across the Golden Gate Bridge and past the town of Mill Valley, and followed the GPS directions to Seventeen Bramblewood Way.

It was not at all what Serena had expected.

Up and down the street were Spanish-inspired stucco palaces that all looked more or less the same, but this was a small New-England-style white Colonial with black shutters and a modest but lush and meticulously gardened lawn in front. The yard was in full bloom—roses, tulips, azaleas, and bougainvillea burst forward in high-spirited technicolor. A freshly painted white picket fence formed a perimeter around the front lawn.

Honeysuckle clusters poured heavily over a wooden trellis that covered a narrow pathway leading up to a Kelly green front door that was rounded at the top.

"Well hellooo, Mary Poppins," said Mallory with a snicker.

"Seriously."

Serena wished she could have disagreed with Mallory, but the truth was, the utter cute-ness of this place gave her the creeps.

"And check out that mailbox. Guess she's a big fan of butterflies. Could we be any more Hallmark?" said Mallory, pointing to the hand-painted white metal box that was covered on all sides with cheery green ivy leaves and indigo butterfly wings. *17 Bramblewood Way* had been carefully painted in black script on the bottom of the whimsical scene.

"Take a closer look," Serena said. "Those aren't butterflies."

Mallory leaned in to get a better view, but still could not see any more clearly. "What are they then? They look like butterflies to me."

"Fairies. They've got little human bodies and faces," said Serena, not sure if this was a good or bad sign.

"Well, better than a skull and crossbones, right?"

"I suppose so," said Serena uneasily. "I guess I just expected something more..."

"Gypsy-fortune-tellerish?"

"Yeah, I guess. I feel like this doesn't fit," said Serena, nervously biting her bottom lip. "Maybe we should have called first, like you said."

"Well, too late for that now. No time like the present, like *you* said. And we'll never know anything sitting here in this car all day. Remember..." Mallory paused for effect before speaking in the fakest Count Dracula voice she could muster. "She vas da one who said it vas time for you to come." Mallory raised one ghoulish eyebrow as if to say, *Vell, vat are you vaiting for?*

"I didn't say anything about her being a vampire."

"But she *could* be," said Mallory, taking her Dracula accent up a notch. "Let's see if she vants to suck your blood."

"If you're not going to take this seriously, let's turn around and go back home."

"Okay, okay," said Mallory sheepishly. "That last one was pretty bad. You know the only way I can deal with being nervous is through humor. I have no idea what to make of what you say you heard in that game, but if you believe it, I believe you."

Serena glanced back to the house and then turned back to Mallory with fresh determination in her eyes. "Okay, then. Let's do this."

Serena and Mallory got out of the car and opened the small, latched gate that led to the front door. They walked slowly and deliberately up the path. The quiet, flowering splendor of the yard almost seemed to demand that they fully take in the details. The saying "take time to smell the roses" sprang into Serena's mind.

"Hey, does this remind you of anything?" asked Mallory, nodding toward the ground. "Ever seen a pathway like this before?"

Serena looked down and stopped walking. The pathway was made out of bricks. *Yellow* bricks. Her eyes followed the pathway all the way up to the door. A *green* door. She looked back up at Mallory, who was now grinning from ear to ear, her short, auburn hair shining brightly in the sun. Serena put two and two together.

"The... Wizard... of Oz?" Serena whispered the words like she was afraid someone else would hear, even though they hadn't seen a single other person since they arrived.

Mallory began humming "We're off to see the wizard" and added a little skip to her step as she continued up the yellow path.

"Kind of strange," said Serena, pausing behind her.

"Or kinda fitting," said Mallory.

Serena rang the doorbell, and within moments, the door swung open. A tall, slender woman in her late fifties with short salt-and-pepper hair stood in the doorway with a beaming smile. She wore an elegant, light gray pants suit that was tailored to perfection. Serena was immediately reminded of an older Audrey Hepburn.

"Well, hello there. I'm so glad you could make it," said the woman, looking directly into Serena's eyes. Serena noticed that the woman's eyes were not brown, but an arresting midnight blue. Before Serena could speak, the woman extended her hand to shake Serena's.

"I am Devania. What a pleasure to finally meet you."

"Nice to meet you, too," said Serena shaking her hand. She cleared her throat and tried to sound natural and not too bewildered. "I am Serena. I umm..."

Serena felt the sharp jab of an elbow in her lower left ribs.

"And... right, yes, this is my friend Mallory." Serena gestured to her left and Mallory gave a quick "hi" salutation before shoving both hands into her pockets without saying a word. Serena could tell that Mallory was trying hard not to crack any jokes. "We hope we aren't intruding on your day."

"Well, of course not," said Devania, as if Serena's statement was completely absurd.

"You see, um... I received a gift certificate from a friend for a session of..." Serena held out the blue card that she was still gripping in her left hand. "Journey... uh... Mag-"

"Journey Magnification. Of course," said Devania. "Why don't you step into the parlor, so we can proceed with things accordingly?" She moved to the left side of the doorway and extended her right arm into the house, inviting Serena and Mallory to enter. She stood regally and continued to smile sweetly.

Serena felt herself being watched so closely by Devania that she did not want to appear to be rude by stalling. More importantly, she didn't want to appear afraid. Serena stepped inside without hesitation and Mallory followed closely behind. It was strange to see Mallory, who normally couldn't shut up, acting like a kid with stage fright.

The parlor felt like an extension of the gardens that lay outside the door. The walls were painted orange—the color of an actual orange. A round wooden pedestal table stood in the center of the room with a large floral arrangement sitting on top. The flowers had clearly come from the garden and repeated the textures, colors, and scents that lay outside the green door. The wall opposite the front door was banked by two curved mustard-yellow velvet couches. In between the couches was another single green door, again rounded on top. The shape of the two yellow couches made Serena realize that there was something weird about this room. *What was it?* It finally hit her—the room was circular.

"The room is... round," said Serena.

"Accurate observation," said Devania, looking around with satisfaction.

Serena felt her cheeks warm. "Yes, sorry... it's just that on the outside, the house looks... square."

Devania took a step toward Serena, her smile broadening. "There are many things that appear quiet different on the outside than they are on the inside, wouldn't you agree?"

Serena nodded. "Why, yes. Yes, there are."

Serena felt another nudge into her ribcage from Mallory's direction. She looked over at Mallory, who was apparently still temporarily mute, because she gestured up to the ceiling using only her eyes.

Serena looked up. A large, round stained-glass skylight filtered rays of multi-colored sunlight from above. Her jaw dropped open as she gazed up at an exquisite glass rendering of an overlapping moon and sun, intertwining colors of the deep inky blues of the night sky with the radiant gold of the sun's rays. As the sunshine poured in from above, Serena felt the colors stream down onto her face with an alluring energy that was almost tangible.

"Beautiful, isn't it?" asked Devania, breaking into Serena's reverie.

Serena realized that her mouth was hanging open and quickly snapped it shut, slightly embarrassed that she'd completely lost herself and her manners for a moment. "Yes...yes, it is. I've never seen anything like it."

"Well, I certainly hope not," said Devania,

eyes fixed on Serena. "That wouldn't do, since I designed it."

"You *designed that*?" asked Mallory incredulously, finally breaking her silence. Her head was still upturned, her mouth open as she stared at the ceiling.

"Yes, I did. I actually designed the most of the inside of the house, including the furniture. Since I work out of my home, I've found it very important that the space be..." Devania paused, a small, mischievous grin spreading across her lips. "...shall we say, perfectly suited to one's life pursuits."

Devania stood calmly, her quick eyes alternating her attention between Serena and Mallory.

Serena and Mallory slowly nodded in unison, neither sure how else to possibly reply to such an indecipherable statement and not wanting to let on that they had no idea to what Devania was referring. Serena shoved her hands down into the back pockets of her blue jeans and tried to look relaxed. She felt her armpits begin to sweat, the surest sign that her anxiety had gotten the best of her. *Great*, she thought, pressing her arms down along her sides to try and hide any stains that might begin to appear on her white t-shirt. Shifting nervously before the perfectly composed Devania, Serena already felt she was in over her head.

"Well," said Devania, clapping her hands

together as if to announce that they should move on. "Shall we get down to business, Serena? I am sure you did not come here to talk about the merits of stained glass and feng shui within home design. Are you ready to proceed with your Journey?" Devania gently clasped her hands in front of her waist and looked directly at Serena with her soft but serious dark blue eyes.

Serena looked at Devania apologetically and said, "Well, to be honest, I have no idea what that means. I'm sorry—I was given the gift without much explanation."

"Well, of course not. There couldn't possibly be, could there? It's different for everybody, and besides, it has more to do with you than with anything else," Devania said, smiling patiently.

Serena drew a complete blank as she tried to think of what to say next. She took a quick look over at Mallory. Serena didn't think it was possible, but Mallory was sweating even more than she was. Serena could even see little beads of sweat on her upper lip. Mallory's expression conveyed something along the lines of *Sorry that I can't help you...I'm just here for the ride.*

"Let me ask you this," said Devania, gracefully shifting the awkward moment. "You are here to address some aspect of your life that you are curious about, that you have questions about, is that correct?" Devania narrowed her eyes slightly as she waited for Serena to speak.

"Yes. Yes, I am." Serena was relieved to be able to finally respond without hesitation.

"Then that's all that is required." Devania held out her hand for Serena to take. "I take it you are ready, then?"

Confused or not, in over her head or not, Serena could tell from Devania's firm tone that there was only one correct response.

"Yes," said Serena. "Yes, I'm ready."

"Luminous," said Devania with a broad smile. She looked over to Mallory with an expression of kindness and concern. "And Mallory, dear friend, this may take a little while, so I want to make sure that you are as comfortable as possible and that all your needs are met as well. Please go ahead and have a seat on the couch."

Mallory sat down on one of the yellow couches without argument, giving Devania a level of reverence usually reserved for doctors in an examination room. Devania proceeded to pull out a tiny silver cell phone out of the left-hand pocket of her suit, and pushed one of the buttons. Within seconds, the green door between the two couches opened and two young women walked into the room, closing the door behind them.

Serena was struck at once by how similar they looked. Both women were dressed in simple, black cotton mandarin-styled uniforms, each with their long, dark hair neatly swept back into a bun held in place by dark wooden chopsticks. Serena could only venture to guess their ethnicities—both women looked so unidentifiably exotic to her. *Perhaps Northern African and Eurasian?* she wondered as they took their places after entering. Both women stood in front the door smiling pleasantly, apparently waiting for further instruction from Devania.

"Serena, Mallory, please allow me to introduce you to my assistants, Jasmine and Iliana," said Devania, motioning to each woman respectively.

"Welcome," both assistants said unanimously, not missing a beat.

"Hi," said Mallory, continuing to look as amazed as she did looking up at the skylight.

"Hi," said Serena. "Very nice to meet you."

"Serena will be spending some time with us today, and I would like you to please take the utmost care of her friend Mallory while she has to wait for us to return," said Devania. "Comprenez-vous?"

"Of course. It is our pleasure," said Jasmine, nodding her head to Iliana. Both women immediately went back through the green door. Moments later, Iliana returned with a small velvet stool while Jasmine brought back a large silver tray carrying a collection of bottles, jars, and pitchers filled with various liquids.

"Shall we start with some hibiscus tea and a

pedicure?" asked Iliana, looking down at Mallory with a look of hopeful anticipation.

"Or perhaps a botanical oil foot massage?" asked Jasmine, equally eager to please.

After a moment of temporary disbelief, Mallory nodded affirmatively to both assistants. "Are you kidd—I mean, yes, please —I... I mean thank you. That would be very nice," Mallory managed to stammer out. She looked at Serena and shrugged her shoulders as if to say "when in Rome," all the while grinning from ear to ear. Iliana and Jasmine did not hesitate for a second more. Iliana began setting up the footrest while Jasmine began removing Mallory's flip-flops.

"And please be sure we aren't disturbed, girls," said Devania, her tone both kind and firm.

"Of course, Devania," said Jasmine looking up, her chin set in way that confirmed that she understood her duty without question.

"Excellent. Onward, Serena?" asked Devania, giving Serena's hand an encouraging squeeze.

Serena looked back at Mallory, who was holding a glass of hibiscus iced tea with her bare feet propped up. Jasmine and Iliana were busily setting up around her with smooth precision.

"Are you gonna be okay?" Serena asked softly, a bit worried about leaving Mallory to her own devices. After all, even if these two women were a pampering spa-dream come true, they were still relative strangers in this whole kooky escapade for her benefit.

But before Serena had a chance to feel any pangs of guilt, Mallory raised her hand and started shooing her away. "Don't you worry about me. I'll be perfectly fine. Now, go. Go journey magnify." Mallory picked a strawberry up from the tray of never-ending goodies and popped it into her mouth.

"Okay," said Serena. "Thanks for being here, Mal."

"See ya after," said Mallory, just as Jasmine placed a cucumber slice on each of her eyelids.

"See ya after," said Serena.

Serena followed close behind Devania as she opened the green door and stepped through the threshold.

Chapter 5

After Serena heard the green door close securely behind her, she found herself in the last place she expected to be—outside again. Her footsteps slowed down as she reoriented herself. She looked down and found herself facing yet another yellow brick path, similar to the one leading up to the front door. This time, however, the path was completely shaded by the overhang of two large oak trees that stood majestically on either side. She looked up to discover that the path, which was at least fifty feet in length, was covered from beginning to end by a long pane of stained glass suspended from the tree branches. Serena felt in awe as she took in the details of the dreamy stained-glass masterpiece that extended out in undulating waves above the path below. *If Marc Chagall had created a magic carpet ride, it would have looked just like this*, she thought.

"Serena, dear?"

Serena was brought back to attention by Devania's soothing, clear voice. She had not realized that her pace had slowed down so much that Devania was now ahead of her and waiting at the end of the yellow path in front of another door.

"I'm sorry. I just couldn't take my eyes off of that—it's just remarkable," said Serena, pointing above her head as she slowly started walking down the path. The rays of sunlight that danced across the starburst of swirling colors somehow made her feel more buoyant, as if her cells were becoming lighter with every step. "Did you design that as well?"

"Oh, no, not that," said Devania, sighing as she looked up with a look of nostalgia in her eyes. "*That* was a gift."

"Oh. Jeez, that's some gift," said Serena, a little embarrassed afterwards that she might have sounded tactless.

"Indeed," asked Devania kindly. "Shall we proceed to the Meta House?"

"The Meta House?"

"Yes. We were in the Genesis Cottage."

"Oh, okay, sure," said Serena, already starting to feel like she was miles away from Mallory and everything familiar. "That's where we will have the... session?"

Devania broke into a high-spirited, crackling laughter. "Why, you make it sound as if you've come in for a root canal!" Serena was slightly startled by the uncharacteristic break in Devania's staid demeanor.

Feeling she had made a faux pas, Serena tried to recover. "Oh, no... I am actually...very—"

"Anxious to get out of those dreary clothes?"

"Huh?" Serena looked down at her jeans and t-shirt as she reached Devania, who had her hand on the doorknob of the next door.

"Yes, I couldn't agree more," said Devania. "Let's carry on. By the way, how are you feeling right now?"

Serena struggled to keep up with Devania's train of thought. "Well... well, actually I feel great, strangely... light. Like I'm floating or something."

"Perfectly natural," said Devania, as if she had just checked Serena's pulse.

Serena could now see that the next door was the color of glittering gold and connected to a wall covered by a thick layer of ivy. Between the camouflage of the ivy and the trees, Serena had no way of making out the shape or size of this next building. Devania opened the gold door and held it open to let Serena enter first this time.

Serena's senses ignited as she entered the Meta House. Like the Genesis Cottage, the room was circular; but this room was much larger and had the luxurious opulence of a seventeenth-century Parisian boudoir. It was covered from floor to ceiling in rich, beaded fabrics in deep shades of red, pink, purple, and gold. Soft light emanated from several crystal chandeliers that hung throughout the room at varying heights. Unlike the traditional chandeliers that Serena was accustomed to seeing, each of these had its own theme of colored crystal facets. One chandelier glittered in shades of blue, another in shades of green, and yet another in golden yellow. In the middle of the room sat a low, circular, burgundy settee as big as a king-sized bed. The most intense aspect of the room, however, was that it had the most intoxicating aroma Serena had ever smelled. She closed her eyes for a moment and tried to identify the strange mixture of heady scents. *Gardenia... cinnamon... tuberose... and black cherries... Where was it coming from?* Serena began to feel dizzy as the pungent infusion swirled around her head. She opened her eyes, took a moment to take in the room again, and thought, *I am in a real life genie-bottle.*

"This room is beautiful," said Serena softly, looking around as if she might disrupt a dream. She heard Devania's voice rise from behind her.

"Not a bad dressing room, is it?"

"Dressing room?" Serena whirled around in the direction of Devania's voice. She gasped and stumbled backwards at the sight of her.

Devania still wore grey, but she was now donned in a steely-hued velvet gown. The luxurious fabric draped dramatically from shoulder to shoulder and into long gothic sleeves that reached almost to the floor. The bottom of the gown spread out around her in a wide pool of sumptuous folds. Somehow, the gown seemed to shimmer, as if the

velvet were inlaid with diamond dust. Serena was
too dumbfounded to speak.

"One can't expect to conduct serious matters
in a business suit, can one?" said Devania with a
satisfied smile.

"How... when... um, I mean... well, I guess
not," said Serena, still wondering if she was
hallucinating.

"So let us find something more appropriate
for your Journey, shall we?" said Devania, and
motioned around her with a wave of her right arm.

Serena looked around and for the first time
noticed that the lush fabric walls of the Meta House
were banked with racks of clothes hanging from
ornate brass rods extending out from the walls.
Long, heavy robes and gowns of rich fabrics and
colors encircled them from every angle. *I'll be
damned*, thought Serena, *it IS a dressing room*. As
she continued to survey the room, her eye caught
sight of a brass rail, fashioned in the same style as
the clothing rods, which extended down part of the
wall into a mysterious hole in the floor.

Serena brought her attention back to
Devania, feeling the intensity of her gaze. "I need
to change, then?" she asked, looking down
apologetically at her jeans.

Devania slowly walked towards Serena. The
skirt of her gown billowed around her as she
moved, causing the dress to sparkle even more
brilliantly. "Yes, my dear. In your case, I think it

will help you to degonify before the magnification process."

"De—degonify?"

"Yes. Helps us to unclench ourselves from our current ego manifestation. Go ahead and pick something, my dear. There is still much to do." Devania extended her hand out toward the wall again, indicating that Serena should choose something to wear.

"But... how do I pick?"

"Well, in my opinion, for the best result you should just close your eyes and walk around the room until you are drawn to one that speaks to you. Simple as that."

Serena looked around with uncertainty. "And then what do I do when one of them—when one of them... speaks to me?"

"Well, then you will take hold of your selection."

"Okay. Okay, sure." Serena tried to sound confident and ready. "That sounds pretty easy. But how will I be able to pick one out with my eyes closed?"

Devania walked behind Serena and gently put her hand on her shoulder. "Here, my dear, let me help you get started," she said sympathetically.

Before Serena knew it, Devania had whipped a black silk scarf from out of nowhere and tied it around Serena's head, covering her eyes. She gently guided Serena towards the wall. Serena stepped forward cautiously, afraid at first that she might trip or lose her balance. She wanted to concentrate, but she wasn't quite sure on what she should be concentrating.

Okay, Serena, just breathe and walk. This is just like... meditation—yeah, like walking meditation. Except in a genie bottle. So I'll just be calm, breathe, walk, and everything will be fine... I hope.

"That's it. You are doing fine," said Devania, as if she could read Serena's thoughts. "Now just feel and listen."

Serena kept walking slowly, now completely clueless as to which direction she was heading. *Just feel and listen,* thought Serena. *Yeah, right—easy for you to say, Devania.*

"It *is* easy."

Serena stopped dead in her tracks and silently gulped. Being under a veil of darkness seemed to make her thoughts even more alarming. *Can she hear me? You've got to be kidding.*

"I assure you I am not. Now shh. Keep walking, Serena," said Devania earnestly.

"Sorry, I'll try to concentr—"

"Not *that* way."

"Then which way, Devania?" asked Serena, still moving forward with unsure, small steps.

"That was not I, my dear," said Devania.

Serena's breath halted. She was afraid to move or speak.

"*This* way."

This time, Serena heard the voice more clearly, coming from her right side. It was feminine, soft, and strangely melodic, as if two voices were being blended together. It most definitely was not Devania.

Serena pushed aside her apprehension, turned to her right, and continued to move with slow resolve. She stretched out her arms for balance as she made her way around the room. Being blindfolded made it difficult for her to be sure how far she had traveled. She slowed down, afraid that she might hit the wall.

"You are getting waaarrrmmer."

Serena was sure, now. She was hearing two soprano voices, speaking together in sweet harmony. Serena considered the statement. Actually, she *was* getting warmer. As she walked towards the voices, she felt a heat radiating out toward her, as if she were walking toward a fireplace. She continued forward, reaching out, the warmth surrounding her and kissing her face like the sun.

"Take hold," urged the voices.

Serena felt like the gentle heat was now penetrating every one of her cells. The strange lightness that she had been feeling since leaving the Genesis Cottage seemed magnified. She felt almost weightless—warm and weightless, like fire.

"Take hold, be true, and let go," the voices

beckoned.

Serena instinctively reached out with both hands and tried to take hold of whatever garment hung before her. She was startled by what she felt next beneath her palms. It was not fabric. The texture felt unfamiliar and strange. Serena wrinkled her brow and took a firm grip with both hands. Her tactile memory clicked into recognition.

"Metal," whispered Serena.

A moment later Serena's hands were empty.

"WHERE DID it go?" she asked aloud as her fingers combed futilely through the air. Serena reached forward again but found there was nothing left to grasp.

Serena dropped her hands back down to her sides. At that moment, she felt something cold and slippery brush against the insides of her arms, sending a shiver down her spine. Serena suddenly became aware that her shoulders were bare and that she no longer felt her jeans on her legs. She raised her hands up to her waist and felt the same metallic sensation she had felt just moments ago. Strings of small metallic beads dropped into her palms and in between her fingers. Serena raised her eyebrows and could feel something heavy pressing into her forehead and temples. She felt the plush carpet beneath her now-bare feet.

"I think we can take this off now."

Serena had barely processed that Devania was speaking to her before she felt the blindfold whisked away from her face. When she opened her eyes, she saw Devania standing before her, as calm as ever, with one had resting at the top of an intricately carved wooden standing mirror. Devania was surveying the length of Serena's body as if she were an architect studying a new design.

Serena followed Devania's gaze down to her own body and then up to the mirror to confirm her vision. She stood frozen and awestruck at the sight of herself.

"Hmm," said Devania, a shrewd smile spreading across her lips. "You must be tougher than I thought."

Serena nodded in dazed agreement as she took in the details of her new appearance. She tentatively lifted her hands up to her neck. It was surrounded by a soft black leather band that fit snugly, like the top of turtleneck. From the very bottom of the front and back of the wide leather neck-piece hung strings of pea-sized metal beads which cascaded down to her waist, leaving her shoulders bare. Serena felt the strings of silver beads that covered her torso with both hands. There were so many layers that the skin underneath was completely covered, and yet the hundreds of strings felt almost weightless. It felt like armor—a strange sort of elegant, fluid armor. The strings of metal beads were attached at the bottom to another broad piece of black leather that cinched around Serena's waist like a corset, covering her midriff. Serena slowly moved her hands to the bottom of her leather-bound waist, where a long skirt of alternating strips of black leather and shining silver chainmail descended gracefully from her hips and down to the floor.

"So, what do you think?" asked Devania, sounding genuinely curious.

Still staring at the mirror, Serena brought her attention back up to the top of her frame. Her hair, which previously had been gathered up into a ponytail, now fell luxuriously around her shoulders. Serena covered her mouth with both hands as her jaw dropped. An iridescent silver crown with a large, radiant emerald centered among dazzling amethyst and pink sapphire stones sat majestically on top of her head. Serena gingerly touched the crown on each side of her temples and recalled the weight she felt around her head before the blindfold was removed.

"I... I recognize this. I've seen it twice now. Something like it at my birthday party and another time when... when I was playing my sons' video game." Serena looked back to Devania expectantly.

"Interesting," said Devania, clearly pleased. "Do elaborate."

"Well, some... strange things have been happening to me. I fainted after blowing out my birthday candles, and then later I started playing this video game that my sons gave me, and... it was surreal... it was as if the characters in the game were talking to me, and one of them was you—well, not you, but her name was Devania and she said to come see me—you, I mean, or her..."

"I see. Lovely," said Devania.

"And that's lovely because... why exactly?"

"Well," said Devania, taking her hand off the mirror and walking toward Serena. "It's a sign of cosmic symmetry, which is quite exciting."

"Cosmic symmetry? And that's a good thing?"

"Yes."

"Are you... connected to the game?"

"Not that I know of," she laughed. "Not any more than that chandelier is connected to that fabric, which of course they are, since they are both energy in different forms."

Serena blinked as she tried to process the sentence. "Okay... right, I get that, but I guess this just feels like much more, somehow." Serena took another look at the magnificent crown in the mirror.

"Do you think it's possible that it's *real*?" asked Serena, pointing up to the top of her head.

"Why of course it's real, my dear. The idea is to get *closer* to reality, not further away from it. Now don't just stand there like a statue. Take a turn around and let me get a better look at you."

Serena turned around slowly, not sure how

easily she would be able to move given the fact that she was now adorned from head to toe in metal and leather. To her surprise, the garment was incredibly lightweight and comfortable. Devania seemed to be studying Serena from every angle. Serena could only guess what she was assessing.

At least a minute passed by before Devania finally spoke. "Well, I must say it suits you. How do you *feel*?"

Serena thought about it for a moment. It was hard to explain how she was feeling, even to herself. *It's a weird combination. I feel buoyant, but strong. I feel somehow cool and but fiery at the same time. I feel radiant... and somehow... more alive.* Serena hesitated before responding. She worried she would sound like an idiot admitting all these bizarre things to anyone, even someone as mystical as Devania.

"Well?" Devania's left eyebrow arched up as she prompted Serena once more.

"I feel bold." Serena surprised herself with her own confession.

Devania smiled enigmatically. "And... anything else?"

Serena recalled how she felt that very morning as she sobbed on the floor of her foyer, weak and ashamed, wiping up her snot and tears with her Christmas socks. The contrast between then and how she felt now almost made her wish... Serena bit down on her bottom lip.

"Serena?"

"I... I just wish my mother could have seen me like *this*," said Serena her eyes becoming glassy with tears. "I know that must sound stupid at my age. She died a long time ago."

"Not at all. Actually, you should know, my dear, that sometimes there are synchronicities... calls from beyond. Another dimension trying to break through to this one. It can feel like someone trying to tell you something. Or *give* you something."

"Me? Why me? I'm just a—" Serena stopped herself. She had started to say she was just a loser-divorcée-soccer-mom, but all of the sudden she thought more about her own mother. She had passed away when Serena was only nine, but before her death she was involved in some kind of international speaker circuit. Her mother used to tell her that she was a 'spirit doctor' and Serena was never sure exactly what that meant at the time. But she flew all over the world talking to academic communities, and deep down Serena always knew her mother's work was somehow very important.

Serena wasn't sure how any of that could possibly have anything to do with her life now, but she told Devania anyway, watching her eyebrows as she did.

"So, when you say something is trying to break through from another dimension, what... or *who* do you think it is?" Serena asked.

Devania took a deep breath and smiled. A look of tenderness glinted over her features as she faced Serena and took her hands into her own.

"I think..." Devania started, and then paused. "I think the next part will be greatly enhanced by your primordial strength."

"What's the next part?" At this point, Serena felt she could not be sure of anything.

"Why, your Journey Magnification. Let's begin."

"Do we begin here?" Serena pointed towards the large settee sitting in the middle of the room.

"Certainly not, my dear."

Devania lifted her arm dramatically and pointed toward the brass railing leading downward that Serena had spotted when she first entered the room.

"On to the next room, then?" Serena felt like she finally might be getting the hang of this.

"Yes. On to The Elemental Chamber."

Chapter 6

Serena stood at the bottom of the spiral staircase, rubbing the goosebumps running down her arms. The stairs had descended much, much further down than she had anticipated. The air was moist and cool, and it was so dark that she could barely make out Devania's shape as she made her way across the room. Serena stayed behind and leaned her back against the cold stone wall. She felt a damp dirt floor beneath her bare feet. The plush warmth of the Meta House seemed like a distant dream.

"Devania?" Serena called out, crossing her arms to stay warm.

Serena heard a match being struck. Within seconds a blaze of fire appeared across the room high up on the wall. She could see Devania moving swiftly along the wall, stopping at intervals to reach up to ignite blaze after blaze.

"Wow. Real torches," said Serena.

By the time the final torch was lit, the room was illuminated with a soft orange glow that instantly dispelled the chill from the air. When Devania returned to her side, Serena was no longer cold, but she stood rigidly, fixated by what had become visible in the center of the room.

In the middle of the round, dungeon-like chamber stood a large, circular stone platform that stood at least five feet high and almost ten feet wide. On one side, a set of stone steps ascended from the earthen floor to the top of the platform. It was covered by a spongy green substance that Serena could not identify. Curiosity got the best of her, and she moved away from the security of the wall so she could take a better look.

"Is that... grass?"

"Mmhmm. From an ancient forest that no longer exists on the surface of this earth."

"Ohh... gosh."

"But hopefully you have a more pressing question?" Devania looked both patient and eager at the same time.

Serena looked back to the strange grassy knoll that lay atop the raised stone area. She had never seen grass that was so intensely green—it was almost fluorescent. *What forest could this have come from?*

Serena was about to open her mouth to ask the question when she saw it. Her breath quickened as she stepped forward to ensure that she was seeing clearly. She blinked her eyes hard.

There was a ball floating in the air. What

kind, Serena had no idea, but there was definitely a spherical object, perhaps the size of a beach ball, floating high above the center of the grassy plateau. It had a shiny surface, like that of a bubble. Beneath the surface was a whirling mass of orange and blue, as if the bubble were filled with densely pigmented smoke. Serena walked cautiously to the foot of the stairs leading up to the top of the platform and stood transfixed as she gazed up at the wondrous globe.

"It looks like a miniature planet." Serena spoke barely above a whisper.

"Ahh," sighed Devania with relief. "Then you *can* see it."

"Yes—I can," said Serena, slightly confused. "Should I? I mean—doesn't everybody?"

"No, they don't. It's actually quite unusual." Devania walked towards Serena and joined her at the base of the staircase. "But I suspected that you would be... shall we say... different."

"What... what is it? A crystal ball?"

Devania leaned back and once more released a decidedly witch-like laugh. "I certainly hope not! It would be pretty unnerving to have to lie down underneath one of those, now wouldn't it?" Devania clapped her hands together and continued to cackle in amusement.

"Lie down? I have to lie down on this?" Serena pointed up at the circular bed of grass.

"Yes. You will lie down and harmonize fully

with the Alchemic Orb, and then your journey will begin. Of course, I will help you get things started." Devania smiled and paused for a moment, giving Serena a chance to grasp her instructions.

Serena looked back up at the Alchemic Orb. The swirls of orange and blue were churning with even more intensity than before, like a celestial storm. The Orb's violent energy seemed to be directed at her, almost daring her. She reached up to her forehead and touched her crown with both hands. It felt like a shield emanating protection from around her head. Serena threw her shoulders back and stood defiantly tall. She looked over at Devania and gave her a quick but resolute nod.

"Luminous. I see you are ready." Devania offered her hand to Serena to assist her climb up the stairs. "After you get to the top, lie down on the grass, directly under the Orb. Your hands should be positioned right above the heart. Keep your eyes on the Orb. Never mind me—I will have my own work to do. But I will be near at all times, my dear."

Serena took Devania's hand and began to slowly climb the staircase. She felt a warm vibration beneath her feet as she climbed, as if each stone step were electrically charged. When she got up to the fourth stair, she hesitated. She realized she would now have to let go of Devania's hand and make the rest of the climb on her own.

Serena took a look back at Devania. She saw the glimmer of the Alchemic Orb reflected in

Devania's eyes as she looked up at her. She released Devania's hand and turned back to the whirling dervish that hung above her. Serena felt the gravity and exhilaration of knowing that wherever she was going next, she was going alone.

SERENA TRIED to keep her eyes fixed above her, but found it difficult to keep still. The grass beneath her felt unnaturally soft—more like miniature feathers than blades of grass. The tickling sensation they created underneath her body was downright unnerving, and she had to try not to squirm. A fierce wind began to blow throughout the Elemental Chamber as soon as she laid down her head.

As if in tandem with the Alchemic Orb, Serena's thoughts and fears swirled ferociously through her mind. She squinted her eyes in an effort to block out everything except the Orb, the interior of which continued to churn like the most ominous of tempests. She could see her mirror image staring back at her from the Orb's shiny surface. As instructed, her palms lay calmly on her chest, but her heart jackhammered madly within her ribcage. She could not escape the eerie thought that she resembled some kind of supernatural corpse.

Serena tried to keep her mind sharp and calm. She tried to anchor her thoughts in the solid, comforting realities that she knew with certainty—

where she was, what time it was, how she had gotten to this place. But she had felt completely unmoored from all familiar parameters of time and space since entering the Meta House. *How long have I been down here?* she wondered anxiously. She tried not to panic, but a fog blanketed her mind and she could not access these reliable checkpoints.

By the time Serena had come to the conclusion that it must have been at least an hour since she had left Mallory behind, she noticed that something had changed. The wind had stopped blowing. The Elemental Chamber had become deadly silent. She could hear only the sound of her heartbeat resounding in her eardrums. Serena found the mysterious calm somehow even more disturbing than the chaos that had preceded it. She got the dreaded feeling that she had just entered the eye of a storm.

To add to her distress, the Alchemic Orb had stopped swirling. Not only had it stopped, it had turned completely black. Serena resisted the urge to sit up in order to get a better look. Instead, she squinted again, and tried to discern what was now floating above her. The Orb no longer had a shiny bubble-like surface. Although still circular in shape, it now seemed to be completely devoid of edges or physical boundaries. It was the deepest black she had ever seen—so dark that it seemed to have *depth*.

Serena thought carefully. She could not be

sure, but she felt like she had seen something like it before... somewhere. She stared into the sheer, unimaginable blackness of the Orb. Her eyes widened and flickered with recollection. She'd never seen one in real life before, but she was almost sure.

I think... I think it's... a black hole.

The strange black hole was so hypnotic that Serena was no longer distracted. She felt a penetrating calm sink into her body and her heart rate slowed. Serena continued to gaze up, locked into the magnetic pull of the black void above her, with only her thoughts to pierce the silence.

It looks like it's getting... closer. Serena's hands began to tremble. *No—no, that's not it. It's getting... it's getting bigger. Which means...*

Serena's mind went completely blank, for she had absolutely no idea what that meant. With each passing moment, the inky depths of the black hole seemed to expand. *What will happen if everything disappears and goes black? Will I be surrounded by nothingness?*

The infinite darkness continued to slowly unfold around her. Time seemed to slow down as well, until even her thoughts stopped forming in her mind. She felt that she was awake, sleeping, and dreaming all in the same moment.

But surely I'm still awake, aren't I?

She felt the sharp slap of a heavy hand hit her cheek. Blood started to flow from the side of her mouth. She then felt the sensation of the burning sun streaming into her eyes. Images of an ancient stone shrine flashed around her. Now she felt herself running. Steel swords held by masked men slashed through the air, narrowly missing her. No—now she stood on a stage made of rock, surrounded by the melody of some kind of exotic music and the smell of burning spices. She was spinning, twirling, jewelry swinging rhythmically from around her neck and ankles... She extended her arms seductively above her head and she was surrounded by a crowd of people. Dancing? Yes, she was dancing. Another shift, and now she was bowing—kneeling before a magnificent stone statue with a huge, sparkling crystal lodged in its center. Another hit, this time to the back of her head. Again her blood—this time flowing under her cheek onto the ground. Her eyes fluttered open and the only thing she could see was a gaping hole where the brilliant crystal used to be. She coughed. Blood splattered roughly from her lips. Her eyes closed and once again she was enveloped by darkness.

"SERENA, MY DEAR, please wake up."

Serena began to stir slowly as a voice gradually entered her consciousness. At first, she could not understand the words, the voice sounded muffled and far away, like a foghorn gently coaxing her to return. Serena opened her eyes and blinked in an effort to focus as blurry sunlight filled her vision. She winced, retreating from the light by turning her head away from it. At that moment, she felt a pounding ache fill her head and a shooting pain raced through the whole length of her body. She had a splitting headache.

"Ooww." Serena let out a low, guttural moan.

"Shhh. Slowly now. Don't move too quickly." Serena could hear clearly now—the distinctive, noble voice of Devania coming from somewhere above her. Devania spoke in hushed and urgent tones.

"Wh—wh—what happened?" Serena tried to sit up, but immediately felt the need to lie back down again. Not only was her head throbbing, but she felt weak, as if all the blood had been drained from her body.

"All in due time, my dear. First things first. Take a sip of this."

Serena kept her eyes closed as Devania gently lifted the back of her head and pressed the edge of a large glass goblet against her lips. As she drank, she felt a warm, tingling sensation travel into her throat and all the way down to the pit of her stomach. The relief from the potent minty brew was immediate—the pain in her head started to subside. Serena took a bigger sip and felt the strength in her arms and legs begin to return. One more sip and she was able to open her eyes. Her vision was almost clear now. Clear enough to see the distraught, uncertain face of Devania hovering above her.

"There you go," said Devania, her expression becoming slightly more relaxed. "Feeling a bit better?"

"Yes, I—I think I can sit up now." Serena pushed herself up awkwardly until she was seated upright. "Ouch," she said, realizing she had put too much weight on her hands and wrists, both of which felt sore and bruised. Serena looked around and tried to take inventory of her new surroundings. She was reclining on a plush, white chaise lounge, so wide that it seemed to be built for at least three people. A mixture of sun and shade enveloped her, for the chaise was positioned outside under a large fig tree within an enclosed garden that she hadn't seen yet. The angelic ring of a windchime called out from somewhere in the distance as a soft breeze blew through the leaves above her. Serena looked down and found that the metallic gown that she had worn in the Elemental Chamber was gone. She was now wearing a long kimono of lavishly embroidered white silk. Devania stood at her side, one hand on Serena's head, the other still holding the goblet, wearing the signature grey suit that she recognized from their first meeting.

"What happened?"

"To be honest with you, my dear," said Devania, taking a seat beside her, "that is precisely what I was about to ask you. I know it's a bit soon, but Serena, do you remember anything?"

"Well," said Serena. "I'm not sure—I mean, yes, but it's kind of jumbled up in my head. But I remember it was like I was me—I mean a different me—somewhere else. But it kept changing and it was hard to keep track of what was happening. And then..." Serena paused, unsure of whether to voice her thoughts aloud.

"Yes?"

"Well, then I—got hurt—really hurt. It was like I—like I..." Serena's voice trailed off and she and looked down, her hands beginning to tremble.

"Like *what*, Serena?" asked Devania, urgency rising once again in her voice. She took her hand to Serena's chin and gently lifted her face, forcing Serena to look at her. "I know it's difficult, my dear. But you must tell me. It may be very important."

"It was like... I died. I mean... was killed," Serena shuddered, her breath catching in her throat. She looked down at her hands, instinctively afraid to meet Devania's gaze.

Devania rose slowly from the chaise lounge. By the time Serena looked up again, she was almost ten feet away, standing with her back to Serena. This was the first time since their introduction that Devania did not look Serena straight in the eye, and the truth of this detail made her beyond uneasy.

"Devania?"

"Yes, my dear."

Devania stood motionless, still facing away.

"Are you—I mean, is everything okay?"

Devania turned around. She looked directly at Serena, her face soft and composed. Serena sighed, relieved that Devania didn't seem troubled by what she remembered. When she began to walk back towards her, however, Serena could see that Devania was not truly looking at her, but rather, seemed to be looking *through* her, as if there was something troublesome distracting her beyond Serena's physical body.

Devania leaned down and gently picked up Serena's left hand. She turned the hand over and slowly traced the lines imprinted on Serena's palm with her index finger. Serena felt an overwhelming rush of fear explode through her. She jerked her hand away as if she had just been burned.

"I'm sorry..." said Serena. "I don't know why I jumped like that... or what happened to me in there."

A look of resignation crept across Devania's face. She drew in a deep breath and then locked eyes with Serena. She gave Serena's arm a gentle squeeze and smiled.

"But everything *is* okay, right, Devania?" Serena asked once more, anxious for her assurance.

"Well..." Devania said, now sitting by Serena's side. "I guess that depends on your perspective."

"Wh-what do you mean?"

"I mean, the fact that your life is in danger is not entirely bad."

"My *life* is in danger?"

"Well, if not at this moment, in the very near future. I believe so, yes."

"So you're saying that's what the dream was telling me? That my life is in danger?" Serena's voice cracked as the volume rose to a level not quite in her control.

"I did not say it was a dream."

"Then... then what was it?" Serena's eyes darted around in panic as if she were searching around the garden for the answer. A look of comprehension swept across her face. "You mean that was *real*?"

"At one time, yes."

Serena closed her eyes and winced. Her heart was beating rapidly and her head had started aching again from the increased blood flow. She sank back into the lounge chair and rubbed her temples.

"Shhh. Take it easy, Serena." Devania held the goblet out to Serena once more, giving her another sip. "Yes, my dear, it was real. And I expect that you will remember more and more of what happened in the days ahead."

Serena felt revived by the minty concoction once again. She breathed deeply and tried to calm down enough to think clearly. Suddenly, she opened her eyes and sat up abruptly.

"What do you mean that my life being in danger is '*not entirely all bad*'? How could that *not* be all bad?" asked Serena incredulously.

"Well," said Devania with an amused smile, "it means that this particular life is going to get *much* more interesting. Only by walking through the fire of two paths—the path that you choose... and the path that is already chosen for you—will you find your truth and your greatness."

"But... how?" Serena asked, unable to hide her frustration.

"Well, what else do you remember?"

Serena closed her eyes. "Come on... come back to me," she said, clearing her mind. She slowed her breath and tried to envision The Orb spreading its darkness before her. Then she saw it—a sparkling flash of light bursting through stone. Serena jumped back, startled.

"Before I got hurt I saw... a stone. An enormous stone in a statue. And then it was gone."

"Was there anyone else there aiding you? Anyone you know?"

"You mean... like my mother?" asked Serena. "No, I think I was alone."

"Well, then, my dear," said Devania, "it seems that whatever is coming for you can only be revealed by you, and no one else. Your work has just begun."

Serena collapsed back into her chair,

thoroughly exasperated by Devania's perplexing wisdom. "Well, that's freaking luminous," she said, rolling her eyes.

Devania stood up and suppressed a chuckle, looking down at Serena with faux-disapproval.

"Devania?"

"Yes?"

"Who *are* you?"

Devania cackled as she reached up and plucked something from a branch hanging above her head. "Let's stick to finding out who *you* are, shall we? Here, my dear Serena. I think it's time to have a fig."

Chapter 7

"And then what did she say?" Mallory shouted from the kitchen. Sitting in the living room, Serena heard the popping of a cork being pulled from whatever bottle of wine Mallory had chosen to open from Serena's liquor cabinet. Not long after, Mallory rounded the corner of the couch with two glasses of her favorite Pinot. She handed one to Serena and plopped down beside her.

"She told me my life is in danger," said Serena.

"What?" asked Mallory. "Seriously? Great job, Devania. Nice way to kick you when you're down. I suppose she meant that the divorce from Tom didn't do quite enough damage? Is he coming back to finish the job? I mean, she really said that?"

"That my life is in danger and I better figure out why," said Serena, taking a small sip. She put the glass down on the coffee table and sat back in frustration.

"Yeah, but what does she expect you to do

with that? I mean didn't she tell you anything else? Like what to do next or something?"

"She said that over time, I would remember more and more from the Journey Magnification, and that eventually I'd know where to go for help and that the steps would quote 'reveal themselves,'" Serena spilled out in one breath, holding her fingers up in the form of air quotes. "Like that's sooo helpful." Serena raked her fingers through her tousled hair.

Mallory leaned back next to Serena and took another sip of wine before putting her bare feet up on the coffee table. She wiggled her freshly painted cherry-red toes.

"God, Serena... I feel terrible. There I was enjoying my free 'spa day' while you were being dragged to hell and back by some crazy conjurer. I mean, are you sure she didn't hypnotize you or something?"

Serena let out an exasperated sigh. "No, she didn't hypnotize me, Mal. She helped me get through to something... to something real."

"Serena... are you sure?"

A lit candle sat in the middle the coffee table next to Serena's wine glass. She stared at the reflection of the flame wavering in the shiny glass bowl. She could see The Orb again, churning with its dark knowledge. Serena covered her face with her hands, and leaned over with her head down above her knees.

"Serena?" said Mallory, tapping her arm. "You okay?"

"No, I'm not okay, Mal," said Serena, her head still buried in her hands. "I don't know what the hell I am." *Or who I am*, she kept to herself.

"Okay... sorry. Then I don't know. It sounds like there's nothing else you can do right now but wait, right? Unless..." Mallory paused and turned to Serena, treading carefully with her next words.

"Unless what?" asked Serena.

"Well... unless you already remember something from the journey-thingie that could help you figure out what to do next?" Mallory looked at Serena apprehensively, leaning forward in an effort to gauge her reaction.

Serena drew her fingers up to her temples and squeezed her eyes shut. "I told you. It's all jumbled up. I can only remember bits and pieces. None of it's clear or makes any sense." Serena felt a stab of guilt right after she told Mallory the white lie. Despite the fact that she knew she could trust Mallory implicitly, Serena could not help but feel like she wanted to protect her from the details and the harsh truth of what she had experienced in the Elemental Chamber.

"Well... okay then," said Mallory, giving up for now. "Then let's just lay low and try to sit tight for the rest of the weekend. I'll even help you do your never-ending pile of laundry tomorrow." She picked up Serena's glass of wine and handed it back to her. "It will be Monday before you know it. Lucky you, back to Dr. Strangelove and all his never-ending research of ancient crap."

Serena sat upright. "What did you say?"

"Ancient crap."

"Exactly." Serena closed her eyes. The image of the ancient statue with the large crystal of unimaginable size slowly resurfaced in her mind. Eyes still closed, she started grinning.

"What?" Mallory took hold of Serena's knee and started shaking it.

A few moments later Serena opened her eyes and turned to Mallory without saying a word, a smile still streaming across her face.

"*What?*" Mallory breathed out with exasperation.

"Nothing. I just remembered something."

Mallory sat up with impatience and perched herself on the edge of the sofa. "Okay... *and*?"

"Dr. Strangelove of Ancient Crap might be just the person I need right now."

Too bewildered and tired to think any more, Mallory shook her head. "Well, then," she said, lifting her glass as if to toast Serena's revelation, "if that's true..."

"Yes?"

"You're in a lot more trouble than I thought."

Serena choked out a little laugh and clinked

her glass against Mallory's. She took a healthy swallow of wine. After she was finished, she stared down at the deep burgundy liquid and tried to push away the memory of blood on her lips.

Chapter 8

Serena made every effort to walk up the marble steps that led to the front doors of Trentsdore Hall of Bennett University as if it were any other Monday morning. The familiar sound of her own quick steps on the smooth stone gave her a boost of energy and confidence that always peaked when she reached the top and looked up.

There, as always, she stopped and took a moment to read the Latin adage inscribed above the heavy wooden doors.

VERITAS NUMQUAM PERIT

On this particular morning, Serena felt compelled to translate the enduring words of the philosopher Seneca, saying them aloud.

"Truth never perishes."

She had read this phrase hundreds of times before on her way into work, but somehow the words felt different on this occasion—weighty and inexplicably laden with hidden meaning. Today, it seemed as if the words had been specifically designated for her and were now intimately connected with the day that lay before her. No, it was more—it was as if the words now gave rise to her very existence, one which had become less and less certain since her Journey Magnification.

Clutching a stack of books and papers in the crook of her left arm, she took hold of the heavy brass handle and heaved the door open. A rush of cold morning air blew in from behind her, propelling her body into the marble-floored hallway.

As she approached the door leading to the cozy set of interconnected offices that housed the small Ancient History Department, a smile crept across Serena's face. It both amused and comforted her to know that upon entering, she would be greeted with the same familiar scene she knew only too well at this point.

"Good morning, Morgan," Serena said as she opened the door to the reception area, a cramped, closet-sized space that contained little more than two wooden chairs, Morgan's small desk, and an anemic ficus tree.

"Morning, Serena," said Morgan, the department's administrative assistant, glancing up from her computer. Morgan still had her dark, curly hair up in a ponytail and her workout headband around her head from her early morning run.

"Is the Professor already in?"

"He sure is," said Morgan, taking a sip from her customary triple espresso without taking her alert, grey-blue eyes off the screen.

"Well, I better get in there then," said Serena.

"Yeah, you better. Because he certainly doesn't listen to me."

"He will," said Serena, knowing all too well the meaning behind Morgan's exasperated tone. "Just give it some time. Old habits—"

"Create fossils," interrupted Morgan. "That guy needs to pick up the pace and join the 21st century." She snickered at whatever she was reading and typed something back quickly. Serena wondered how Morgan could constantly be instant messaging, even at nine a.m. on a Monday.

"Well, see ya later," said Serena, smiling as she walked passed her. Serena couldn't help but empathize with Morgan's impatience.

"See ya," said Morgan, clicking away with one hand and taking another sip from her white cardboard cup with the other.

Just down the hallway beyond reception, she came to the office door of her boss, which stood slightly ajar. Serena had always felt that this door gave her a sort of ironic preview of things to come. The frosted glass window was etched with black magisterial letters proclaiming:

Dr. Julius LeMott, Ph.D.
Professor of Ancient History

When she pushed the door further open, however, she found the esteemed Dr. Julius LeMott in a disheveled tweed coat and half-buttoned mismatched shirt, most likely already stained with this morning's coffee. Several mountains of books and papers were piled up to his shoulders on his desk. As always, he was searching frantically for the notes that he would need to prepare for his Monday afternoon lecture. Serena could tell by the beads of sweat that had already formed underneath the wispy strands of grey hair on Dr. LeMott's nearly bald head that things were not going well.

Even though Serena stood waiting inside the archway to his office, Dr. LeMott continued to sift through papers, completely absorbed by the chaos that surrounded him. His round face was becoming red and moist with perspiration, causing his glasses to slide down to the tip of his small pug nose. Dr. LeMott was forced to push his glasses back up to the bridge of his nose with his index finger every few seconds so they didn't slide off his face completely. Giving up on the mess in front of him, he then rolled his chair back and leaned his portly body down behind his desk and started searching the remaining piles that surrounded his desk on the floor.

"Ahem."

No response. Dr. LeMott continued to search on the floor, his khaki-clad butt bobbing up and down in the air like a buoy. She tried again, this time a little louder.

"Ahem. Dr. LeMott?"

She was immediately sorry she had said anything at all. Startled, Dr. LeMott sprang back up reflexively and hit his head on the underside of his desk. He lost his balance and fell back into his chair, his glasses hanging precipitously from his left ear.

"Ouch!" He rubbed the top of his head vigorously, as if trying to remove a stain.

"I'm sorry Dr. LeMott—I didn't mean to startle you." Serena rushed towards the front of his desk. "Are you okay? Do you need any help?" Serena tried to find a place to put down the stack of paperwork that she was still holding in order to assist him. There wasn't an inch of spare space to be found on his cluttered workspace.

"Oh Mrs.—I-I mean rather Miss Rayborn!" exclaimed Dr. LeMott cheerfully as he tried in vain to collect himself by smoothing out his hair and straightening his clothes. "I-I didn't see you come in. Why, good morning, good morning. Please sit—do sit down." Dr. LeMott stood up, his face flushed with embarrassment, and extended his arm toward one of the worn leather armchairs in front of his desk, inviting Serena to take a seat. He continued to babble nervously, peppering Serena with questions, his glasses still swinging from one ear.

"How are you this morning? Is there anything I can do for you? My, you do look quite nice today if you would permit me to say so, Miss Rayborn. Quite nice. I do like that blue on you. Always a joy to see you first thing in the morning. Now then, did I ask you if you would like a cup of coffee? No, I didn't, did I? How thoughtless of me. Would you care for a cup? Or would you rather have tea? I'd be only too happy to—"

"Thank you so much Dr. LeMott," interjected Serena gently, "And good morning to you, too, but I am fine. If anything, it should be me asking you if you need anything this morning. Are you sure your head is feeling all right? Do you need any ice?"

The color in Dr. LeMott's face rose once more. He waved his pudgy fingers in the air as if he were swatting away fruit flies. "Not at all, not at all. Don't give it another moment's notice. I am fit as a fiddle. Perfectly fine, perfectly fine." Dr. LeMott gave the sides of his rotund belly a firm pat for emphasis.

"Well, then, I thought that perhaps you could use some help finding... I mean putting together your notes for today's lecture?" asked Serena, shifting her gaze down to the disorderly mess that dominated the room. She suppressed a giggle and tried to look sympathetic.

Dr. LeMott looked around his desk

sheepishly. "Ah, yes. Quite. Well, I must admit that today I could use a bit of assistance. I know my notes are right here someplace... I just had them yesterday... but I have no desire to trouble you. I know you are very busy doing the research for the segment on Ancient Urbanism..."

"No trouble at all. Why don't you take a little break and let me take a crack at it?" It was now Serena who extended her arm towards one of the leather chairs, gently but firmly suggesting that Dr. LeMott take a seat.

"Why, that is indeed kind of you Miss Rayborn, th-thank you," said Dr. LeMott as he awkwardly scooted his body around to the other side of the desk. "I do say that I don't know what I would do without you."

"No need to thank me. It's a pleasure," said Serena as she slid behind the desk, switching places with her unwieldy Professor. Serena dropped the stack of books and papers that had been burdening her arms onto Dr. LeMott's chair and leaned down to begin her own search for the missing notes.

"But you know... this is exactly the type of thing you could ask Morgan to help you with. That is her job, after all.." suggested Serena with as much diplomacy as she could muster. "And you know, Morgan's also a tech whiz—a wonder with the computer. She can help you transition over to digital files, which would make it so much easier than keeping track of so much paper..."

"Yes, I know Morgan is quite capable, but you know I'm not really comfortable with just anyone going through my work... years of research that only certain people can truly understand or appreciate..."

Serena glanced up at Dr. LeMott and gave him a knowing, cheerful smile. She had heard the Professor say this more times than she cared to count.

"Yes, I see. Well, at least think about it. Please have a seat, Professor. I'm sure this won't take very long. I know my way around here pretty well." Her long brown tousled hair fell around her shoulders as she conscientiously worked her way through each pile with systematic care. Dr. LeMott obeyed Serena's instruction and sat down.

"You know, Dr. LeMott, I know I've suggested this before... Instead of Morgan, perhaps it wouldn't be a bad idea for you to let me org—um, I mean to say, re-organize your office." Serena bent down behind the desk and continued to hunt. "It wouldn't take me much time at all and you'll be amazed how much time it will save you in the future." *How much time it will save both of us*, thought Serena as she flipped through the stacks of papers on the floor. "Do you think I can finally convince you to let me to do that?"

Dr. LeMott just sat there, dazed by the unexpected view of Serena's suspended derrière.

"Dr. LeMott? Professor?" called out Serena

from under the desk. Serena peeked over her shoulder at the Professor and was suddenly aware of what had become the object of his attention.

"Oh, yes!" shouted Dr. LeMott at an unnatural pitch. His face reddened and he looked down and began twiddling his thumbs in his lap. "I—I know I've been a bit resistant in the past, but I can't say that I don't agree with you. I mean, I know that the place could use a little straightening here and there. Although I admit I do like to keep things as they are. You know me, not one for a lot of change..."

"Yeah, you and me both," mumbled Serena as she got down on her knees to get a better look underneath the desk. "But sooner or later we've all got to..."

"Yes?" Dr. LeMott sat up to full attention.

"Got it!"

"Excuse me, Miss Rayborn?" The professor stood up and peered over the desk. Serena's hands reemerged at the edge of the desk, one gripping several sheets of heavily annotated notepaper. She pulled herself back up to standing and dramatically handed over the papers to Dr. LeMott with a look of triumph.

"Voila. I believe these are the notes you were looking for, Professor." Serena's eyes beamed with victory.

"Why yes, yes. These are the very ones I was looking for. I do thank you Miss Rayborn. Don't know—I say, I just don't know what I would do without you," Dr. LeMott said, blushing once more as he flipped through the recovered notes.

"Not at all," said Serena, as she re-collected her pile of paperwork and started walking back towards the door. "Well, I'll just let you get back to work now."

"But was there something else you wanted to say, Miss Rayborn?"

"Excuse me?"

"You were saying 'sooner or later we've all got to...' Got to what?"

"Oh, nothing really," said Serena as she shifted the load in her arms to the other hip. "I was just going to say that at some point... I mean to say that we've all got to... I guess we've all go to give into change if it's good for us."

"Right you are, Miss Rayborn." With a look of childish guilt, Dr. LeMott surveyed his disorderly domain. He let out a sigh of surrender. "Quite right. Whenever you have some spare time, I say we whip this place into shape." The Professor nodded affirmatively and rocked back and forth on his heels with enthusiasm.

"Great. I'll get started on it later this week then. You won't regret it," Serena said, giving Dr. LeMott an approving smile.

She turned around to continue out the door, but then stopped in her tracks when she realized that this just might be the opportunity she was hoping for to ask Dr. LeMott for a little help of her own. She felt uneasy as she turned back around. She had not been prepared for the chance to present itself so soon. Serena could feel a small apple form in her throat as she tried to remember the speech she had started putting together in her head last night. Professor LeMott was already seated at his desk again, squinting at the recovered notes, clearly in an effort to decipher his own handwriting. *Just bring it up casually, Serena. Casually.*

"Um, Professor? If you don't mind, I just had one other small question."

Dr. LeMott looked up expectantly, like a puppy that was just tossed an extra treat. "Why certainly, Miss Rayborn. Of course—anything at all. What is it?"

"Well, I was just wondering if... in all your extensive study of ancient history, if you ever explored, or maybe I should say traced... the use of ancient stones?"

Dr. LeMott crinkled his brow in confusion. "The use of ancient stones? What—you mean for example, like the Rosetta Stone? Well, of course such stones are of monumental import—"

"No, not exactly," Serena interrupted sweetly. "I guess I was referring more to, say, precious or semi-precious stones. Like the kind that might be found placed in statues." Serena pretended to examine her fingernails and tried to look slightly bored, as if it were any other trivial topic.

Professor LeMott's eyebrows arched up over his round mole-like eyes. "Oh, I see. *Those* kinds of stones. Well, let me see... Well, yes I guess they do come up now and again in the process of tracing the use and significance of various historical landmarks, temples, and shrines..." He put a stubby index finger up to his lips and looked up, contemplating further. "And of course they are mentioned quite frequently in historical folklore. Lots of mysticism around precious stones, you know. But I must admit that's not my area of interest or expertise. We purists tend to focus on, shall we say, the more practical aspects of ancient historical enterprise." He gave Serena a self-satisfied nod.

"Oh, I see. That makes sense, of course. Well, thank you Dr. LeMott," Serena said, trying to sound indifferent. Once again, she turned to head towards the door.

Dr. LeMott frowned, as if disappointed that he had not succeeded at impressing her. "B-b-but what I mean to say is that area of historical research is traditionally more in the domain of the Relics folks."

Serena stepped back and swung her head around. "Relics folks?"

The Professor smiled, seeming pleased to

have gained Serena's attention. "Why, yes. As in the department of Ancient Relics and Antiquities. We have one here at Bennett, you know. Well, if you can call one man a whole department."

"One man?" Serena restrained her voice and tried not to seem too eager.

"Well, he's only one man, but Dr. Riley is actually quite highly regarded—one of the best in his field. Which is why Bennett pretty much gives him free rein to do anything he wants," said Dr. LeMott, his voice dropping ever so slightly into a mumble that betrayed a tick of envy.

"I see..." Serena paused, forgetting herself as she started to think about what she would have to do next.

"Well, if you want," continued Dr. LeMott, "that is to say, if it would help in any way, I'd be only too happy to make your introduction. Always helps to have a person of, shall we say, the appropriate stature make a call to smooth the way." Dr. LeMott sat back in his chair and gave himself a grandiose pat on the chest. He beamed at Serena with an impish grin.

"Oh, thank you, Dr. LeMott," said Serena, trying to disregard how ridiculous her boss looked when he made self-aggrandizing gestures. It was like watching an obnoxious version of the white rabbit from Alice in Wonderland. She choked back another giggle. "That would be very kind of you."

"No trouble at all, no trouble at all. It's the very least I can do for you—I-I mean to say someone who has been as valuable to the department as you have been, Miss Rayborn," said Dr. LeMott, the color rising slightly in his cheeks.

"Well, thanks again. I really appreciate it." Serena turned around, hoping a graceful exit would forestall further inquiry.

"Oh, and Miss Rayborn? I hope you don't mind my curiosity... is there a particular reason you needed some information from the Relics Department? I was just wondering if it was something specific?"

Damn. So close. Serena turned around slowly to buy herself enough time to think of something plausible. *When in doubt*, she thought, *talk about the kids.*

"Oh well, you know, it's really no big deal. It's for Asher. You see, he has to pick some kind of ancient artifact and do a report about it. He's hoping to find one that once held treasure or something. He asked me to do some 'grown-up' research at the University for him. You know, to make sure that his topic is the coolest one in the class." Serena shrugged her shoulders, a dismissive smirk on her face.

"Kids," said Dr. LeMott. "Wonderful imaginations."

"Yeah, gotta love'em. I personally think mine have been playing a little bit too much *Tomb*

Raider, but I try to be as supportive of their academics as I can." Serena smiled innocently, hoping that would put an end to the subject.

"Well, good for you. No sense in keeping their feet on the ground if it's going to extinguish their love of learning."

"Exactly." Serena took a couple steps into the archway of the door.

"I'll call over to Dr. Riley right away and let him know you'll be stopping by. If there's anyone who would enjoy finding you a report topic worthy of *Tomb Raider*, it would be he."

Serena cocked her head to one side with a quizzical look. "What do you mean?"

"Well, Dr. Riley is brilliant, no doubt about it. Whether he's a realist or not is another question. But that doesn't seem to be any deterrent when it comes to book sales..." said Dr. LeMott, his gaze drifting away to another part of the room. Lost in his thoughts, the Professor seemed to forget for a moment that she was still standing there.

Serena cleared her throat.

Dr. LeMott snapped back into focus. "Well, no matter, no matter," he said as he started flipping through his rolodex for the number. "But I just feel I should warn you that Riley can be a bit... on the *Dungeons and Dragons* side, if you get my meaning." He raised a disapproving eyebrow.

"Got it," Serena nodded and gave him a thumbs up to confirm.

She closed the office door behind her and leaned against the wall with a sigh of relief. *This is good. Progress. Well, maybe. Sort of.*

She laughed silently to herself as she replayed Professor LeMott's "warning" in her head. *Dungeons and Dragons? I'm already there, Professor.*

Chapter 9

Serena pressed her ear up against the door into Hamilton Hall to make sure class was still in session. According to her trusty graduate course schedule, Ancient Artifacts and Modern Technology would be in progress for another ten minutes. Serena had mulled it over all day, and she thought this would be the best way to determine whether she would even bother approaching Dr. Riley at all. *No sense in making a complete fool of myself.* No, she decided, if she did not get a good vibe from him during his lecture, she would find some other way to get some answers. She could hear a male voice, a rather husky but gentle one, speaking rapidly. She could not understand a word being said—they ran together into one indistinguishable murmur. She pushed the door open and prepared to make a beeline to the first available seat in the back row.

She was in luck. Upon entering, she immediately spotted an empty seat just to right of the long middle aisle that led down to the front of the small, rather intimate lecture hall. She quickly tiptoed over to the seat. In spite of her efforts to be as stealthy as possible, her seat let out a loud squeak as soon as she at down. A couple of female graduate students further down on the same row looked up briefly at Serena, but they were so engrossed in their note-taking that they barely seemed to register her presence. Serena tucked her purse onto her lap and sank down into her chair, hoping to make herself as inconspicuous as possible.

The lecture, which she could now hear clearly, was being given by a guy in low-slung jeans and a form-fitting white t-shirt. He faced a large whiteboard and was drawing, with what seemed like incredible speed and accuracy, a diagram of some kind of ancient structure. His face was obscured from view, but Serena could already see from his bronzed arms and lean, muscular back that he was all wrong. He was too young.

"And so, in 1961, archaeologists digging at the Palatine Hill in Rome uncovered a previously unknown room. In a niche of this room there was a painting, the subject of which was so startling that no explanation satisfactory to any system of belief has yet been offered." He turned around to make sure his audience was still following.

You've got to be kidding me, thought Serena. Not only was this guy too young, but he was waaaay too good looking. Serena shifted uncomfortably in her seat.

"The painting itself, believe it or not, depicts in its center what appears to be a modern spacecraft—a rocket, in fact. It stands on a launching pad, and cables appear to be running from it. There is a tall wall in the background, the purpose of which is unclear," he continued, now facing his students.

Serena continued to take physical inventory. Height: around six feet. Weight: about one-seventy. Face: Abercrombie and Fitch meets James Dean. His t-shirt and jeans, hip and modern, gave him a slight rock n' roll air. She looked down at his feet: well-worn Adidas sneakers. His rich, dark hair had a stylized unkemptness that could only be described as sexy. He could not be more than twenty-eight years old. Looking at this guy was like watching some daytime soap opera star *pretend* to play the part of a professor. Serena surveyed the class. Male or female, they were all riveted. They seemed to be actually buying that this guy was legitimate.

"So of course, the big question is what exactly was it that the Roman artist painted? Was it imagination? Was it reality? Why a picture of a rocket ship would appear on the wall of a hidden room dating from ancient times is, of course, anybody's guess. But, curiously, there may be many more links between places of worship and space travel than one might first dare to think..." He glanced down at his watch and gave a sigh of regret, "and judging by the time, I guess we'll have to save that controversial discussion for the beginning of our next class. Have a great week, everyone. I'll be reachable via email if you have any questions about your term paper outlines."

The energy of the lecture hall shifted instantly as the fifty or so students began closing their notebooks and packing up their backpacks. The room suddenly became noisy with the sound of desktops being stowed and students standing up to leave. She heard the sound of laptops clicking closed in various parts of the room. Before she knew it, the two graduate students to her right were heading her way so they could exit the row. She had forgotten how quickly students could move when class was over, like bats escaping hell. She stood up abruptly to get out of their way, and in the process, spilled the entire contents of her purse on the floor.

She winced as her wallet, cell phone, brush, tampons, pens, change, and various other random items scattered in every direction. A tube of lipstick, now free and with a mind of its own, bounced down the center aisle and landed a few feet in front of Dr. Riley.

He looked down at the object, suddenly recognized what it was, and looked upwards to locate the owner. He looked directly at Serena, clearly did not recognize her, and smiled with confused curiosity. *Perfect*, thought Serena. *Smile:*

George Clooney. The two women that were on their way out had stopped briefly to help Serena gather her things. She groaned inwardly as she thanked them and placed her personal items back into her purse. She knew there would be no way to get out of having to make an already botched introduction to Professor GQ.

Serena took one more look underneath the nearby seats before standing up to smooth her skirt. She threw her reloaded purse over her shoulder and started walking down the center aisle towards the front of the lecture room. Dr. Riley had already moved from behind the podium and was now in the process of picking up Serena's errant lipstick. Serena felt her cheeks get slightly warm. The sight of him touching one of her most personal items made her feel strangely self-conscious. She tried to shrug the feeling off by putting on one of her most self-assured faces, complete with a friendly yet impersonal smile. By the time she arrived in front of Dr. Riley, she felt composed and confident that she could deal swiftly with the situation. Unfortunately, Professor GQ was the first to speak.

"Hello." The irresistible smile again. "This must be yours?" he asked while holding the object up in front of her like a carrot. He did not attempt to hand it over.

"Yes. Yes, sorry. Spilled out while trying to get up. Thanks so much." Serena extended her hand out to retrieve the lipstick, even though it still hadn't been offered. Serena focused her line of sight down on the small object in his hand, even though she knew very well that Dr. Riley was still looking directly at her eyes. She could not help making a mental note. *Eyes: Amber.* She tried to keep her demeanor cool.

He looked back down at the lipstick and turned it over, bottom side up. "Do you mind?"

Serena's arm dropped slightly at the question. "Excuse me?"

"Do you mind if I read it to see what color it is?" The smile broadened.

"Oh. Oh, well, why of course not." Serena felt the heat in her cheeks begin to flare again. *Cheeky bastard.*

Dr. Riley brought the bottom of the lipstick closer to his face so he could zoom in on the practically microscopic words written on the bottom. His eyes flashed back up to Serena and twinkled with satisfaction.

"So?" he asked, as if the question were obvious.

"So what?" asked Serena, this time not hiding her annoyance.

"So what's the name of the color?"

"Are you really asking me the name of my own lipstick?"

"You must admit it's the best way to establish that you are the true owner." His grin softened and he waited with a look of dutiful innocence. Serena cleared her throat before answering.

"Goddess."

The corners of his eyes turned up along with a smile of approval. "Correct. Proof positive," he said before handing over the lipstick. "By the way, I am—"

"Professor Riley. Yes, I know," said Serena rather curtly, determined to regain control of the conversation. She clipped the lipstick out of his hand and shoved it back inside her purse.

"Oh, I see. Are you a student?"

"No, um, I actually work here at Bennett. My name is Serena."

"Serena..." he said and looked up as if the name rang a bell. She could see the dots connecting in his brain, his amber eyes searching for the connection. "Serena Rayborn? Dr. LeMott's research assistant?"

"Yes. I guess he called you then?"

"Yes. Yes, he did." He paused and narrowed his eyes slightly, as if surprised.

Serena read his thoughts and jumped at the opportunity to expose them. "Expected someone younger?"

He smiled, as if pleased with her for catching him. "Well, yes, maybe just a little." He paused, and a mischievous grin broke across his face before he shot back, "Expected someone older?"

Serena's professional composure gave way to laughter. "Well, yeah, I guess you could say that." She held out her hand to shake his, "Serena Rayborn, late bloomer."

"James Riley, early bloomer."

Serena paused mid shake. It was her turn for the dots to connect. "James Riley? As in, like Dr. J—"

"As in like Dr. James Kenneth Riley, the world-renowned historian and anthropologist." He paused for effect. "Yeah, he's my dad."

Serena's mouth opened without the sound 'ahhhh' actually coming out. She released his hand, embarrassed that she was still clinging to it.

"But if you don't mind, please call me James." He gave her a conspiratorial wink.

"James, then," said Serena, tempted to curtsy without quite knowing why.

"So..." said James and walked back behind the podium to collect his jacket and notebook. "Dr. LeMott mentioned that you wanted some advice about some kind of research project? He was pretty vague."

"Yes, well, um... I did not really discuss it with him. I was hoping, that is to say I thought..." Serena stopped mid-sentence and tried to quickly reconsider her options. She watched James' movements carefully as he shrugged on a trendy black leather jacket. *Thought you would be a hell of a lot less attractive*, she thought, finishing the sentence in her head. *But still, he* is *the son of the great Dr. James Kenneth Riley, for goodness sake. And if the apple doesn't fall far from the tree...*

"Thought... what?" asked James, now standing in front of her again. His perfect eyes blinked at her expectantly.

"Thought you could perhaps give me some guidance about how to research a subject that I think might be related to your field." She swallowed hard, not sure what else she should say at this point.

"What's the subject?"

"Well, that's the thing. I'm not entirely sure myself. But I do know that there's a large stone that I'd like try to trace the origin of." Serena tried to keep her tone even and serious.

"A stone? Huh. What kind?" James took a small step forward, his focus a bit more intense.

"Well, it might be a crystal. Or a big... a big diamond. I'm not sure of that either." Serena stopped again so she could carefully formulate her next words.

"A large diamond. Intriguing. Where did you see it?"

"Well, that's the weird part," said Serena, her voice faltering slightly.

"Did you say the *weird* part?" James cocked his head and his shiny, styled locks to one side.

"Yeah. The weird part is that I saw this

stone... or diamond or whatever... in like a dream."
Serena looked down to the tips of her shoes.
Avoiding his reaction seemed like the best course of
action right now.

"In like a dream," said James, enunciating
each word with care. His husky voice was
measured and slow.

"Yeah."

"Well in that case..." said James. He started
to walk slowly toward the exit.

I knew it, thought Serena, now looking up at
him to confirm the reaction she feared. *I sound
crazy.*

"In that case, maybe you should elaborate
while we walk and talk. I'm dying to get outside
and get some spring air." In one swift motion
James retrieved a pair of stylish aviator sunglasses
from his pocket and put them on, still walking up
the aisle.

"Sound good, Goddess?" He made a quick
motion with his head towards the door. He flashed
Serena a smile that could make a nun swoon.

Serena let out a small sigh of relief and
managed to stay on her feet. "Sounds excellent,"
she said.

THE LATE afternoon sun dipped behind the
thick foliage of the trees that surrounded the
Graduate Quad of Bennett University. As Serena
walked, a dizzying array of bikers and

skateboarders whizzed by. She was always amazed at how deftly the students seemed to book around the maze of the campus. They weaved around each other on their various forms of non-motorized transportation with the precision of the most efficient of ant farms. She let out a small sigh of contentment. The constant buzz of the campus always lifted her spirits in a way that few places could. It was the sort of eternal optimism that only a backpack full of course books and a student ID could conjure. It was written on the face of every student she passed: The future is not set. Anything is possible.

"What are you thinking?"

"What do you mean? Nothing." Serena could now see in her peripheral vision that James was watching her, but she continued to look straight ahead.

"You are smiling like you like are in on a private joke or something," James said, slowing his pace a bit.

"Joke? No it's... it's just that I like the feel of the campus. The students look so..." Serena caught sight of a young woman with long, braided auburn pigtails riding by on a pink town bike with a basket full of books. She sang happily along to a song that only she could hear through earbuds connected to a cell phone that was hooked onto her waist.

"Stressed and naïve?" asked James with a snicker.

Serena stopped in her tracks to give him a semi-stern look. She was grateful that he had on sunglasses. "Actually, I was going to say *free* and *hopeful*." She resumed walking, leaving him slightly behind. "Where would you like to sit?"

"How about over there?" asked James, pointing ahead of her and to the right.

"The Raven?"

"Yeah, I love that fountain."

"So do I," said Serena, the words slipping out before she could stop them.

"Really? So we already have one thing in common. Shall we?" asked James, heading in the direction of the fountain.

"Sure," said Serena, following his lead.

Serena and James took their seats at one of the corners of the low hexagonal cement wall that surrounded the thirty-square-foot fountain. They sat for a few moments in silence as each took in the view of the dark grey metal sculpture that rose majestically from the middle of the pool of water. Sprays of water shot through the rough-hewn planes and arches of the fifteen-foot otherworldly modern form. Serena shivered as the tactile memory of her chainmail dress suddenly clicked into her mind. Luckily, James did not seem to notice.

"So..." said James with a cool casualness before turning towards Serena and removing his sunglasses. He placed them beside him on top of the notebooks that he carried over from the lecture. "You were about to tell me more about the stone you saw in your... I believe you said, 'like a dream'?"

Serena was comforted by the fact that there was no hint of mockery in his tone, but found it unnerving to have to converse directly with James at close range. The late afternoon sunlight only served to highlight the liquid amber of his eyes and the richness of his dark brown hair. The rushing sound of the water cascading next to them made Serena feel like they were enclosed in their own little world. *Stay focused*, she reminded herself.

"Yes. You see, I was hoping to find out whether the stone I saw might have actually existed at some time, but I have very few leads to go on in terms of identifying it, and I am a bit stuck. It's really outside my field of typical ancient historical research, so I am afraid that the sources that I normally use are not really helpful. And I tried doing some research online for large white gemstones or diamonds, but the topic is too broad—of course thousands of results came up." Serena spoke quickly, hoping that by doing so she would gloss over any suspicious holes in her story.

"Professor LeMott said that looking into the origin of stones that would be found in say, statues, would be more in the 'Relics' domain. So he thought you might be able to help." Serena stopped abruptly, practically panting. She hadn't taken a single breath since she started speaking.

James narrowed his eyes slightly as he studied Serena's face. She could see him taking in her details, his eyes examining her like she was a piece of fine art. Like a painting that he was trying to determine was the original or a very good forgery. She pushed her nervousness aside and forced herself to meet his inquisitive gaze head on. She was relieved when James' cocky smile returned and he took a deep breath.

"So... anything else you want to tell me?"

"Like what?"

"Oh, I don't know, like exactly what the stone looks like and a description of the location where you saw it. Those types of little details tend to help."

"Yes, I'm sure they do. But you see the problem is I only saw it for a few seconds—not enough time to see where it was." Serena stopped short again, not quite sure what to say next.

"I see. Well, how big was it?"

"Oh, okay. Yes, of course. Hold on." Serena closed her eyes tightly. She held on to the edge of the stone wall with each hand and tried to let the image of the stone resurface within her mind. She inhaled deeply and saw the stone flashing through the darkness of her thoughts like a comet. She opened her eyes. She tried to ignore the intensity with which James was now staring at her.

"This big," she said, using both hands to

make an O-shape the size of a lemon.

"That big?" James leaned forward and used his own hands to reproduce the size.

"Yeah."

"Huh. That's big. I'd say at least a hundred carats. And you said that it was in a statue?"

"Mmhm. An ancient statue, I'm pretty sure. Maybe from Asia or South America or Africa...I don't think it was European. But I could not tell what it was a statue of. Maybe a person, or maybe some kind of animal."

"Was the stone at the bottom or the top?"

Serena closed her eyes. It came back faster this time. "The top."

"Anything else?"

Serena felt her stomach turn a bit. She was not overly anxious to close her eyes to recall the rest. She looked directly at James, studying him in very much the same way he had inspected her moments ago, unsure of what else she should confide. A light breeze blew through the fountain, blowing a spray of cold mist over them, sending a sudden chill through Serena.

"No, that's pretty much it."

"You hesitated."

"No, I didn't." Serena folded her arms protectively in front of her.

"Okay... I guess if you say so," said James, arching an eyebrow. He looked back up at the fountain, this time focused on something other than the structure. He leaned his head to one side and took his chin in his right hand, thinking. Serena wished she could make his thoughts visible. And she wished she could make the rest of him invisible. He was distractingly gorgeous.

A particularly loud skateboard whooshed behind Serena, making her jump a little. She looked back and saw the culprit zooming away, a skinny undergrad with jet-black hair streaked with electric blue throughout. He moved across the plaza with remarkable agility, made even more impressive by the fact that he was talking into a cell phone at the same time. When she turned her attention back to James, his eyes were waiting for her.

"Mind if I ask you a pretty obvious question?"

Serena swallowed hard and kept her arms tight. "Sure—I mean go ahead."

"What makes you think the stone in your dream really existed? I mean, you seem like a relatively sane person. Am I missing something here?" James' smile was roguish, but his eyes were serious.

Serena bit her lower lip a little and turned away from James to look up at the fountain. She watched the water rushing down the smooth, metal surfaces of the imposing structure. Without warning, the sound of scraping blades echoed through her brain. She blinked hard and saw swords, almost the same color and texture as The Raven, blazing past her, threatening to slice her to pieces. Since leaving Devania, she had kept her mind busy—busy trying to make plans of how she would figure this thing out. For the first time, she felt how alone she was. Tears sprang into her eyes involuntarily. Her body shuddered with fear and she looked back at James. She didn't care what his question was and she didn't care if he saw her cry. She was scared.

"Hey... hey don't worry about it. Let's pass on that question, okay?" said James, lowering his voice to a hush.

Serena nodded, her body quivering as gust of wind swept up her spine.

"You cold?" asked James.

"Yeah, I guess a little. Sun's setting."

"Here, take my jacket," said James, starting to pull one of his arms out from its sleeve.

"Oh no, you keep it on. I'm fine. But thank you."

He leaned forward and reached out for Serena's hands, both of which were still tucked up under her arms. He gently pulled apart her crossed arms and took both of her icy hands and folded them into the warmth of his.

"Cold hands," he said, giving her hands a reassuring squeeze. He smiled at her kindly and openly.

"Yeah, my hands always seem to be cold,"

said Serena, surprised that she didn't feel the need to pull them away.

"Listen..." said James, slowly releasing her hands from his grip. "I really would love to help you, but I don't think we have enough to go on. Even knowing the continent on which the statue was located might point me in the right direction. But without anything more... sorry, I just don't think so." Serena appreciated the fact that James looked sincerely apologetic.

"Oh, no worries," she said, desperately wanting to change the mood she had created. She quickly wiped the wetness from beneath her eyes with the backsides of her hands, still feeling the heat on them from his grasp. "I knew it was a long shot. Just thought I'd see if there was any way to find out more. It's really no big deal." She wished she believed it.

James gave her a knowing smile, as if he was being tolerant of her bad acting. "Well, if you remember anything else that you think might be relevant... well, please let me know. Okay?"

"I will. Thanks." Serena smiled back, anxious to move on. She'd had enough embarrassment for one day. Serena tried to think of something to say to break the awkward, tear-stained silence that now sat between them.

"Why do you think it's called 'The Raven'?" she finally forced out, pointing over to the center of the fountain.

"New topic, huh?" said James, chuckling. He looked over to the sculpture. "No one knows for sure. I've had my theories. You don't think it's an abstract interpretation of a raven?"

"No. I used to think that's what it was. But not today."

"Why?"

James watched Serena with searching eyes as she once again turned away to look up at the fountain. Another small gust of wind pushed through the Quad, sending a burst of cool spray over them. James took a moment to wipe the moisture off his brow, but Serena sat motionless, her hair swirling up wildly, enthralled by the twisted wrought-iron form before her. Suddenly, she turned back to James, her eyes wide and brimming with revelation.

"I think it's Edgar Allen Poe's poem "The Raven." It depicts an experience. A tortured one." Serena locked eyes with James, her face troubled, but certain.

James opened his mouth to speak, but then closed it again before he uttered a sound. Without taking his eyes off Serena, he nodded ever so slightly in unspoken agreement. They both turned to see the final rays of sunlight shine down onto the pool below, illuminating to each of them, for the very first time, the bright copper pennies that lay far below the surface.

Chapter 10

Serena stood in front of her refrigerator with the door open and let out a loud sigh of frustration. She knew that if Asher and Drew were there, she would have no problem having a dinner of macaroni and cheese, broccoli, and applesauce. She had realized long ago that she had neither the time nor the energy to fix separate meals, first for the kids and then for herself. So whatever the boys ate, she ended up eating. The downside to that arrangement was, of course, hitting home right this moment: she had no adult food. She had chicken nuggets, pizza bagel bites, fish sticks, and tater-tots galore, but not a single thing from which to make a respectable adult meal. She crouched down, hoping that the view from there would somehow change the situation. *Forget it*, she thought, giving up. She grabbed the already not-so-fresh loaf of bread along with the peanut butter and jelly.

As Serena spread the peanut butter on a slice of bread she felt some of the tension drain out of her shoulders. It felt good to do something routine and normal, something she had done a hundred times before for the kids. Her brain needed a break from worrying about Devania's premonition and whatever impending doom might be waiting around the corner. She let herself relax and smile as she thought of how Drew liked his sandwiches overloaded with grape jelly with the crusts cut off, whereas Asher preferred mostly peanut butter with just a smidgen of strawberry jelly. She went back to the refrigerator to find something to drink. She surveyed the collection of random photographs that covered the front door. Drew and Asher's faces—smiling, silly, proud— looked back at her and she felt a lump of longing rise in her throat. She pulled open the door and tried to think of what the boys would ask for next. She grabbed the carton of milk and poured some into an adult-sized glass.

Serena sat down on the couch in the living room, put the glass of milk on the coffee table, leaned back, and took a bite out of her PB&J. She was exhausted from all the mental energy it had taken to try not to reveal anything about the fears that had consumed her thoughts all day. She crossed her legs and took another bite. She was thankful to finally be in yoga pants and a t-shirt and to just not think for a moment.

She leaned her head back against one of the cushions and closed her eyes, but something hard poked into her left hip, making it impossible to relax. She reached down into the cushions and pulled out a hard, rectangular plastic device, opened her eyes, and sat up again. She looked down at the black GXG controller in her hand and then back up to the seemingly harmless GXG game console that sat underneath her television, both reminders that no matter how many peanut butter and jelly sandwiches she made from here on out, things were not normal anymore. She let out a small sigh of defeat.

One thing was for sure—she needed some more answers and she was running out of ideas as to where to find them. She wondered if she dare turn on the GXG and play *The Rings of Prophesy.* Perhaps Zahra would lead her in the right direction again. She reminded herself of Devania's counsel— that eventually she would find the help she needed and that the next steps would reveal themselves with time. She rolled her eyes and leaned forward to exchange her sandwich plate for the glass of milk on the coffee table. She took a huge gulp and then jumped involuntarily, splashing milk halfway up her nose. As she tried to wipe the milk off of her face and set the milk back down again, she realized what had rattled her. The doorbell was ringing.

Serena scrambled up from the couch. According to her email, UPS was finally supposed to be delivering the spring clothes that she had ordered for the kids from Land's End. She slid through the foyer and up to the front door in her socks, something she always told the boys not to do. The thought of this made her smile as she opened the door. She liked the feeling of secretly breaking her own rules. The smile, along with the blood from her face, drained away at the sight of Professor GQ standing at her doorstep.

"It's you." Serena furrowed her brow and took a step back, embarrassed that she was wearing the most unprofessional clothing she owned. She automatically attempted to brush her hand through her hair to straighten it out and realized it got worse. When she arrived home, she was lazy and had decided to pile her hair up into a messy bun. Which meant she had a huge ball of tangles on top of her head.

"Wow. I'll try not to take that reaction personally," said James, leather jacket on and smiling.

"No... I mean hi... Sorry. It's just that... what are you doing here?"

James held up a square red leather object in his hand.

"My wallet?" Serena turned and looked around for her purse. There it was, sitting on the side table in the foyer. She turned back around and looked at James again, confused.

"I assure you, it's not in there," said James, following her logic. "You accidentally left it on the floor of the lecture hall this afternoon. It must have fallen out when you dropped your bag. When the janitorial staff couldn't find a student by the name of Serena Phillips, they brought it over to me since I was the only teacher who had a class in there today."

"Serena Rayborn. Rayborn. Need to get that changed." Serena shifted uncomfortably and crossed her legs, feeling as awkward as she had in seventh grade gym class.

"Sorry. Serena Rayborn, then." James smiled as if he was going to burst out laughing at any moment. "I must say your license doesn't do you justice."

"What do you mean?"

"I prefer the milk mustache." James pointed up to his top lip and grinned even wider.

Serena could feel the temperature in her cheeks increase to what felt like one hundred and fifty degrees. Leaving the door wide open, she sprinted to the boys' bathroom, switched on the light and looked at her "Got Milk?" reflection in the mirror. She turned on the water, wet a hand towel and scrubbed the dried milk from her upper lip. She didn't know whether to laugh or cry.

When she returned a minute later, the front door was still open, but James was now waiting in the foyer. Serena walked up to him coolly, and with as much dignity as she could gather, calmly extended her hand out for her wallet.

"Hope you don't mind that I stepped inside," said James, giving her the wallet. "And sorry if I caught you off guard with the hand delivery. But I obviously did not have your phone number." James took off his sunglasses and his smile gave way to a look of contrition.

"No, not at all. Sorry I ran out like that. It's just that I was eating—oh, nevermind. Thanks for returning my wallet to me. That was really nice of you. Even if you had to violate my privacy to do it," said Serena, half-jokingly.

"Well, I couldn't very well have you driving around town without a license, after all."

"Couldn't have that on your conscience, huh?" Serena asked, putting her hands on her hips and cocking her head to one side.

"Nope." James took a quick survey around the room and looked beyond Serena into the adjoining living room. "Very cool place."

"Thanks." Serena looked around at her own surroundings and wondered what it must look like from an outside perspective. James stood in front of her, not budging, and looked at her patiently as if waiting for a cue. Serena looked towards the open front door and then back to the living room. She wondered if she still had the smell of peanut butter and jelly on her breath.

"You want to come in for a minute?" she asked tentatively, not sure what else to say without being rude.

"That would be great," said James and turned around instantly to close the front door.

Serena ran into the living room, picked up her sandwich plate and glass of milk and rushed into the kitchen to deposit them in the sink. When she returned, James was standing in the archway of the living room holding his jacket, his back to her.

"Please go ahead and have a seat," said Serena, coming around his side and stepping into the living room. "Anywhere is fine."

James took a seat on the right side of the couch and waited for Serena to join him. Serena walked slowly as she tried to figure out whether she should sit on the couch next to him or in the roomy armchair just to the left. She cupped her hand up to her mouth so she could do a quick breath check. *Chair*, she decided.

"I really like this place. How long have you lived here?"

"Oh, not long, a little less than a year. I moved in here just after my divorce." Serena pulled her legs up onto the cushion of the chair so she could sit cross-legged.

"Sorry to hear that. I mean about the divorce, not the house," said James, his voice low and kind. He sat forward, leaned on his knees with both elbows and took one more look around the room "Well, it's turned out great."

"Thanks, we like it so far."

"Kids?"

"Yeah, two boys, Drew and Asher." Serena picked up a framed photograph that sat on the wooden end table between the chair and the couch and turned it around so James could see it. "This is from Halloween last year. They were ninjas."

James leaned in closer to get a better look and his eyes became soft. "They look like you. They're beautiful." He looked back to Serena and his face flushed slightly. "I—I mean, they must be a lot fun at that age," he said, leaning back into the couch.

"Yes, they are. Twelve and seven. They are with their dad this week for Spring Break, so it's much more quiet around here than usual." Serena could not help but feel a pang of satisfaction at having seen James embarrassed for the first time.

"So," said James, his tone clearly switching the conversation in a premeditated direction, "I must admit I was hoping that I could talk to you a little more about that stone you are trying to research."

The muscles tightened in Serena's jaw. "Well, like you said, I know I need a lot more contextual information to research it properly, so don't worry about it."

"Well, that's just it. I've been thinking about it, and perhaps you have enough, but you just don't know it yet. If... that is to say, if you can remember a little more about your dream." James narrowed his eyes, his expression becoming uncharacteristically serious.

"Well, that's all I can remember about what

the stone and the statue looked like. Really."
Serena did not like the way James was looking at
her. She suddenly felt like she was sitting in the
principal's office lying about something that could
get her suspended.

"Okay. But there must be something else."
James scooted a foot closer to her on the couch and
waited patiently.

Serena looked down at her hands and
twiddled her thumbs. She could feel her throat
constricting, like someone was squeezing it closed
with a fist. She looked back up at James, his face
now a mixture of softness and hardness. Soft like
he would do anything to help. Hard like he was not
going to let it go.

Serena steadied her gaze at James and
crinkled her brow a little—she knew he did not
know what he was asking of her. The corners of
James' eyes curved upward with sympathy. He
gave her a quick nod, as if to give her the go-ahead
to jump off a diving board. Serena took a deep
breath, keeping James in her sight until her eyes
were totally closed. She exhaled, emptying her
lungs completely. She inhaled again slowly and
could feel it this time more than see it. Her arm
outstretched above her and her hips swinging
rhythmically to the right. A drumbeat reverberated
in the back of her head. Her eyes fluttered back
open.

"I think I was there. Where the stone was."

She stopped and her mouth closed like a trap door. She was breathing hard now. It felt like she had just been under water. The rest of the words felt stuck in her throat. She pushed them out. "And I think I was dancing."

To her surprise, James barely skipped a beat. "Show me."

"What do you mean 'show you'?"

"I mean, I would like to see what the dance looked like. Can you stand up and show me what you remember?"

"You're kidding."

"Hardly."

Serena smiled sweetly and then slowly shook her head from side to side. *No Way.*

"I see. Well, then let me know when you want stop being such a scaredy-cat. Then maybe I can help you," said James, visibly irritated. He arched his eyebrows up and gave Serena a look of challenge. His message was clear: *I dare you.*

Serena sat up and carefully set her feet down on the floor. She stood up tall and put her hands on her hips, indignation seeping out of her pores. She pulled a large bobby pin out from her bun and let her hair drop around her shoulders. However unruly she must have looked, she felt more protected with her hair down.

"Want to help me move this coffee table? I need more room."

James was up from his seat in seconds. He

pushed the coffee table out from the center of the room towards the french doors which led out to the back patio. By the time he got back, Serena was already standing in the center of the area rug in the middle of the room. James sat back down on the arm of the couch and waited, his eyes wide and unable to hide his anticipation. Serena looked down at her feet to establish her balance and then back up to James. She extended both arms over her head like a ballerina and gave him an affirmative nod.

"Okay, here goes," she said. Serena took a deep breath and closed her eyes.

A loud chiming sound rose up from somewhere below her head, the beat of a drum guiding the rhythm. Not only could she hear the chiming, but somehow she could also *feel* it. It felt heavy—a 'ching-ching' sound pulling down on her legs. Disorientation set in as the sounds of other instruments began to fill in the spaces in between and around drumbeats. Music, familiar and foreign at the same time, enveloped her, making her dizzy. Just then the heaviness disappeared and a lightness started to take over her body. She no longer felt lost in space, but suddenly grounded, anchored by exotic music and the singing accompanying it. Singing? Yes, there was singing. She suddenly realized that the 'ching ching' was reverberating from her. She stamped her feet rapidly and with precision: the chiming sound was being generated by her own feet. Her arms were riding the wave of the music, snaking gracefully in predetermined directions around her. She was using her hands and fingers to make gestures that were so exact that it felt like some sort of sign language. She stepped forward, back, and then around. More chinging as she lifted her left leg high into the air. Quick staccato steps found their way out of her legs and she looked up as her arms rose gracefully above her.

A glint of steel caught her eye. Before she knew it, a metal blade was falling fast from above her, perfectly positioned to make contact with her exposed neck. The sound of a scream pierced her eardrums just before she fell to the ground in a crumpled ball.

"Serena!"

Serena lifted her head up from the carpet and tried to blink her eyes back into focus. James was on his knees beside her and pulling at her, encouraging her to sit back up. Her stiff, defensive body resisted. She kept her arms hugged into her body and tucked her chin down into her chest. She was cold.

"You are shivering. Come here, let me help you up to the couch."

Serena did not move, but felt her weight propelled upwards regardless. James carried her, fetal position and all, up to the couch and sat her down. He grabbed the throw blanket that was hanging off one of the armrests and threw it around her shoulders. He sat directly in front of her, took hold of her chin, and gently pushed it up. Serena continued to look down, her body shaking.

"Look at me Serena. I need you to look at me."

Serena brought her eyes up to meet James. As much as she thought his usual cavalier appearance riled her, she hated seeing him like this, his irresistible golden-brown eyes anxiously searching her face. He put his right hand on her forehead and then gently pinched her wrist between two fingers of his left. He was taking her pulse.

"You—you don't have to do that. I'll be—"

"Shh." James continued to squeeze her wrist, fully absorbed by the counts of her heartbeat. Serena sat still and did not say another word. Finally, she could see the worry ebb away from James' face. He released her wrist and put one hand on each of her shoulders and gave them a squeeze.

"I'm sorry," said James. "I should not have asked you to do that."

"No. It's okay. I'm feeling better now."

"You sure you're okay?"

Serena nodded. She was grateful for the blanket. She was warmer now and feeling almost normal again.

"You... you screamed. Why?" James' eyes were filled with concern again. He searched her face for the answer.

Serena bit down on her lip. She was inches away from James' face. She did not want to lie to him, but she could not handle tackling the whole truth with him right now.

"I-I remembered something else. Something not good. But I don't want to talk about it right now, okay?" Serena gave James a fragile smile and hoped he would give her a temporary reprieve.

"Okay. No arguments from me right now." James took an index finger and gave her a gentle nudge at the bottom of her chin. He looked over to the center of the room, where Serena had collapsed just minutes ago. Serena could see James' mental processes flowing. A smile, the one she was so glad to see again, started to spread across his face.

"What?"

"I can help you find your stone."

"What do you mean? Did you see something? Something that made sense?" Serena sat up at full attention and looked at James anxiously. She let the blanket drop from her shoulders. She was buzzing with warmth now.

"Yup. You are quite a dancer. Incredible, really."

"I am? What did I do?"

"You danced the Bharatanatyam. Extremely well, I might add."

"The WHAT?"

"The Ba-ha-ra-ta-nat-yam. An ancient dance originally performed in temples by Devadasi."

Serena covered her face with her hands and shook her head vigorously. "You are officially giving me a headache. What does that *mean*?"

"It means—assuming the stone is ancient— that if the stone was located in the same place where you—well, let's just say right now for argument's sake that it was you that performed that dance—then that narrows down where it's located considerably." Now it was James who was out of breath.

"How narrow?" Serena got up onto her knees on the couch, her body buzzing like a neon sign. James took hold of her shoulders and gave each a gentle pull until she was completely still.

"India."

Serena did not move. The news did not give her the satisfaction she thought it would. She now had a place—a real and specific place from which to start putting together the pieces. But instead of feeling excited, she felt a heaviness begin to press down on her chest. She looked back over to the center of the room and thought of James picking her up from the carpet. She could not help but imagine what the carpet would look like if what she remembered had actually occurred right there. A dark red pool of blood seeping slowly into the beige fibers below. Blood from her death. A death that she now knew happened to her in India. Not just her death, but her *murder*. The terrible, inescapable acknowledgement made her cringe.

"Serena, you okay? This is good news, no?" James leaned over to get within her line of sight, his face bright and eager. She was grateful that James seemed to have enough enthusiasm for both of them right now. Serena managed to give him a weak smile.

"So what do you think we should do now?" she asked.

"You have a computer here?"

"Sure."

"A laptop?"

Serena nodded.

"Go get it."

SERENA STOOD waiting impatiently over the stainless steel teapot that sat on the front gas burner of her kitchen stove. She could hear the sound of James' fingers ticking away vigorously on her computer keyboard. The unbelievably rapid clicking sound was so unfamiliar that it was hard for her to believe that he was working on the very same laptop that she used every day. She looked though the archway of the kitchen that opened up into the dining room. James sat at the dining room table, his back towards her, full energy and attention on the screen in front of him. James would pause for a moment when a particular image would catch his attention for some reason, and then would continue working at lightning speed. What exactly he was looking for, she had no idea.

Serena pulled the teapot off of the stove before it had a chance to let out its angry squeal. She did not need anything to make her nerves more ragged than they already were. Having James comfortably outposted in her dining room made her nervous for some reason. She poured the water into two mugs that held silk bags of the most expensive black tea she could find in her pantry. Serena gingerly took one hot mug in each hand and headed towards the dining room to join him. She stood behind him for a moment and watched him work with the intensity of a surgeon. It was then she realized that it was the first time that a male above the age of twelve had spent more than two minutes in her new home. It was no wonder she was skittish.

"So how's it going?"

"Pretty well," said James without looking up. "It's going to take a while."

Serena put the mugs down on the oval oak table and took a seat beside him. She waved an attention-seeking hand in front of James, who was now fully absorbed in reading the small print of what appeared to be an article from the *Journal of Ancient Near Eastern Religions*.

"Care to share with the class?"

"So glad you asked. I was just about to." In

a flash, James brought up a new website page and turned the laptop towards Serena. "Go ahead and take a quick read so I can bring you up to speed."

Serena looked at the screen and frowned. "Are you kidding? *Wikipedia*?"

"Just for starters. You need the fast and dirty CliffsNotes version right now, not a dissertation. Come on, read." James nudged Serena in her arm with his elbow. She tried to ignore the slight tingle she felt from the contact with his bare skin.

Serena let out sigh. "Okay. Devadasi... originally described as a Hindu religious practice in which girls were 'married' and dedicated to a deity. Devadasi was the name given to the group of women who danced in the temple premises and who served their God through dance and music. In addition to taking care of the temple and performing rituals, they learned and practiced..." Serena stopped for moment to make eye contact with James. "Ba-ha-rata-natyam and other classical Indian arts traditions and enjoyed a high social status."

"Good. Okay. Now skip to down to here," said James pointing toward the bottom of the screen.

"The popularity of devadasis seems to have reached its pinnacle around the tenth and eleventh century AD. The rise and fall in the status of devadasis can be seen to be running parallel to the rise and fall of Hindu temples. The destruction of temples by invaders began during the second millennium AD, starting from the northwestern borders of the country and spreading through the whole of the country. Thereafter, the status of the temples fell very quickly in North India and slowly in South India. As the temples became poorer and lost their patron kings, and in some cases were destroyed, the devadasis—"

Serena stopped suddenly so she could read the last sentence to herself before saying it aloud. She could feel James' eyes fixed on her, but kept her eyes locked on the screen. "The devadasis were eventually forced into lives of poverty, misery, and prostitution, and in some of the worst cases, were put to death."

Serena sat back in her chair and rubbed her temples with her fingertips. She could feel a tension headache coming on. She reached forward and picked up her tea from the table and took a sip. Finally, she looked back at James, whose inquiring eyes were waiting for her to say something.

"I don't suppose there's any good news yet," said Serena flatly.

"Well, no, I guess not yet," said James, slightly deflated. "But what it *does* mean is that we have a place to start. You see, from what I can tell, it seems that there were very few temples that had idols that would have been adorned with the kind of extraordinary Varja stone like the one you describe."

"*Varja* stone?"

"Sorry. Sanskrit for diamond."

"So you think it's an actual diamond?" asked Serena, perking up. She picked up the mug of tea that she had prepared for James and passed it to him, a small peace offering for having been so snippy.

"Ha. What they say about diamonds must be true. One mention of the word and look at her smiling now," said James teasingly. "Well, I mean assuming, of course, that it really existed at all, then yes, I think it was a diamond."

"And so what kind of temple would have had a diamond like that?"

"A rich one."

"Huh?"

"One located in close proximity to a serious diamond mine," said James. "India is famous for them, as I'm sure you already know from your background in Ancient History."

"Yes... I do," said Serena. She looked around the room, turning the facts over in her mind. "You think that we can find the temple?"

"Whoa, wait a minute. The exact temple? Given that it would have been destroyed almost a thousand years ago with little to no records, I'd say probably not."

Serena sat back again despondently, her head starting to throb again. She was tired. And she was starting to feel incredibly stupid for thinking that this could possibly go anywhere. She put her right hand up to her forehead, covering her eyes. Her head literally felt too heavy to hold up anymore.

"But hey, cheer up, it's not over yet," said James.

"No?" Serena kept her hand up, but could see James through her spaces in between her fingers.

"Depending on what else emerges from that precious memory bank of yours, we might be able to narrow it down to a pretty small region. And from there, who knows." James reached over and gave Serena's shoulder a small squeeze. He pulled her hand down and away from her face and held it for a moment. "Okay?"

Serena felt something in her stomach begin to churn. She was nauseous. No, she was nervous. When she realized what the strange percolating feeling was in her gut, she gently pulled her hand away from James. He picked up his cup of tea to take a sip, uncovering a stained spot on the table from the time Asher and Drew had experimented with making a volcano. No matter how much she scrubbed and scrubbed, she had never been able to get the stain out. James gave her a fresh smile and put the cup back down, not noticing the stain at all. She loved that he didn't see the damage that she could see. *But, he would see it eventually—all of it,* she thought, her mood sinking.

She tried to settle herself by taking another sip of tea. "So what now?"

James pushed his chair back and stood up. "Now? Sleep. That's what's now. You are exhausted."

Serena blinked her heavy eyelids. "You can tell?"

"Yes, Miss Rayborn. I could tell an hour ago. You've been through a lot today and you need to get some rest, or else you're bound to get a headache."

Serena smiled broadly at James, her head already throbbing.

"In the meantime, I'll take a look at my written sources and see what else I can dig up. Can you come by my office tomorrow?" asked James as he walked into the living room to retrieve his jacket.

"Sure. I can come by after I'm done at the Ancient History Department. Around four, okay?" Serena let out a huge yawn as she shuffled into the living room behind James and watched him toss his leather jacket over his shoulder.

"Perfect," said James.

Serena noticed that even though it was long after sundown, James put his sunglasses on the top of his head like he was headed out to a barbeque. While she felt like a rumpled potato sack at this point, he still looked like a Ken doll. The words *too cool for school* came to mind. Serena trailed after

James as he walked towards the front door, her yawns now overcoming her in back-to-back waves. When he got to the front door, he spun around and looked down at Serena with the authority of a police officer.

"Rest. No more dancing," said James, playfully wagging his index finger at her.

"Yes, Sir, Professor Sir," said Serena, giving him a mock salute.

James opened the door. "See you tomorrow at four, Goddess."

James walked down the moonlit pathway towards his parked car. Even in the dark, Serena could tell was some kind of late model sports car. She squinted and tried to figure out the color and model. Black. Audi. Convertible. *Yup, fits him like a glove*, she thought. With a yawn so huge that it threatened to crack open her jaw, Serena went inside and shut the door. She heard the low rev of the engine's ignition turning over and the sound of wheels rolling away on the asphalt and out into the night.

Chapter 11

The clock on Serena's desk read 11:30 am. Only a
half hour before she was supposed to meet Mallory
for their weekly lunch-time walk around Satellite
Trail. Somehow, in the two-plus hours since she
had arrived at the University, she had not managed
to get a single thing done related to the research she
was supposed to be working on for Dr. LeMott.

Since the moment she had woken up, India,
diamonds, and death were the only things on her
mind. And so, what was intended to be a little five-
minute detour on the computer had turned into a
full-blown web-surfing session that had taken all
morning. And the worst part was that she felt like
she had gotten no closer than where she and James
had left off the night before. Sure, she now knew
quite a bit about the history of diamond mining in
India, but she was absolutely nowhere near finding
the temple that she believed sealed her fate
hundreds of years ago. The printer that sat at the
front corner of her desk continued to churn out
pages of material that she hoped would eventually

lead somewhere.

Serena was sitting in the back cubicle of the office that served as the multi-purpose workroom for research and for the teaching assistants of the Ancient History Department. Out of the four dreary cubicles, Serena usually chose one of the two rear ones because they were adjacent to a window that overlooked Bennett's sculpture garden. The sculpture garden was a source of pride for the University, not only because of its impressive collection of modern sculpture, but also because of the colorful rose trees that served as the elegant border. The view gave Serena relief from her claustrophobic work quarters—but sitting in the back also meant that there was a chance that someone would pop out from behind the partition in front of her before she noticed them. Usually this was not too much of a problem, but today she was definitely bending the rules about the appropriate use of school resources.

"Miss Rayborn, are you back there?"

Thankfully, this time Dr. LeMott had given her warning.

"Yes, Dr. LeMott, right back here," said Serena, leaning her body over the partition so he could see her. Dr. LeMott was standing just inside the doorway, both hands hooked onto either side of his jacket lapel, rocking to and fro on his feet like one of those classic toys that "Weeble Wobble, but don't fall down." Catching sight of her, Dr. LeMott smiled and gave his typical nervous and over-animated wave. Serena returned the smile, leaned back, closed the webpage she was currently printing out, and got up from her seat. Better to meet him at the door than have him heading back to check up on the non-existent progress she was making on her research into the ancient urbanism that she intended to plow through today.

"Good Morning, Professor LeMott. Just getting back from teaching your Roman Empire class?" Serena made sure her smile remained intact as she reflected on how he never ceased to amaze her with his wardrobe choices. Sometimes, she thought it was a real pity that she could not just speak her mind. *Oh Julius, how could you have possibly matched up that blue striped shirt with that green and yellow polka-dotted tie?*

"Why, yes; yes I am. I say, Miss Rayborn, you know my schedule better than I do. I hope you don't mind the interruption. I just thought I would drop by to see how you are today. When I didn't see you this morning... Well, I presumed it was because you were knee deep in all that ancient urbanism research I piled on you."

"Oh... yes... yes, I did want to get straight to work this morning. Trying to make some real headway, you know." It was times like these that Serena wished she were a much better liar.

"Of course, of course," said Dr. LeMott. "Well, don't work yourself too hard, my dear."

182

"Thank you, Dr. LeMott. I'm doing just fine." Serena felt like a kid who had just lied about cutting class. "Actually, I am on my way out to lunch right now to meet my friend Mallory. So see? No need to worry." She blinked her eyes innocently. She was laying it on so thick that she almost felt guilty.

"Oh, good. Very good to hear you won't be cooped up in here all day. Well, let me get out of your hair and let you be one your way." Dr. LeMott straightened his tie and patted his lapel once more before turning and walking out the door.

Serena let out a small sigh. On one point she was not lying. She needed to leave right now or she would be late meeting up with Mallory. She walked back to her desk to gather her things before heading to the bathroom for a quick change into shorts and sneakers.

"And oh, Miss Rayborn?" asked Professor LeMott, "Just one more thing..."

Serena picked up her purse from where it was hanging on the back of her chair and looked back towards the door. No sight of Dr. LeMott this time. He was calling to her from somewhere further down the hallway.

"Yes?"

"I was just wondering if you were able to meet with Dr. Riley, yet? I called him to make your introduction."

"Oh, yes. Yes, I did actually meet with Dr.

Rilely and he was quite helpful. Thank you so much for putting me in touch with him." Serena was careful. Her instincts told her *the less you say, the better*.

"Oh, very good. Glad I could be of assistance. Were you two able to come up with a scintillating topic for your son's report?"

Serena's heart started to drum hard within her chest. She was glad that he couldn't see her. "Oh, we're working on it. He's made some good suggestions. We'll come up with something special."

"Lovely. Lovely to hear." And just then Serena saw Dr. LeMott lean his chubby little head back into the doorway of the office. "Just out of curiosity... what did you think of him?"

It took only a second for Serena to think of the perfect generic response.

"He's rather young."

"Yes, I couldn't agree more... but quite accomplished, I suppose. Well, I say, don't let him steal you away from me," he said with a skittish laugh.

Serena felt like she was standing on a frozen lake and just heard the sound of the ice cracking under her feet. "Very funny, Dr. LeMott. Why, of course not."

"Just joking, Miss Rayborn, just joking," said Dr. LeMott, waving his hand in the doorway once more and chuckling awkwardly. "Well, please

don't let me delay you one minute more." He gave
Serena a disturbingly rodent-like smile before
waving goodbye and disappearing from view again.

Serena tiptoed to the hall and looked to the
right to make sure that Professor LeMott was
actually leaving this time around. A giggle rose
within her as she watched his body bounce down
the hall like a more durable version of Humpty
Dumpty, his shoes squeaking loudly with each
jaunty step.

SERENA AND Mallory both rejoiced when,
after climbing the steepest portion of Satellite Trail,
they caught sight of the oak-shaded picnic table
that signaled the impending reward of lunch. After
almost three miles of power walking, they were
sweating and out of breath, not to mention
ravenous.

"You asked them not to put sprouts on my
tuna, right?" asked Serena, picking up the pace as
she came within the final few feet of their usual
resting station.

"Yes, yes, I told them. And don't change the
subject," said Mallory, following close behind.

"I'm not changing the subject. I'm just
starving and you know I can't stand sprouts."

Serena sat down at the picnic table, snapped
open her water bottle, and took a generous gulp.

"Okay, then; if you're not changing the
subject, please explain why you think that this

Professor... what's his name again?"

"Riley," said Serena, restraining herself from saying *GQ*.

"Right, Riley. Why you think that if this Professor Riley finds the temple where this supposed diamond from your Journey-whatchamacallit is located, that it will help you figure out why your life is in danger? I still don't get it."

Mallory sat down on the bench next to Serena, took off her backpack, and unloaded the sandwiches that she had procured for them from the Bennett Campus Café.

"Well, I guess I don't know for sure." Serena unwrapped her sandwich and inspected it for a potential sprout invasion.

"I see..." said Mallory, removing her sunhat and sunglasses. She squinted at Serena suspiciously, her chestnut hair wet and disheveled. "And there's not some *other* reason you are in dire need of his help? Huh?"

"I see where this is going and the answer is no." Serena could see Mallory's train of thought from a mile away.

"No?"

"Stop looking at me like that. No."

"Hmm... methinks the lady doth protest too much," said Mallory before taking a big bite out of her BLT. "So what's he like, anyway?"

"What do you mean?"

"I mean like, for example, what's he look like? Hmmm?"

Serena stared down at the tuna sandwich that she was holding and continued to chew as if she had not heard the question.

"Hellllooo? Did we just go into bad cell range?" Mallory gave Serena's shoulder a hard poke. "C'mon; what's he like?"

Serena looked up and rolled her eyes, hoping she could steer Mallory in a different direction. "Mallory, please. What's that matter, anyway?"

"The usual academia fossil? Decrepit, boring, and crotchety?"

"You're awful," said Serena, looking back down and taking another tuna-filled bite. "Not exactly," she mumbled, her mouth full.

"Then exactly what?"

"Well, for starters, he's young."

"How young's young?" Mallory's blue eyes blinked wider with the alertness of a cat eyeing a milk dish.

"Maybe twenty-eight," said Serena, trying to sound indifferent.

"No way."

"Yes, way."

"Crikey. Then I don't suppose he's got grey hair yet."

"Not even close."

"And he must still be in pretty good shape."

"I think so... hadn't really noticed." The lie was so palpable, Serena thought her nose might start to grow.

Mallory took another bite and looked up as if to examine the branches of the large oak tree that was providing their umbrella of shade. Serena knew that Mallory was flipping the new information around in her head like a pancake. A Harlequin Sherlock Holmes, she would soon come back for more detail.

"Smart but dorky?" she finally asked.

"Smart but cocky," said Serena before polishing off the last bit of her sandwich.

"*Interesting.*"

"Try annoying," said Serena dismissively. She balled up the paper wrapping and took another sip of water.

"Okay... if you say so," said Mallory. "But I must say, the young Professor must be pretty interesting if he's willing to help you do all this because of Sorceress Devania and her Magic Carpet Ride." She popped the last bite of her BLT into her mouth and cracked open her Powerade.

Serena bit down on her lip and wiped the crumbs off of her lap in preparation to get up. "Ready to go?" she asked, clapping her hands and looking around impatiently.

"Waaait a minute. You didn't *tell* him?"

"Well... no. I mean, at least not yet. I told him that I was trying to do some research about a dream I had."

Mallory's mouth hung open, and her eyebrows curved up so high they looked like Mickey-D's golden arches. "*That's* what you told him?"

"Okay, listen, what the hell else was I supposed to say?" said Serena, throwing up her hands. "I'd only just met him and I didn't want him to think that I was psycho and I..." She let out a heavy sigh and sat down again on the wooden bench. "I really need his help, Mal. The stuff I remember from the journey is..." Serena fell silent and looked out toward the golden rolling hills that lay out in the distance.

"Pretty scary?" whispered Mallory.

Serena turned back and nodded slowly, her face without a trace of humor.

Mallory nodded with uneasy comprehension. "And he... he's cool with it? This supposed project to research a dream?"

"So far, yes. I think he's giving me the benefit of the doubt because I'm a historical research assistant, thank goodness."

"But you are going to tell him, aren't you, Serena? I mean if you really are in some kind of serious... oh I don't know, I guess cosmic *crisis*, I mean... don't you think you should tell him?" asked Mallory, her voice full of worry.

"I don't know. Hopefully I won't have to, depending on what else I find out. We'll see."

"When do you see him again?"

"Today at four."

"Oh, really? That soon, eh? " Mallory smiled and took an elastic out of her pocket and tied her short hair back into a mini-ponytail.

"Hey, the sooner the better, right? Like you said, cosmic crisis." Serena swung her legs over the back of the picnic table bench and stood up. "Let's go. I need to get back and get some actual work done before I go and see James."

"His name is James?"

"What?"

"Dr. Riley. You called him James."

"I did?" Serena thought for a moment. "I guess I did."

"Yup." Mallory stood up and put the trash remains from lunch in her backpack and zipped it up before swinging it onto her back. "Huh. So what kind of James is he?"

Serena took one more sip of water and snapped the top closed. "Excuse me?"

"You know what I mean. Is he a James Taylor or a James Bond?"

Serena rolled her eyes and picked up Mallory's drink. "I'm not even going to dignify that question with a response."

"Ha. I know what *that* means," said Mallory, putting on her sunglasses and baseball cap.

"Yeah. It means it's time to get going.

We're going to have to take the short-cut back."
Serena jiggled Mallory's half-empty bottle in front
of her. "Want the rest of your Powerade?"

"Yes, Serena. Shaken, not stirred."

Serena handed her the bottle and said, "He's
not even old enough to *play* James Bond."

"Oh, yeah, that's right..." said Mallory.
"Scary."

"Thanks for the reminder, Mal."

Chapter 12

For once, Serena had the luxury of being able to walk slowly. Professor LeMott had run off to his faculty meeting at three o'clock, and she knew that she would be much better off if she were already gone by the time he returned. That way there would be none of the last-minute requests that always seemed to keep her in the office just a few minutes late at the end of the day. More importantly, she would be able to avoid any questions about why she was leaving a bit early or whom she was rushing off to see. So at three-forty-five p.m., Serena closed the office door, shut off the lights to make it clear that she was gone for the day, and slipped quietly out the back exit of Trentsdore Hall.

According to the campus directory, Dr. Riley's office was located in Meade Hall, which was directly adjacent to Trentsdore, only a two-minute walk away. Suddenly, Serena found herself in the unusual position of being ten minutes early. For whatever reason, the building was relatively quiet

and sparsely populated that late afternoon. Serena
could hear only the clicking sound of her own
footsteps as she walked down the long hallway that
forked off to the right side of the main entrance.
Just before she left, she had scribbled down Dr.
Riley's office number on a yellow Post-It and stuck
it on top of the stack of notebooks and print-outs
that she now held in her arms. Serena looked down
at her hurriedly scrawled note. *Meade 135.* She
looked up at the number on the next door that she
passed on her left. 115. She slowed her pace. She
had plenty of time. Even enough time to take an
unrushed drink at the water fountain that was
coming up on her left. She was still feeling a bit
dehydrated from her mid-day walk with Mallory.
Serena switched the stack of papers over to the
other arm and balanced them on top of her left hip
as she pushed down the metal button with her right
thumb. She closed her eyes as she leaned over and
took leisurely sips. There was something about
drinking from a water fountain that she found
instantly soothing and calming. And calm is what
she needed in order to stay grounded enough to
face James again.

"Thirsty?"

Serena opened her eyes. Husky. Brash.
James.

Still leaning over, she released the button
and tried to lick her lips dry. From the trajectory of
his voice, he was standing right behind her. She

tried to remember whether she was wearing one of her "good" skirts or one of the ones that was less than flattering from the rear view. Either way, she thought, best to turn around as quickly as possible.

"Hi, Dr. Riley," said Serena as she wiped off a drop of water that was making its way down to her chin. When she turned around, she found James looking every bit his usual self, except somehow even more so today. He wore a snugly cut burgundy t-shirt, jeans, and what looked like very expensive brown leather sandals that could not possibly have been American-made.

"C'mon. James. Remember we agreed?" He took a sip from a Peet's coffee cup, the edges of his mouth upturned. Even drinking, he could smile with his own brand of mischievous delight.

"Yes, of course. James."

"You know, I have bottled spring water in my office if you'd like."

"Oh no, that's okay. I like the fountain water."

James lowered his coffee and wrinkled his sun-kissed brow. "Really? I thought no one liked fountain water."

"Well, I guess it's not the water I like. It's the... the... oh, nevermind; it's hard to explain." Serena shrugged her shoulders, suddenly feeling silly.

"No, I get you. You like the way it feels to drink from the fountain, huh? There's a certain zen-ness to it. Right?"

Serena just stood there for a moment, dumbfounded by the accuracy of James' response. His matter-of-fact acuity could be truly unnerving. Somehow, she felt foolish all over again.

"Yes... yes... actually, that's exactly it," she finally said.

"Right." James took another sip of coffee, smile unbroken. "Great to see you. Let me show you back to my office. Can I help you with that?" He reached out for the paper bundle in Serena's arms.

"Oh, no, thanks I've got it," said Serena, pulling her stack of papers a little closer to her chest. "I tried to do some more research, but I'm afraid I wasn't able to get very far. Thought I'd bring it with me anyway."

James gently pried the stack away from Serena arms. "C'mon, let me take it. My office is just down here," he said, lifting his coffee cup towards the back of the building. "I've got some stuff to show you." Serena released her grip and followed close behind James as he headed down the hall.

"So how long have you been a professor at Bennett?"

James slowed his pace for a bit so Serena could walk by his side. "Almost a year and a half now. And you? How long have you been working with Dr. LeMott?"

"Oh, for just over two years. I've been helping him research his next book."

"For over *two years*?"

"Yes, I know... that sounds like a long time. But there's quite a lot to do and Dr. LeMott has been kind enough to get the research grant extended twice so I could see the project through until the end."

James stopped walking and turned to look directly at her. "Well, I don't know about that, but it's pretty clear that he's very fond of you, if you don't mind me saying so. When he called, he went on and on about how dedicated and talented you are, and how I was supposed to... wait now, how did he say it? Oh, yeah, how I was to 'do my utmost to assist dear Miss Rayborn.'"

Serena laughed. James had nailed Dr. LeMott's formal accent to a T. She looked around and tried to ease into another subject. "I was surprised that they did not put your department in the Classics building. No wonder I haven't run into you before."

"Yes, they quote 'temporarily' decided to house me in the Anthropology building instead. Temporarily a year and a half ago. To tell you the truth, I think it's a conspiracy. I don't think they thought that I quite fit in with the other ancient history folks." James pointed to the open doorway behind Serena. "Well, anyway, here we are."

Serena turned around and looked into the

room behind her and almost gasped. "*This* is your office?"

"Yup."

"Gee, I can't imagine why they thought you wouldn't fit in, James."

Serena could not take her eyes off the opposite wall, which consisted of floor-to-ceiling windows that reached up two floors—at least thirty feet. Afternoon sunlight poured into the room and a lawn of bright green lay just on the other side of the glass, giving the impression that one could walk straight through and directly out into the spring air. Lofty eucalyptus trees could be seen interspersed around the grounds in the distance, their branches swaying in the breeze.

Serena walked inside and looked from left to right in dazed amazement. The room was enormous. She took a few steps forward and found herself in a comfy sitting area, a Mission-style chocolate leather couch banked on each side by two matching chairs. In the center stood a glass and wrought iron coffee table covered with a variety of educational journals and magazines along with a laptop that was switched on and humming with life. The whole lounge scene sat on a huge, faded Persian rug.

"So come on over here. I've dug up some stuff for you to look at."

James walked from behind Serena's right side to the center of the room and placed her papers down on a long rectangular dining table made of rich toffee-colored wood. The table was surrounded by eight tattered but once-exquisitely-upholstered lima-bean-green chairs, one placed at each end and three along each side. Strewn across the table were several stacks of books. Some were new, but most looked so old they could have been on loan from the Smithsonian Museum. Notebooks and papers of various sizes and shapes were also organized at various places along the length of the table. Two large flat-screen monitors were set up at each end of the table, connected to computers that sat on the floor discreetly below. Beyond the table, the front area of the room had two more leather chairs that faced a large black chalkboard that was covered in a strong, fluid script that Serena could now easily identify as James' handwriting.

"James, what is this place?"

"My office. Come over and have a seat and take a look at these," said James, already opening up several books in front of one of the chairs.

"I see that it's your office *now.*"

"Oh, you mean before," said James, looking around the room as if he had not considered the question in a long time. "Originally, it was built as a study lounge of sorts for the Anthropology faculty. But they abandoned the space when they rebuilt the North Wing. The new one over there is much more modern, space-efficient, and high-tech. But I knew this was the right space for me as soon as I saw it."

"No desk?"

"Nah," said James, walking around the table to check something on the computer at the end closest to the chalkboard. "I believe in working in 360 degrees, so desks don't really do it for me."

"How silly of me," said Serena, thoroughly enjoying the sight of James buzzing around in his native habitat. "And the furniture? I assume that the University didn't give you an expense account at Crate and Barrel."

"Nope. Pottery Barn."

"Seriously. What's the deal?"

James walked back over to Serena and laid a large leatherbound book on the table in front of her. "Most of this furniture used to be in my father's study. He passed some of it on to me when he moved and downsized," said James, scanning the room nostalgically. "His books alone were reason enough for me to ask Bennett for this room."

"What do you mean?"

"Turn around," said James, and pointed behind her.

Serena turned around and found herself face to face with a wall of books. She looked up and down the length of the room and stepped back so she could appreciate the sheer volume. From floor to ceiling, this side of the room was wallpapered with finely bound books—the kind of books she had only seen in the Special Collections of libraries. Old, handsome books, bound in brown, red, and black leather with pages like parchment. She walked towards the wall again and saw a particularly large volume of cracked leather that was so exquisitely worn that she could not resist reaching out and touching it. She leaned down and looked closer. The words WORLD ATLAS were emblazoned in gold along the spine. She closed her eyes and leaned forward. For some reason, she just had to know what it smelled like. She took a healthy sniff. It had the scent of a well-worn saddle.

"I used to look through that one for hours as a kid. Guess you can tell by how beat up it is. It belonged to my grandfather."

Serena turned back around. James was sitting on the edge of the table with his arms crossed, his eyes locked on her with a look of good-natured self-assuredness. In spite of his Calvin Klein demeanor, in these surroundings, James exuded an old-world sophistication that belied his youth. Serena looked back down at the atlas and its aged splendor and then back to James. It was undeniable. James had been imbued with an inherited accumulation of knowledge and resources that had given him a certain grain and finish that was unmistakably... Brahmin.

Serena walked over to the table and took a seat beside James. They both sat, arms crossed, looking up at the wall in silence.

"It's a beautiful collection, James," said

Serena softly.

"Thanks. Not that I can take much credit."

"You said your father moved. Where is he now?" asked Serena, turning towards him.

"He moved to London after he retired," said James, still looking up at the wall.

"Oh. So he doesn't teach at a university any more?"

"No. He hasn't for a few years now. But he still writes. He's in the middle of writing his, oh, I don't know, fifteenth book right now."

"Only number fifteen? Some people just have no ambition," said Serena, playfully nudging James in his ribcage with her elbow.

"Yeah, tell me about it. I actually co-authored his last book with him. Talk about a test of the father-son relationship."

"Ahhh. So that's how you got this cushy gig," said Serena, looking around the room once more. When she looked back at James, however, he wasn't smiling. His jaw was set into a hard line and there was a wounded look in his eyes. She had never seen him look like this before. A lump rose in her throat. She had stepped over a line.

"I meant... I'm sorry James... I was kidding. I of course didn't mean—" She put her hand on James' shoulder.

James stood up quickly and turned around to face the book that he had laid out for Serena to review. "That's okay. It's not like you're the first person to ever insinuate—"

"That is NOT what I was suggesting. It was just a joke. A bad one. I'm sorry." Serena searched her brain for something else to say that would not involve her sticking her foot further into her mouth. "Oh, and by the way, I happen to know that you've published two of your very own books. Not bad for a guy who's not even thirty yet."

"I see someone wasn't just researching diamonds."

"I googled you, of course."

James looked over at Serena and the edges of his mouth started to soften. By the time he turned to face her, his grimace had been replaced by a full-blown smirk. "You're one to talk anyway."

"What do you mean?"

"Well, let's just say that I'm clearly not the only one that may have a little bit of an inside track in the job department." James briefly looked her up and down from head to toe and shook his head. "Poor old Professor LeMott never stood a chance."

Serena's face suddenly felt like it was on fire. "Take that back," she said, giving his arm a strong shove.

"Why, my dear Miss Rayborn," said James, taking Dr. LeMott's accent to a whole new level of absurdity, "I do, I do say I shall need you to stay on for another year so you can help me do the alphabetizing for my index..."

"SHUT up." Serena raised up a balled fist

that threatened to come crashing down on James' head. She was trying to be serious, but she could not manage to keep a straight face.

"Okay, okay, I'm sorry, I'll stop," said James, raising his hands in mock defense.

Serena felt her face begin to return to its normal temperature. Still miffed, she gave James a little punch in the arm and placed herself squarely in front of the book he had opened. "So let's get to it, Dr. Riley. What do you have for me? This looks like quite the book of spells."

James, still smirking, came back to Serena's side and flipped through the pages of the large, rectangular book until he got to page 189.

"Not exactly," he said, pointing to the title of Chapter 9.

Serena sounded out the word in her head and took a stab at it. "What's Gol-conda?"

"Golconda was a region that was located in the present-day states of Maharashtra and Andhra Pradesh."

"Okay..."

"Central India."

"Got it."

"It's the region where India's most prized diamonds originated. First discovered there during the fourth century, and by the fourteenth century, most of the diamonds entering Europe were being mined from there. The Hope, the Koh-I-Noor, the Orlov, the Sanc, the Darya-e-Nur... they all came from the mines in this region."

"So you think that my stone—I mean the stone that I saw came from this region Golconda?"

"Possibly, but don't get excited. It's kind of a stab in the dark, but I want you to take a look. This book has some really old descriptions and sketches of some of the more prominent structures and temples from the region dating back to the eighth century. Maybe something will... come up for you." James hesitated and looked up at Serena. "I'm still not sure how this whole memory thing works, so you'll have to forgive me if I improvise a bit here."

Serena looked up at James and met his gaze. Only then did she realize how close they were— their faces were inches apart. She caught the subtle aroma of his coffee on his breath and something else emanating from his hair... mint and... patchouli?

"Well, that makes two of us, so improvise away." She looked back down at the page and traced the word Golconda with her index finger.

James walked over and grabbed the nearest chair, sliding it right behind Serena.

"Please have a seat and make yourself comfortable."

"Thanks," said Serena, caught a bit off-guard by the gentlemanly gesture. "Anything else you want me to look at?"

James reached across the table and slid two

other crackling volumes across the table towards Serena. "Well, I pulled a couple of other books that might lead us in the right direction. This one, for example, was written by Jean-Baptiste Tavernier, a French explorer and merchant who became one of the most pre-eminent diamond dealers of the seventeenth century, and one of the few to chronicle where he traveled and what he saw in detail, particularly in the Golconda region. Be careful with that one... I'm fairly certain that it should be in a museum somewhere."

Using only her index finger and thumb, she lifted the scaly brown cover. The brittle leather made the sound of dry leaves being crushed as she opened it. She looked up over her shoulder at James and gave him a small scowl.

"It's in French."

"Oui. You don't like French?"

"No, James. I don't *speak* French."

"Oh. That's okay. I can translate for you. Or I'm sure we have a more recent English translation of it somewhere around here..." James carefully lifted up the book and began to slowly leaf through the pages as if he was handling pieces of delicate lace fabric.

"You speak fluently?"

"You mean French?"

"Yes."

"Sure."

"When did you learn?"

"Hmm?" said James, barely registering the question as he continued to examine the book.

"French. When did you learn?"

"As a kid. International School of New York. We were required to become fluent in at least four languages."

"Oh, my God."

"It's really not that big a deal."

"No I mean... James... oh my God. Stop. That's it."

James froze mid-page turn and looked over to Serena, sitting to his right.

"What's it?"

Serena stood up. She took hold of James' hand, which was still suspended in mid-air holding up one of the pages, and set it down on the table. She pushed the page down slowly until it lay flat. She pointed to one of several black and white illustrations depicted on the page.

"That's it," she said, so definitively, her voice sounded almost mechanical.

"Now wait a minute, Serena, hold on. I thought Tavernier's writings might help us zero in on the region where the temple was located. In no way did I mean to suggest that there was any way..."

James took a breath and tried to speak more slowly, "You see, Tavernier only illustrated the most notable diamonds from his travels—most of which have become the most historically renowned diamonds in the world. The chance that the diamond you saw is in this book is astronomically small." James pointed to Illustration #4 on the page and shook his head from side to side, emphasizing his definitive no.

"But you are not saying that it's impossible."

"Um, actually, for our purposes that's exactly what I am trying to say."

Serena leveled a dispassionate look at James and then turned away from him abruptly. She placed her hands down on the table, one on each side of the book. She closed her eyes and sat very still, her body becoming taut and rigid, as if it had suddenly become filled with some foreign and unnatural substance. She looked alive and yet bizarrely inert at the same time.

"Serena, what are you—"

"Shhh. I know it's here. Give me a second."

"A second to what? I don't know what you are trying to do, but please believe me and don't—"

"Shh. Give me a paper and pencil. Quickly."

James let out an exasperated sigh before walking down to the end of the table and grabbing a pencil and one of his notebooks. He brought them back to Serena, who was still sitting in the chair motionless, the pads of her fingertips pressing down into the table.

"Put the pencil in my right hand and a blank page underneath," she said firmly.

James shook his head once more before

following Serena's instruction. He stood next to her quietly, crossed his arms and waited.

"Serena... you are freaking me out," said James after about thirty seconds of silence. "I can't even tell if you are breathing. If you want to write at least open your..."

But Serena's right hand had started to move. While the rest of her body remained as immobile as a marble statue, her right hand had come alive. Eyes still closed, her hand drew systematically across the page with the robotic accuracy. James leaned over and watched Serena sketch, his eyes growing more and more startled with each line she laid down. She continued feverishly, with astounding speed and detail. It was geometric. It was faceted. It was a blueprint. An exact blueprint of the cut of a diamond.

Chapter 13

Serena suddenly stopped drawing and her eyes popped open, her body coming back to life with a little jolt. To her surprise, her recall had left her energized and very lucid, instead of drained and disoriented like on previous occasions. She was proud to have controlled the shift better this time. She looked down at the yellow notebook paper that lay underneath her hand, and smiled broadly with satisfaction and awe at her own work.

"So... *now* what do you think?" she asked, but when Serena looked up to find James, he was gone. Serena looked around. No sign of him.

"James?"

"Up here."

Serena got up from her seat and turned around. "Where?"

"Here."

James was waving to Serena from the top of a ladder that stood at the upper left-hand corner of the wall of books. He had a pencil in his mouth and was making his way down to the floor, clutching a book at his side that was so thick she thought it might topple him over. James, however, snaked his way nimbly down with no problem. Upon reaching the bottom rung, he pushed off with his left foot and came sliding towards Serena along the wall, one hand still holding onto the ladder. Serena stepped back and giggled at the sight of James cruising toward her like some kind of surf-hipster-historian. Apparently, the ladder was on wheels.

"Having fun?" she asked when he finally came to rest in front of her. James hopped off the ladder and removed the pencil from his mouth.

"Almost," said James before heading straight to the table and laying the beefy black book down. With a renewed sense of purpose, he started furiously flipping pages. James took labored breaths with the turn of each page. In the middle of his search, he stopped short and looked at Serena. He placed his hand on the back of her neck.

"You okay?" he asked, giving her a concerned pat on the back.

"Yeah. Much better this time around. What's going on?"

"I want you to look at something else. Think you're up to it?"

"I think so."

"Good enough. Here," he said, pushing the thick black book in front of Serena. Serena crinkled her nose at the sight of it. If the last book looked like a book of spells, then this one looked like its evil-twin book of curses. Someone must have set fire to the cover at some point; the pages were stained a mottled brown, and the edges gnarled up like it had been though some form of hell. It smelled strange and foul, like it had been dredged up from some dark, dank place.

"Wow, where'd you get this thing? Mordor?"

"Never mind that for right now. Come on. Look through the drawings in this chapter." James took Serena's arm and pulled her closer to the table.

"What exactly am I looking for?" she asked, ignoring the quiver that was traveling down her spine.

"I can't be sure exactly. Just look." James picked up the pad of paper with Serena's picture and studied it more closely, tracing the lines with his index finger. She could only guess, but from his focused expression, it looked like he was calculating something.

"You're not going to say anything about my drawing?"

"Not yet."

Serena sat back down with a pout. She looked down at the page opened in front of her. It was covered in a language that appeared to be about as far from English as you can get.

"Sanskrit," said Serena with a sigh of frustration. She looked up at James. "If you tell me you speak Sanskrit, too, I'll kill you."

"Well, then better move on for both our sakes," said James with a smile and quick nod towards the book.

Serena kept turning the pages. Sanskrit, more Sanskrit. Really tiny Sanskrit. Then Serena finally came to a series of pictures of ornate stone buildings that were drawn in meticulous detail. Serena scanned the structures more closely. They comprised a large complex of buildings that were surrounded by a series of towering walls. The walls had numerous gates and entrances leading into the central portion of the compound. These magnificent entrances arched up high into the enclosing walls. Serena's breath slowed as she leaned down to examine the drawings more closely.

"What kind of architecture is this?" she asked, pointing to one of the large dramatic entrances.

"Hindu-Islamic," said James, peering carefully at Serena. "Why?"

"It feels familiar."

"It *feels* familiar?"

Serena looked up at James and shrugged her shoulders sympathetically. "Yes. I don't know how else to describe it. Is it some kind of fortress?"

"Sort of. Do you think you remember seeing it before?"

"No, but it reminds me of something else I remember."

"What?"

"Peacocks."

"Peacocks?"

Serena let her eyelids close slowly like curtains being drawn down over a movie screen. "Peacocks and lions. Etched into stone. Two peacocks over two lions." Serena blinked her eyes open. "That's it. But no diamond."

James ran over to one of the computer screens at end of the table towards the front of the room, grabbed a keyboard, and started typing vigorously. The screen was facing away from Serena, leaving her clueless as to what James was working on. She walked slowly over toward where James was standing, treading lightly with each step. His eyes were roving over the screen with the single-minded focus of a hunter. He was searching for something. Something specific. Suddenly, his eyes narrowed and he stopped typing altogether. His gaze flicked back up to Serena with a look of certainty. Whatever it was, he had found it.

"Come here," he said.

Serena came around the corner of the table and looked at the web page that James had opened. This time, there were no ancient renderings. It was a clear, crisp color photo. A photo of a large, ornately adorned stone doorway that curved up to a point at the top. The etchings underneath the point left Serena completely speechless. Inscribed in the rock below were two peacocks facing each other, each with a glorious fan of tail feathers. They stood majestically over two smaller lions that looked ready to do battle with each other.

"Serena?" James reached out to Serena and gently shook her arm.

"When was this taken?" asked Serena, the words tumbling out awkwardly.

"Two thousand seven. But it was built during the fourteenth century." James hesitated for a second. "You've seen it before," he said, both stating it and asking it.

Serena nodded her head. She wanted to ask more questions, but the words would not come. Her head was swimming.

James stroked her arm gently. "Serena, this is Bala Hissar Gate, the main entrance to Golconda fort, which was located in the Kingdom of Golconda in India. As you can see by this recent photo here, it very much still exists, although in ruins.

"From everything you are telling me, the diamond you saw is indeed the same diamond depicted in Tavernier's book, and it was believed to have come from a shrine in the Mahakali Temple, located inside this fort."

Serena's mind was flooded. She felt lightheaded. Her hands had begun to tremble. She clasped them together to make them stop.

"Here. Sit down," James said, gently guiding Serena back to her seat. Serena sat and looked back down at her drawing on the yellow pad of paper. She looked back up to James and then back down again.

"But how did... how did you know for sure that this was it?" she asked, pointing to her work. "This could be any number of diamonds, couldn't it?"

"No, it couldn't. The diamond that you drew is a distinct variation of a triangular Old Mine cut. It has nine main facets instead of eight, along with nine corresponding pavilion main facets," said James pointing to various parts of the blueprint. "But more importantly, and most extraordinarily, this diamond—your diamond—has a number of non-symmetrical facets scattered around its crown and pavilion. This can be one—and only one—diamond."

Serena stared down at the paper in silence. She sat back in the chair and let the all the information that James was pouring into her brain settle into cohesion.

After all the facts had clicked into place, she looked directly at James. "Does it have a name?"

James grabbed the yellow pad of paper and a pen and scribbled something in all caps below her drawing. He passed the pad to Serena and crossed his arms with a knowing smile.

Serena took the pad and after reading it, looked back up at him. She could not help feeling pleased.

"Eye of Fire," she said, smiling with gratification.

Serena looked around the room as she tried to pick out her next question. "Do we know where it is?"

"We?" asked James, smirking.

Serena rolled her eyes. "Oh, for heaven's sake, do *you* know where it is?"

"I have no idea. But given it must be one of the most infamous diamonds in the world..." said James as he walked back towards the computer. He pulled up a chair and sat down and started briskly typing again. "It shouldn't be too hard to find out."

Serena picked up the yellow pad of paper and walked over to James, once again thrown into full information-retrieval mode. She looked back down at the words he had written under her drawing. She felt a knot of anticipation grow in her stomach as she wondered where they would lead. But by the time she reached James, his look of neutral concentration had changed. He looked irritated. Actually, it was worse. He looked *pissed*.

"What is it? What's wrong?" asked Serena, putting her hand on James' shoulder and turning toward the screen to see what had disturbed him.

"You know how I just said it shouldn't be too hard to find out where it is?"

"Uhh... yeah?"

"Well, let's just say I might have been dead wrong about that."

"Why? What do you mean?" Serena peered

over James' left shoulder at the computer screen and tried to see what could have possibly deflated his enthusiasm so quickly.

"Here," said James standing up and moving aside so Serena could sit down in his place. "Take a look for yourself." He pointed to the third paragraph down on the screen.

Serena sat down and let out a small sigh before she started reading aloud.

"Nothing is known about the history of the journey of the Eye of Fire from India to the West. According to legend, in the early seventeenth century, the Sheik of Kashmir was forced to give the Eye of Fire as ransom to the Sultan of Turkey, who had abducted his beloved Princess Rasheedah. The first authenticated fact, however, about the history of the diamond is that it was part of a collection of jewels belonging to Sultan Abdul Hamid II of Turkey, the 34th Sultan of the Ottoman Empire. Discontent with the Sultan's despotic rule, however, led to a military revolution in 1908. After this revolution, the Sultan faced exile and was forced to dispatch most of his valuable jewels to Paris through a trusted agent. These jewels included the Hope Diamond..." Serena paused and took a small breath before continuing, "and the Eye of Fire."

Serena stopped reading and tried to fully absorb what she had just learned. She looked up at James, who was hovering above her right shoulder. "Can you believe this?"

"I know. Seriously Arabian Nights," said James.

Serena looked back at the screen and thought for a moment. She crinkled her brow.

"What?"

"Well... the Eye of Fire doesn't seem to be bring very good luck, does it?"

"Now that you mention it," said James, quickly re-reading the last paragraph to himself. "No, it doesn't."

"Hmm," said Serena.

"Hmm," James said, looking back down at Serena and nudging her shoulder with his own. "Keep reading," he said, as if she hadn't gotten to the good part.

Serena turned back to the screen and picked up where she had left off, this time reading a little faster. "The next time the Eye of Fire resurfaced was immediately after World War II, when it was acquired by a Dutch diamond dealer who sold it in 1946 to the renowned New York diamond dealer Steven Turlington. One year later, Mr. Turlington negotiated the sale of the diamond to Mrs. Gwendolyn Whitmoor, daughter of the famous Terrence 'Boss' Quincy, the publisher and co-founder of the *Los Angeles Herald*—"

"Okay, now skip down to here,' interrupted James, pointing to the bottom of the page.

Following James' index finger, Serena continued, "Mrs. Whitmoor, who became a recluse and was thought to have gone mad, died in her eighties. In accordance with her will, her famous collection of jewelry, including the Eye of Fire, was auctioned off, the proceeds of which were to be distributed among various charities. At this auction, the Eye of Fire was sold to an anonymous buyer for an undisclosed sum. It is thought to be one of the most highly priced diamond transactions ever known." Serena stopped speaking, but her eyes continued to scan the page.

"The Eye of Fire is still believed to be owned by the same unidentified buyer." Serena sat back in the chair and crossed her arms in a huff.

Serena looked up at James, who now also had his arms crossed and was standing a couple feet behind Serena. His face looked grim as he continued to concentrate on the screen. Serena got up from the chair and took a step back, her eyes still focused on the computer monitor.

"So nobody knows where it is? A diamond this historically significant and some anonymous buyer scoops it up and nobody knows where it is?" She threw her hands up in the air in frustration. "Well, that's just great." Serena turned to James, who was now holding his index finger up to his pursed lips. He stared down at the computer keys, deep in thought.

"What?" Serena tilted her head towards James and waved a hand in front of his face in an attempt to regain his attention. "What are you thinking?"

"Well," said James slowly. "I was thinking that just because the diamond was sold to an unknown buyer doesn't necessarily mean that no one knows where it is." James turned to Serena, a flash of wickedness in his eye. "*Somebody's* got to know *something*."

Serena bit down on her lip and followed James' train of thought. They stood together silently for a few moments before Serena walked up to the keyboard, quickly typed something into the search field, and pressed return. She scanned the screen and clicked on one of the search results at the top. She took a step back so both she and James could have a full view. The Eye of Fire, which appeared in a dazzling close-cropped color photograph, was set within a circle of small round diamonds and hung from a lavish chain of even more diamonds that were about the size of small pearls.

"So there it is," said James. "Unbelievable." He slowly turned away from the monitor and looked at Serena, whose face was transfixed as she looked at the screen. "Is that really what it looks like? It's beau—"

"Beautiful, yes," said Serena, her breath catching in her throat. She closed her eyes and gulped hard. She felt a heavy ache start to press down on her chest. A wave of prickling tension started to build out of the knots that were forming in her stomach. She opened her eyes and tried to relax as she let herself focus on the brilliance of the Eye of Fire. As each moment passed, she could see a new sparkle, a new glimmer emanate from the diamond, making it appear almost three-dimensional. She breathed deeply and felt a tingly sensation envelop her entire body. The radiant diamond sparkled so intensely she felt the urge to squint. Then she heard a strange, melodic whisper that seemed to float out from the very electricity pulsing through the LCD screen.

"Zahra," she repeated, her breath heavy behind the word.

"What?" James stepped closer to Serena's side and gently tapped her forearm. Serena continued to stare forward, still entranced. "Serena, what did you say?" James gave her left shoulder a gentle shake.

Serena blinked hard. "Nothing," she lied.

James crossed his arms again and shifted his weight to one side. He had a skeptical scowl on his face. He made it clear that he was waiting. Impatiently waiting.

Serena gulped slightly. She knew she should trust James by now, but she couldn't help feeling like this whole thing was going to push him over the edge at some point. She looked directly into James' eyes and thought that now, more than ever, she did not want him to leave her alone in this.

"Okay," said James thoughtfully, "How 'bout I tell you a secret first? Will that make it easier?" James stepped towards Serena and slowly leaned forward until he was hovering right next to her ear. She could feel his breath softly blow through her hair. She shifted uncomfortably. His smell always seemed to make her breath go shallow.

"Ready for the secret?" he asked teasingly.

Serena gave a small nod.

"You can't scare me away," whispered James. He stepped back, the corners of his mouth upturned, but his amber eyes as serious as ever. He wasn't kidding. A smile of relief unrolled across Serena's face and she felt her diaphragm relax. He had said just the right thing.

"I said... Zahra," Serena looked back towards the shining diamond on the monitor. "I'm pretty sure that's my name. Was my name. Is my name."

James did not respond. He looked at her as if he was trying to translate what she had just said into English. Serena felt the nerves in her stomach start to tighten again. To her relief, James finally spoke. He pointed toward the screen.

"You mean, then? You were called Zahra... back then?" James asked excitedly, his eyebrows arched high.

"I'm pretty sure." Serena looked down demurely. She found it easier to keep talking without looking directly at him. "Something... or *someone* has been speaking to me using that name since last Friday, which coincidentally was my birthday."

"You've... you *heard* it?"

Serena kept her focus on the intricate pattern of the Persian rug that lay underneath their feet and nodded a strong affirmative. She waited a few moments for him to respond. James said nothing. He was waiting for her to look at him. She could feel it. She looked up to find James' eyes waiting for her.

"See. Still here," he said smiling softly.

Serena stepped forward towards James, her smile broadening as she moved. To her surprise, James' body tensed visibly as she got closer. She leaned in until she was close enough to whisper into his ear. "So guess that means you are coming, then?"

"Coming?" asked James clumsily, caught off-guard. "Coming where?"

"I was thinking... how about checking out the diamond's last known address?"

"Its what?"

Serena turned abruptly and skipped back to the computer. "Which is..." Her fingers danced across the keyboard. She stopped and studied her search results. "...in southern California. Remember, it said that Gwendolyn Whitmoor was the last known owner. And according to this, her estate is in... Santa Barbara." She looked back over her shoulder and flashed James a devious grin. "Like you said, *somebody's* got to know *something*."

James looked at Serena as if she had just done a flip over his head and landed in front of him. He just stood there with his mouth half-open, his expression a mixture of shock and delight.

Serena stood up, put her hands on her hips and cocked her head to one side. "Well, what do you say Professor? " she asked sassily. "Road trip?"

It took James all of three seconds to regain his cocky composure.

"I say I'm driving."

Chapter 14

Serena was grateful the sun had finally broken
through and was burning off the fog that covered
the rural farmlands of Salinas Valley that spread
out into the distance. She watched through the car
window as the crops sped by alongside the highway
like rows of green, leafy dominos. She and James
had started out at six a.m., speeding off into a
chilly, low-lying cloud cover that made an already
tenuously sane trip seem even more hazy with
doubt. James had wanted to put the top up on the
convertible, but Serena told him no, and welcomed
the fresh air as a way to keep a feeling of clear-
headedness. Still concerned that she would be
chilled, James compromised by giving her a merino
wool blanket that he kept in his trunk, and turned
on both the heat and the seat warmers. For the last
three hours, Serena felt safe and cocooned, in spite
of the fact the James had been driving at no less
than eighty-five miles per hour. Serena pulled the
blanket from around her shoulders and stretched to
welcome the first rays of warm sunlight onto her

skin.

"Too hot?" asked James without taking his eyes off the road.

"No, I'm perfect," said Serena, stretching her arms out above her head. "It's just nice that the sun is finally coming out." She looked over at James, who had somehow known exactly how to dress for their impromptu trip to Santa Barbara. True to form, he exuded ease in a steely grey cashmere sweater topped off with a navy blue wool scarf. "What time do you think we'll get to Rosethorn Manor?"

James' eyes flickered over to the digital clock on the dashboard and then back to the speedometer. After a moment of mental calculation, he said, "I'd say in about an hour if we don't hit any traffic. By about ten a.m." James glanced over at Serena. "What time did you tell them we'd be there for the tour?"

"Well, the young woman I spoke to, Paige, said that any time before noon would be fine. According to her, Rosethorn Manor only does private tours now, and I got the distinct feeling that they are not all that busy." Serena leaned down and pulled her purse out from beneath her legs. She dug out her cell phone and studied the screen.

"Expecting a call?"

"No," said Serena, as she began typing into the tiny keyboard, "but my friend Mallory has been texting me like a fiend. I left her a message telling her I was going out of town for a day, but I guess I was a little too vague. I better get back to her before she sends out the National Guard."

"She worries, huh?"

"Yeah, she does. Especially since..." Serena stopped typing on her cell phone for a moment and looked pensively out of the window onto the rolling fields that had turned from green rows to straw-yellow strands of wheat. "The night of my birthday... the night I first saw the Eye of Fire." She could feel James eyeing her thoughtfully in her peripheral view.

"Well..." said James, "just tell her that you're doing a little field research with a *very* respectable colleague. That ought to ease her mind."

Serena rolled her eyes and let out a little snicker.

"What's so funny?"

"Oh, nothing," said Serena as she tried to hide her amusement. "It's just that I don't think there's going to be any way to convince Mallory that it's a good idea to take off to Santa Barbara with some guy that I met a day ago, regardless of how respectable he is. Sorry, James." Serena smiled. She wanted to give him a pat on the shoulder, but she held back. *Especially not a guy that looks like you and drives a car like this,* Serena mused to herself.

"First of all, I am not just *some guy*," said

James, his words dripping with fake offense. "And I'll have you know that you've known me for *two* days." James looked over at Serena with a raised take-that-smarty-pants eyebrow.

"Sorry—*two* days. I stand corrected, Professor. Forgive me." Serena gave him an even more exaggerated roll of the eyes.

"Forgiven." James put his sunglasses on to combat the morning sun and flashed her his most charming of smiles. Serena found it vaguely annoying that although the wind blew through his hair, tousling it every which way, he still looked coolly coifed. She, on the other hand, had been forced to gather her unruly mane into a ponytail hours ago. Serena felt a nervous sensation in the pit of her stomach. She rolled her eyes at him one more time for good measure in response to the feeling.

"The bigger question is what did you tell Professor LeMott? How did you manage to convince him to survive without you for an *entire day*?"

Ignoring James' sarcastic tone, Serena bit down on her bottom lip and tried not to look as guilty as she felt.

James looked over and analyzed her in a millisecond. "What? You lied?"

Serena nodded. "I called him last night and told him I was sick with some kind of stomach bug. I didn't want to, but I obviously couldn't tell him the truth, and telling him anything else would have led to too many questions. He tends to be very worried about my welfare." She looked over at James. "Plus, I'm a terrible liar. Thank goodness he couldn't see my face over the phone. And at least the kids are gone with Tom this week so I don't have to figure out how to explain all this to them, too."

James looked over at Serena sympathetically. "Yeah, you're about on par with Doris Day in the lying department." James gave a small chuckle. "By the way, I mean that in a good way."

Serena looked at James suspiciously. "*You* know who Doris Day is? Isn't that a little before your time?"

"If you hadn't noticed, before my time is my specialty." James gave her a sideline smirk. "Lucky for you."

Serena took a breath and smiled at James' bravado. Truth was, at this moment, she did feel lucky that it was James was who had decided to become her covert partner in... what, she still wasn't quite sure. A sudden burst of cold wind poured over the top of the passenger side window, sending a chill down to the tops of her feet. She pulled the blanket back up over her shoulders and snuggled back down into the warm leather seat. James accelerated a little, gripping the wheel a bit tighter. The open highway rolled towards them and

Serena felt as if they were being propelled down a solid river of blackness. Serena squinted in the morning sunlight and tried to imagine the Eye of Fire, shining at the end of the road like the sun through deep space. It dawned on her how strange it was that she should feel lucky now, of all times in her life.

SERENA LET out a sigh of relief when she finally spotted the wooden sign for Rosethorn Manor on the side of the winding country road. James turned left onto the gravel, tree-lined driveway. Serena sat up at attention as he slowed down to about ten miles per hour, which seemed unbelievably slow after the warp speed he had been driving for the past five hours. Tall trees with hand-sized leaves shaded them from either side as they ascended up a gently sloped hill, and she soaked up the energy from the vibration she felt from underneath the tires as they rolled over the small, crumbly rocks. Serena drummed her fingers along the sides of her seat, impatient to finally see the destination that had brought them all this way.

"California Sycamore," said Serena excitedly, looking up at the majestic trees passing them on either side.

James lifted up his sunglasses to the top of his head and squinted at the leaves. "Hm. Yup, I think you're right. Been moonlighting as an arborist?"

"Well, flowers are more my thing these days. But yeah, I've loved trees ever since I was a kid. Spent hours in them during the summer."

"Hours in them?"

"Yeah. I was like a monkey. I loved climbing. I even made my Dad build a treehouse for me." Serena eyes moistened a little at the memory, and she turned her face more towards the window to obscure James' view.

"Seriously? I never would have guessed."

"Don't sound so shocked, James."

"I'm not. Well, I am... I guess I just mean it's hard for me to imagine you..."

"Being that wild?" Serena looked at him with a teasing smirk.

"Well... yeah," said James chuckling. "Or that dirty." He gave her a playful wink.

"I must admit, it's been a long time," said Serena wistfully as she looked up at the tree branches as they waved at her in the wind.

"And may I ask where you were living, back when you were this wild, dirty, tree-hugging monkey?"

"Northern Virginia, actually." Serena looked over at James and paused, half-expecting him to give her some kind of smart remark about it. But he just sat there with a look of genuine curiosity, waiting for her to elaborate. "We lived in Virginia until my mother died when I was nine. Then we moved to the heart of Washington, D.C.

So there were no more climbing trees after that."

James turned to her as if about to ask her something, but then seemed to have second thoughts. She could tell he was trying to determine whether he was about to cross that elusive line that separated respectful interest from prying. James tried again, choosing his words carefully.

"I'm really sorry, Serena. How did she die?"

"In a plane crash."

Serena could feel James' whole body wince as her words fell. All her life, she had tried but had never quite found a way to soften the impact of that sentence. Over time, she found it had become easier just not to say it at all. "She traveled a lot for her work. She was... well, she was thought of as a... well, I suppose you are familiar with Shamanism?"

"You're mother was a *shaman*?" James' foot hit the break involuntarily and they slowed down to a crawl.

"Well, yes," said Serena nervously. "Yeah, she was. So as a part of her work, she traveled to remote places all over the world to study with all kinds of other... well, when I was little, she called them 'spirit doctors.' On one of these trips, she was in a small prop plane that crashed in the Andes Mountains."

"My God," said James, his brow creased with dismay at the image. "That's awful, Serena. I'm so sorry."

"Yeah, it was," said Serena, with what she

knew sounded like too much composure, "but it was a long, long time ago."

James fell silent and seemed to turn his attention back towards his steering. He continued to drive with a second-nature smooth precision, but his thoughts were clearly still focused somewhere in the Andes. With each turn of the wheel, she could practically feel the next question that was coming.

"And you didn't think it might perhaps be relevant to mention that your mother was *a shaman*?" James looked at her like she was a student whom he had just found cheating on a test.

"James... it's been a long time since I've thought about that part of my life." Serena looked down at her hands and was reminded of how her father had always said that her hands looked just like her mother's. "And my mother's very peculiar vocation wasn't exactly something I thought would ever have anything to do with me. And I still don't think it does."

"Are you serious? You mean to tell me that you really don't believe that your mother being a shaman might have *anything* to do with what's happening to you now?"

"No... I mean... I don't know. James, I really haven't thought about it."

"And it kinda sounds like you don't want to."

Serena was silenced by James' reproach. She knew he was right. The reality was that the thought *had* occurred to her and she'd dismissed it without fair consideration. Memories of her mother inevitably were accompanied by a well of pain, and she wanted to avoid it, plain and simple. Serena looked out the passenger side window without saying a word.

"Hey," said James. "I'm sorry. That was harsh."

"But true," said Serena. "I guess I just want to get a better idea of where this is leading before I let my mind start going down *that* road. It's a painful one for me, James."

"Understood."

She reached up to her ponytail and yanked out her hair elastic with one pull of her index finger. She shook out her long chestnut hair and combed through it with her hands. A bluebird took flight from a branch above the car, its bright blue wings splashing deftly through the air as it headed in the opposite direction. Serena turned around in her seat and followed the bird's path until it was out of sight. She felt James tap her forearm.

"Well, I'd wager *that* road won't be any weirder than *this* road," said James. "Serena, look."

As soon as Serena turned back around, she saw it. The gravel beneath the car had turned into a wide road of smooth concrete and was now straight as an arrow. The sycamore trees were gone, and two long rows of green hedges dotted with lemon-yellow camellias had taken their place. In the distance stood Rosethorn Manor, a huge, crème-colored opulent structure that immediately reminded Serena of a Jane Austen manor.

"Whoa. Are we still in California?"

"My thoughts exactly," said James, stopping the car to halt. "Why didn't you tell me?"

"What do you mean? Tell you what?" Serena looked back and forth expectantly from the mansion to James.

James looked at Serena with a you-can't-be-serious look of disbelief. "That Rosethorn was a replica of the Petit Trianon."

"The what?"

"The Petit Trianon. At Versailles."

Serena plugged the words into her brain and looked closely at the imposing, elegant, cube-shaped house. Neoclassical, she was pretty sure. Leading up to the immense pillared entrance was a meticulously tended formal garden composed of two rectangular sections of flowers. The gardens were separated by a large lawn that looked as if it had been mowed just seconds before. In front of the sprawling lawn stood a simple but stunning ground-level fountain which shot a single spray of water up into the air about fifteen feet. As she took it all in, a phrase flashed into her mind.

"Let them eat cake," said Serena. The Petit Trianon, the infamous sanctuary of Marie Antionette.

She looked over at James who looked

pleased as punch that she had finally made the connection. Something to the side of the road caught his attention and he put the car back into drive. A little sign marked "Guest Parking" pointed to a smaller lane that veered off towards the right. James was already heading in that direction.

"I had no idea... I was so focused on getting us here that I must have missed that detail." Serena tried to consider what, if anything, this meant. James had reached a small, shaded parking lot and pulled into one of the "Visitor"-designated diagonal spaces. There was only one other car in the rustic lot, a light blue Toyota Prius in a space marked "Manager." She looked over at James, wondering what was going through his head as he put the car into park.

"Kind of bizarre, huh?" she finally said.

"Let's stay positive and call it eccentric."

"Right, eccentric. Then I have a good feeling about it," said Serena, unbuckling her seatbelt. She leaned down and started gathering her things. By the time she sat up again, James had freed himself from the driver's seat and was on his way to the passenger side to open Serena's door. This was precisely the kind of thing that James did that kept Serena constantly on edge. The little chivalries. She had long become comfortable with the fact that these had become extinct in her life, along with the girlish feelings of thrill that came with them. *Damn him*, she grumbled in her head.

"So, have you ever seen the real one?" asked James, as he pulled open her door.

"What—you mean the real Petit Trianon?" asked Serena.

"Yeah."

"Yes, I have. Just once. You?"

"No, actually," said James, taking Serena's hand as she stepped out of the car. "Just lots of pictures of it. I've never been to Versailles."

"Really?"

"Now look who sounds shocked," poked James.

"It's just that I thought... I thought—"

"That I'd been everywhere?"

"Well, yes," she admitted guiltily as she struggled to straighten out her sweater, "I guess so." James grabbed a blazer out of the back seat. Black corduroy. *Classic*, thought Serena.

"Just about everywhere," said James coyly, "but not quite. So when was the last time you saw it? A long time ago?"

Serena shook her head in the affirmative, a little too slowly for James not to notice a look in her eye that he couldn't identify. "What?" he asked, almost suspiciously.

"I went there on my honeymoon. To France, that is. I saw it then." Serena felt a tense knot form in the center of her throat muscles.

James moved a little more slowly as he shrugged his coat over his shoulders. "Hmm," he

237

said, and then with a smart casualness that almost disguised any trace of discomfort, "You've got me two for two then. I've never been on a honeymoon, either."

Serena and James stood for a moment looking at each other. She felt a strange sensation of undesired separateness after being bonded in the intimate confines of the car for so long. Serena stepped closer to James, not quite sure what she was going to do when she reached him.

"Well... I have no doubt you are going to thoroughly enjoy both, one day," Serena finally said. She reached out and readjusted James' scarf, which in reality was already perfectly positioned.

Chapter 15

The sign outside the door read *By Appointment Only*, but since Serena had telephoned beforehand and informed the manager of their impending arrival, she figured that they qualified. Serena felt silly as she rapped on the huge double-doored entrance set deep within Rosethorn's pillared façade. It seemed like a mansion like this should have some kind of tuxedoed footman permanently on the lookout for guests. She knocked a little bit harder, but the impact of her fist was negligible compared to the depth and weight of the monstrous door. James looked at her slyly and then pushed down on the heavy brass door handle, shoved open the door, and quickly stepped inside a large formal reception room. James' trespass made Serena nervous, but rather than play by the rules and sit outside alone, she tiptoed in behind him.

"Hello?" James announced loudly as he looked around.

Standing right behind him, Serena could see that like her, James could not help but gaze up at the ceiling, which looked like it was at least thirty feet high. On each wall of the cavernous rectangular room hung a series of massive mirrors, each bordered thickly with swirling gold gilt detail. The mirrors hung on walls painted in soft shades of eggshell and trimmed in a rosy pastel, which gave the room a light, airy feel in spite of the fact that there were no windows. There were only two pieces of furniture in the whole room. Sitting kitty-corner on the right side was a single white antique desk, and behind it was a wingback chair upholstered in a red and cream-colored tapestry depicting a scene from the French countryside.

"Maybe we're too early," said Serena uneasily.

James crossed to the left side of the room to examine one of the mirrors more closely. "Fantastic. It's like this place was lifted straight out of seventeenth-century France," he said, leaning down to appreciate the meticulously decorated frame. Serena joined him at the wall. Their reflections looked back at her from the mirror and she felt a fluttery twinge in her chest. Somehow, seeing them pictured together at the same time cemented the realness of their partnership in a way she had not quite appreciated until that moment.

"Yeah, I feel like I should be wearing a big white wig and a corset." She laughed, noting that her hair was still a mess.

James turned to Serena with a grin. "Now

that I would pay to see."

"So would I."

Serena and James knocked into each other as they turned around. They found themselves face to face with the speaker, a petite young woman with flaming brick-red dreadlocks gathered into a ponytail high on the top of her head.

"Sorry, I didn't mean to startle you guys. I'm Paige. Paige Quincy." She extended her hand out to shake James' hand first.

"Hi, I'm James. James Riley."

Serena was grateful that James had to move first. Her mind was still struggling to make sense of Paige. Perched on the top of her head, just above her forehead, were a set of dark-lensed goggles. Old-fashioned welding goggles. She wore a tailored, Victorian-style white shirt with tails that hung down to her calves like a tuxedo, over snug, low-slung brown cargo shorts. Layered on top of her shirt was a tightly fitted, dark-brown leather vest. On her feet, she wore knee-high, granny-style leather boots that laced up the front and were adorned with all kinds of strange, antiquey-looking accessories. She looked like a Mad Maxian pixie.

Paige turned her focus to Serena and continued. "And I take it you are Serena? I think I spoke to you yesterday on the phone." Her voice was surprisingly alto for such a tiny person.

"Yes, very nice to meet you," said Serena, trying to keep her eyes respectfully concentrated on

Paige's face instead of her outlandish attire. But as she shook her hand, Serena could not help but stare at the watch on Paige's wrist, which was unlike any she had ever seen. It was a large, brass cuff, elaborately embellished with pretty swirls of silver components, crystals, and pearls. Set in the center of this fantastic design was a classic white clock face. Silver metal wings extended out from both sides of the face, giving the watch the impression that it could take flight at any moment.

"Wonderful watch," said James, politely stepping in on Serena's behalf.

"Thank you," said Paige, looking down at her wrist with pride. "Watches, like so many things, I'm afraid, are becoming more and more a thing of the past." She looked from Serena and then to James. "People just use cell phones now," she said, letting out an unexpectedly bubbly laugh.

"Guilty," said James with a smile, pulling his cell phone from his jacket pocket.

"Exactly," said Paige giving James a good-humored, generous smile back.

"Yes, it's beautiful," said Serena as she looked back up at Paige's gratified face. She released Paige's hand, embarrassed that she had kept hold of it for so long. As she pulled away, Serena's finger grazed the edge of one of the wings extending from Paige's watch. She felt an electric shock travel up her arm. She jumped, startled.

"You okay?" asked Paige, immediately

dropping Serena's hand.

"Yes... yes... I think so," said Serena, shaking the sensation out of her arm. She looked over at James, who was reaching out to her as if he were afraid she might fall.

"You sure?" he asked, worry knitting his eyebrows.

"Yeah. Yeah, I'm fine." Serena rubbed her arm and looked down at the shiny silver wings that sprung gracefully from Paige's wrist. Something inside her veins had started to hum.

"So, welcome to Rosethorn," Paige said, looking right at Serena.

"Thank you. We are happy to finally be here," said Serena, looking around the reception area once more.

Paige gave Serena a quizzical look. "I take it you guys aren't local, then?"

"No, we live several hours north of here, just outside of San Francisco."

"Vacation?" asked Paige matter-of-factly.

"Um, no," said Serena taking a step closer to James, making it clear that he was her accomplice. "We're just down here for the day to see Rosethorn." Serena knew her explanation sounded insufficient, but she had no idea what else she should say. She could have kicked herself for not using the time in the car to prepare more for their introduction.

"Wow, that's a pretty long drive. And

touring Rosethorn is the whole reason you guys came down here today?" Paige looked at Serena and James skeptically. "'Cause to be honest with you, even the locals don't really care about this place anymore." She gestured towards the empty room with a sweep of her arm. "Well, except for the occasional Marie Antoinette freak." Paige cocked her head to one side as if to question whether Serena and James fit into this unsavory category.

Serena let out a nervous laugh. "I can imagine. But no, we are most definitely not Marie Antoin—wait, did you say your last name was Quincy?" Only after the question spilled out did Serena realize she might have sounded a little too interrogating.

Paige took a reserved step back and folded her arms. "Um, yes, I did." She glanced over to James with a puzzled expression.

"I'm sorry... let me explain." Serena tried settle her tone down. "We are actually here because we are interested in the previous owner of Rosethorn, Gwendolyn Whitmoor, whose maiden name, I believe, was also Quincy?"

Paige's dark, quick eyes hopped back and forth between Serena and James. "Yes, it was. Gwendolyn Whitmoor was my aunt. I'm her niece."

"But—you look so young," said Serena.

"My father was the youngest of five siblings. My Aunt Gwen was the eldest, but she was always closest to my Dad."

Serena and James stared at each other in silence, neither quite sure of what they should say next. James gave Serena a quick nod, encouraging her to keep going. Serena did not say anything or move, however, until she heard a soft knocking sound coming from the floor.

When Serena looked back to Paige, her hands were resting on her hips and she was tapping one solidly footed boot. "Is there something I'm missing here?" she asked, directing the question at Serena.

Serena decided there was no point in stalling any longer. "Well, yes... Actually, I wasn't completely up front on the phone when we spoke. Getting a tour is not the main reason we came all this way to Rosethorn. You see, we know that your Aunt had quite a famous collection of jewelry."

Paige stopped tapping her foot. A shrewd smile crept onto her face. "Ah, I see. Yes, there's no secret about that." Her eyes flitted to James and then landed soundly on Serena again. "And by the way you are asking, I am guessing you are probably aware that her entire jewelry collection was auctioned off after her death. Nothing remains here at Rosethorn." Paige caressed the glass face of her watch with a pitch-black lacquered nail.

"Yes... we are well aware of that," said Serena, worried that with every word Paige's patience was wearing thin. "But we thought by coming here we might get a little more insight into…" Serena stalled, unable to find a delicate approach.

"Into exactly how the jewelry was disposed of," said James without restraint. "In particular, the Eye of Fire."

Paige's eyes narrowed and her mouth stiffened. She raised a haughty chin and swept both arms behind her back, interlocking her hands. It reminded Serena of the way people hid their hands behind their backs before they crossed their fingers to cover up a lie. A defensive move. Paige definitely did not trust them.

"Interesting. That was my Aunt Gwen's very favorite piece. She wore it every day until the day she died," she said. "But I suppose you know that, too. Along with the fact that it was acquired at auction by a buyer who was apparently just too powerful and important to allow the rest of us mere mortals to know who he or she is." She looked hard at Serena, her eyes tinged with a mixture of insolence and grief.

At that, moment Serena saw it. Paige was angry. Actually, she was *really angry*. Perhaps it was because the Eye of Fire was in someone's hands that she didn't know. Or maybe it was because she had not become the rightful owner of her aunt's favorite piece. Or both. Serena could feel the beginning of a potential alliance if she handled this right. She glanced over at James. *Strike while this iron is hot*, his expression read.

To her surprise, Paige struck first. "So what the hell is going on? Why, pray tell, are you guys so interested in the Eye of Fire?" Paige fired her questions directly at Serena.

Serena decided that with Paige, blunt was probably best. "A few days ago, I had a vision of the Eye of Fire. Before that, I had never even heard of it. I'm trying to figure out why. I'm trying to figure out what the vision means. So we came here hoping to somehow find out what happened to the diamond."

Paige smiled and raised her eyebrows. She looked over to James for a more sensible explanation. "A vision. You guys are serious?"

Serena gave a strong nod. "Completely."

Paige crossed her arms in front of her again, this time taking one hand up to her chin, as if she were trying to judge whether she and James were worth dealing with for one second more. After a few moments, her expression softened. She slowly extended her hand out to shake Serena's hand again. Unsure how else to respond, Serena stepped forward and took Paige's hand once more.

"Serena," said Paige with a smile mid-shake, "it was a pleasure to meet you and James." She then dropped Serena's hand as if she were holding a scorpion.

"Now get your bloodsucking asses off Rosethorn property," she snapped before turning and leaving the room.

SERENA BUCKLED her seatbelt and threw her purse on the floor of the car.

"God dammit, Devania!" she screamed at the sky.

"Look, Serena," said James. "It's going to be okay. We'll figure this thing out eventually."

"*Eventually?* You don't get it. I don't have time for eventually, James. I need the answers to reveal themselves *now*, not later. The kids come back at the end of the week and what the hell am I going to do now?" She leaned forward and pressed her forehead against the dashboard.

"Serena?"

"What, James?" answered Serena weakly.

"Who's Devania?"

Serena turned her head to face James in the driver's seat, her head still against the dashboard. She felt too drained to hide anymore.

"She's a mystic. A sage. I did my Journey Magnification with her, and that's when I saw the Eye of Fire."

"I see…" he said. Serena suspected that James couldn't really see at all, but was trying his darnedest.

"The Journey Magnification showed me… well, the me from the past. And that's when it happened."

"You mean, that's when you saw the diamond?"

"Yes, but no, that's not what I mean. That's when I was... I was killed. I was *murdered* in that temple, James. Brutally. And if I don't figure this out..." She looked back down to the floor as tears welled up in her eyes. "I might not live to see the end of this."

"No—that can't be," said James, shaking his head.

"Yes, it can be."

"And you believe this because this woman Devania told you to?"

"No, not just because she told me. Because of everything. My kids' video game *knew* I was Zahra and told me to go to Devania. I could feel my death happening to me, James, in every cell of my body. And ever since, I've felt it... I don't know how to say it. I've felt something, I don't know what, *coming* for me."

"Jesus," said James. "Serena... I had no idea."

Serena sat back up and wiped her face off roughly with the sleeve of her sweater. "I should have known better. This is absurd. Par for the course for me."

"What do you mean by that?"

"Meaning, I'm clearly some kind of deranged idiot who can never seem to get it right. You know, pick the right road, for once. With the exception of Drew and Asher, sometimes I feel like that's all my life has been—one big wrong road. But this time... I just thought..." She squeezed her hands into fists and looked down at her lap. She refused to be further humiliated by sobbing in front of James.

"What, Serena?" asked James softly, in what must have been the sweetest voice she had ever heard. "Tell me what you thought this time."

"I thought," said Serena, glancing up at James' imploring amber eyes, "I thought I felt something real in there. When I shook Paige's hand, I thought I felt something way down inside of me that knew. That knew I was in the right place."

James didn't respond. She could tell he wanted to say something, but he let Serena's words just sit in the air between them. She was inexplicably grateful for the silence.

Serena unclenched her fists and put her hand on top of James', which sat poised on top of the gear shift waiting for their departure.

"Drive," was all she could manage to say. The sting of disappointment that she felt in the pit of her stomach was so sickening that she thought she might throw up.

"Just drive, James," she repeated.

"Okay," he said, pushing the key into the ignition switch.

James turned over the engine and headed out of the parking lot onto the same paved road that lead them into Rosethorn. Serena took a deep breath as she felt the wind hit her face and blow through her hair.

An object flew by her face and hit the car with a loud THUMP. Startled, James slammed on the brakes, throwing them both forward in their seats.

When Serena and James turned toward each other, they saw that a long, silver arrow was suction-cupped to the inside of the windshield right between them.

"What the—" said James.

"It's an *arrow*," said Serena.

"I see that, but where the hell..."

James and Serena turned around and looked behind the car. There was Paige, about fifty feet back, strolling toward them carrying a brass-and-steel-colored bow contraption that was even more alien-looking than her clothing.

"Sorry," said Paige reaching the passenger side of the car. "I prefer not to run if I don't have to."

"We were just leaving," said James sharply. "Sorry again for wasting your time."

"About that..." said Paige with chagrin. "Serena, why didn't you tell me?"

"Tell you what?"

"Who you were. That you are Violet Rayborn's daughter."

Serena felt her heart start to pound. Although she did not look at him, she could feel James leap forward a little in his seat. She opened the door and climbed out of the car and stood facing Paige in the middle of the road.

"What difference does that make?" asked Serena.

Paige looked at Serena like she had made a bad joke. She stood there for a moment, trying to figure out how to answer Serena's question.

"It would have made a great deal of difference to my Aunt, who had great respect for your mother's field. Violet Rayborn was a reknowned shaman," she said finally.

Serena stood there, feeling dazed by what Paige had uncovered. James got out and walked around the car to stand at her side.

"She must have googled *you*, Serena."

Paige smiled. "And you are sure what you saw was the Eye of Fire?"

Serena smiled back. "Positive," she said. She wanted to leave no room for argument about the facts this time.

"Okay, assuming I believe you, why should I tell you what I know?" asked Paige, throwing her unorthodox bow up onto her shoulder.

"Because," Serena said. "I think you want to know who acquired the Eye of Fire... even more than we do."

Paige smiled as if Serena had passed a test that Paige had been certain she would fail. "That's entirely true. But unfortunately for both of us, I have absolutely no idea who bought the Eye of Fire.

The buyer has never come forward, and as far as I know, there is nothing in any public record which gives any clue as to who they are."

"I see," Serena said with sigh. She stepped closer to Paige, and something inside her began to buzz.

"By any chance did your Aunt Gwendolyn— did she leave you anything—anything at all?" Serena asked the question without quite knowing why she was asking it.

Paige blushed. She glanced over to James as if to ask if he knew, too. Serena knew she had hit on something. Paige was definitely not the kind of girl who blushed.

"She gave me this," she said, slowly extending her arm between Serena and James. "This was hers. I reworked it. I added the watch face, the wings, and the gold and the pearl work. But the base of the bracelet was hers. It's the only piece that wasn't auctioned."

"So you make jewelry? Then you must have jewelry-making tools, like a magnifier?" Serena could barely suppress her excitement.

"Yes and yes," said Paige, her head cocked to the side. She seemed pleased by Serena's childish enthusiasm.

"Then would you mind if we took a closer look? Please?" asked Serena, pointing to the watch. She stopped, afraid that her excitement was becoming just plain overbearing. Serena tried to put on her most enchanting, persuasive smile.

Paige's eyes bounced from Serena to James. Finally, her focus settled on her wrist. She affectionately touched one of the wings with her finger, as if she were smoothing down real feathers. When she finally brought her attention back to Serena, her staid face gave no hint of a decision in their favor.

"Guess we're going to be doing that tour after all," Paige said at last, a smile starting to form at the outer corners of her eyes.

"Well, then..." said Serena. She reached into the car and pulled the arrow off the windshield with strong yank and handed it to Paige.

"In case we need to fend off any more bloodsuckers."

Chapter 16

Serena stopped trying to keep track of which way they were going after the eighth turn down yet another dimly lit hallway. While the upper floors of Rosethorn were grand, spacious, and logically organized, the tunnels below the mansion were a helter skelter maze that seemed made for the purpose of getting someone lost. Serena now appreciated Paige's wry humor in calling it a 'tour.' After she scampered down the stairs, she called back a quick, "Stay close!" before leading them down a labyrinth of twists and turns. Then suddenly, at a seemingly random stop, Paige stopped short, whipped out a key, and opened a nondescript door to her right.

"Don't be shy, go ahead and take a seat," said Paige. She flicked on the overhead light in a room about the size of a large walk-in closet.

Serena looked around the room. It couldn't have resembled Paige more. Small, but every inch of the walls was covered with vintage wall clocks, antique pocket watches hanging from chains, and other old and bizarre mechanical-looking items that Serena couldn't easily identify. Paige walked over to a brown wooden desk that sat in the corner of the room and turned on a brick-red Tiffany table lamp the exact shade of her hair. She immediately started pushing things off to the sides of the desk, which was covered with all kinds of circular metal pieces, miniature tools, and curious gadgets.

"Go ahead, Serena. Take a seat," said James, motioning toward a compact distressed loveseat that sat to his right against the wall opposite the desk. The tattered blue loveseat resembled the furniture she had seen on the upper floors of Rosethorn, but this piece looked like it had been through a war. Serena sat down and instantly felt like she was too low to the ground. James sat down next to her and she could feel the whole side of his body brush against hers as he struggled to fit into what little space was left. She suppressed an involuntary giggle that bubbled up inside her. It felt absurd to be squished in like sardines on a shabby antique loveseat somewhere within the tunnels of a mansion of an eccentric deceased woman. James turned to Serena and picked up on the same humorous irony of their situation. The corners of his mouth turned up and his body started to shake in unison with hers. He was giggling now, too, and doing his best to stifle it.

Paige turned around to see what was going on. She laughed out loud at the sight of Serena and

James. "Wow, you guys look *really* cozy. Sorry, that loveseat was made in 1672. People used to be a lot smaller."

"No, it's perfectly fine," said Serena, trying to be polite. But then it occurred to her that she was not lying. She liked being that close to James. He was warm, which felt wonderful, especially since touching the watch had sent a persistently cold, odd-feeling current through her body, from her fingertips down to her toes. She could feel the taut muscles along the sides of his arm and leg flex as he moved. She could smell his delicious spicy scent. She noticed that James sounded husky even when he giggled. It had become quiet—all she could hear was the ticking sound of one particularly loud wall clock. Suddenly she realized she was no longer giggling. She was just breathing hard and staring directly at James' lips.

"Ahem," said Paige.

Serena's attention snapped over to Paige. She had a satisfied smirk on her face that said, *Busted.* Serena sprang up from the loveseat so abruptly that she almost lost her balance. She pointed to the watch, which Paige had removed from her wrist and placed on the desk.

"So are we ready to take a closer look?"

"Yeah, let's get to it," said Paige, her expression still amused. She stood up and moved to the side of the desk, giving Serena enough room to trade places with her and take a seat in the chair.

She was relieved to be facing away from James.

Paige walked over to the left wall of the room and unhooked a bronze and glass apparatus that hung from the wall. "Put this on," she said, holding the contraption out to Serena. "Two hands. It's kind of heavy."

Serena took the instrument. Paige was right to warn her. It was heavier than it looked. She slowly turned the awkward metal apparatus over, trying to figure out exactly what to do with it. It looked like a hybrid between a headlamp and a welder's mask. It reminded her of something Sherlock Holmes would have worn.

"Here, let me help you with that," said Paige, taking it back from Serena and carefully placing it on top of her head. It felt like a weighted metal cage, but it was surprisingly secure. A transparent shield extended halfway down her face.

"What on earth is that thing called?" asked James. His voice was coming from a different place, somewhere higher up behind Serena. She still couldn't see him, but she could tell he had gotten up from the loveseat.

"Good question," answered Paige. "I'm not sure. I actually haven't really formally named it since I built it. In my head, I think of it as the M3, which stands for multi-use magnification mechanism. I use it when I'm building jewelry, developing photos... all kinds of projects. How does it feel, Serena? Ready to take a look?"

"Ready," said Serena nodding her head with a wobble. It was not easy to move her head gracefully with the M3 weighing it down. "What now?"

"Go ahead and pick up the cuff and look at it, watch-face side up."

Serena picked up the watch. She felt a cold tingle penetrate her fingertips again. Her body shivered in response.

"Y'okay?" asked Paige.

"Yeah...I just feel a weird, cold sensation every time I touch it. But it's okay. What happens next? The watch looks exactly the same to me."

Paige reached out toward the left side of Serena's head and turned a small, silver dial on the M3. In an instant, the watch zoomed in and appeared to be at least fifty times bigger. Serena could see each and every detail of the watch and truly appreciate Paige's workmanship now that she could study it up close. Silver and maple-brown crystals cascaded outward from the antique watchface in a wavy design that flowed all the way around the bronze cuff. Serena could even count the feathers on the silver wings—two rows on each side with ten feathers on each. A single white pearl hung from the center of the very bottom of the watch face. The watch seemed to have an endless amount of intricate beauty.

"Wow," said Serena. "Paige, you did an extraordinary job. It's exquisite."

"Thanks," said Paige, now leaning over Serena's shoulder. "It took a while. But since it was the only piece of jewelry I had to remember Aunt Gwen by, I wanted to make sure I got it right. I think she would have approved of my modifications, even though it *is* steampunk."

"Steampunk?" Serena turned to Paige awkwardly, her head still adjusting to the weight of the M3. She could sense that James was now standing on her right and was also looking over her shoulder down at the watch.

Paige stood up straight, put her hands on her hips, and cocked her head to the side. She flipped up the visor on the M3.

"Seriously? You don't know what I'm talking about?"

Serena slowly shook her head from left to right.

"Perhaps you can explain?" asked James, who seemed to be equally baffled.

"Ha!" exclaimed Paige with a clap of her hands, her elfin frame bouncing up and down. "Well, if you have no idea what I'm referring to, I must say I'm truly impressed by your open-mindedness so far, you guys." Paige stepped back and performed an exaggerated curtsy. "This," she said grandly gesturing to herself from heels to hair, "is steampunk." Then with a sweep of her hand she pointed all around the room. "And all that is steampunk." Finally, with one finger she pointed back down at the watch. "And now, thanks to me, *that* is steampunk. A supreme steampunk original, if I do say so myself. Think futuristic plus Victorian plus wild west."

"Ooohhhh," said Serena. "You mean it's like an artistic genre?"

"Bingo," said Paige, smiling down at Serena. "'Or as some of us like to think of it, a *subculture.* 'Steam' is a reference to a neo-Victorian age of steam-powered machines. Punk, as in... well, ya know... punk!"

"Cool," said Serena, fascinated, and then turned towards James to see his reaction.

"I agree, very cool," said James, equally intrigued. "By the way, maybe this is a good time to ask," he said, pointing to something on the wall beyond Serena's line of sight, "what is *that*?"

"Ray gun," said Paige matter-of-factly.

"*What*?" Serena and James asked simultaneously.

"Custom-painted ray nerf gun for cosplay. I made it for Comicon."

"Nice," said James, clearly impressed.

"Thank you," said Paige with a look of satisfaction. "Anyway, let's get back to the matter at hand." Paige skipped back to Serena, flipped the visor down, and leaned over her left side again. "Serena, aside from that strange, cold feeling, anything else about the watch catch your eye, now?"

Serena looked back at the watch, pleased that she now had a word for its distinctive, fanciful design. *Steampunk*, she thought, as she gazed at each cursive number on the clock face. Then she noticed a little word in black ink that was so small she almost did not see it, even with the help of the M3.

"On the watch face... there's a tiny cursive word. What does it say?"

"Sun."

A red strobe-light flash blinded Serena. The watch, which had felt icy cool from the very first time she touched it, suddenly was burning hot. Serena dropped it and pushed herself away from the desk. She stood up and stumbled backward in the small room, falling into James. Paige and James reached out simultaneously to steady Serena.

"Are you okay? Zahra, what happened?" asked Paige, her voice coming urgently from Serena's left side.

At the same time, Serena heard James' even, steady voice on her right. "Easy there. Let's get you back to the couch. I've got you."

Serena could feel caring hands guiding her, coaxing her to sit down. With the help of James and Paige, Serena found herself seated on the loveseat again. Her head suddenly felt lighter. Paige had removed the M3. She kept her eyes closed and rubbed her hands together. Her fingertips had started to sting.

"Zahra, you feeling better? Whoa, Riley, look—I think she burned her hands!" exclaimed Paige with dismay.

"Yes, I think you're right," said James, gingerly pulling open Serena's hands to examine them.

Serena opened her eyes slightly in order to get a look for herself. To her surprise, her vision was fine. Still a little splotchy with red spots from the flash, but otherwise her eyes felt normal. Her fingertips, on the other hand, had turned red and were throbbing a little.

"Paige, why did you call me that?" asked Serena, ignoring her hands for the moment. "How do you know to call me that?"

Paige crinkled up her face. "What do you mean? Call you what?"

"You called me Zahra."

Paige looked dumbfounded. "I did?"

"Yes," answered James right away. "You've been calling her Zahra since she asked you about the word on the watch face. Since you told her it said... Sun." James said the word cautiously, as if just saying it aloud might somehow burn Serena again.

Paige stepped back and took a seat on the edge of the desk. She shook her head, bewildered. "Okay, now I'm confused. I didn't even realize that I was calling her that. And if I was, I have no idea why."

"Probably because that was my name," said Serena, " and I think your watch knows it."

Paige shook her head vigorously, confounded. "What do you mean *was* your name? You mean you changed it?"

"I mean as in that used to be my name... in another time and place."

"What?" Paige perched forward and lowered her voice. "You mean in like... the *past*?"

Serena and James both nodded.

"When? Where?"

Serena's voice dropped down to a whisper. "Fourteenth century, we're pretty sure. In India."

Paige looked over her shoulder and stared down at the watch, which sat on the desk just behind her left hip. "Radical," she said after a few moments.

James gave Serena's hands a reassuring squeeze before walking back over to the desk. With one swoop, he picked up the watch without trepidation. Both Paige and Serena recoiled slightly at the sight of him daring to touch it again. He turned it over in his hands, testing out the weight and temperature for himself. Serena could tell by the intense set of his jaw that his mind was working furiously.

"Paige, tell me, why is the word 'sun' written on the face?" he finally asked.

"That word is inscribed on the back of the

original bracelet. No idea why. I used the original bracelet as the base of the brass cuff and built around it." Paige pointed to various areas of the watch as she explained. "I thought it would be cool to keep the word as a reference to the original piece."

Serena saw James' dark amber eyes flicker up from the watch to meet hers and she knew exactly what he was thinking. She shook her head a firm 'no' at him. There was no way she could ask Paige to do what he was suggesting.

Paige, however, did not miss the exchange. "No, what?" she asked Serena. She crossed her arms with a huff, offended that she was being left out.

"Nothing, nothing," said Serena. She continued to rub her sore fingers together.

Paige's jaw tightened with understanding as she studied Serena. "Ahh. I see. You want to see the original inscription. You want me to take it apart."

Serena did not want to admit to Paige that she was right, but she knew that it was the only way. "Is... that... possible?" she asked gingerly. "It's so exquisite and dear to you."

"Why, of course it's possible," said Paige, her poker-faced expression melting into a huge, compassionate grin. "And if what you are saying is true, which I assume is likely since I don't think you are stark raving mad, I would say it's imperative, wouldn't you?"

"Why, yes... yes, I do," said Serena, trying keep the enthusiasm in her voice at a respectful level.

Paige held her hand out to James. "Give it to me, Riley."

James smiled at Paige's spunky impertinence and handed the watch over. She swiveled around on her boot heel, plopped down in the chair at the desk, put on the M3, and immediately got to work. James and Serena watched with amazement as Paige picked up one tool after the other, tinkering with the watch cuff with the speed of a robot. After just a few minutes, Paige sat back, peeled the M3 from her dreadlocks, and exhaled as if she had just deactivated the most complicated of bombs. "Okay, it's ready. Time for you to take another look, Serena."

Serena got up and peered over Paige's shoulder. She gasped at the sight on the table.

"Oh... Paige," she said, putting her hand over her mouth. "I'm sorry."

Paige's brass cuff was disassembled into various pieces scattered across the desk, and the watch face had been removed. Serena felt a wave of sadness and guilt seeing Paige's formidable masterpiece suddenly looking so helplessly naked with all of its internal gears exposed.

"It's okay," said Paige. "It's for an important cause. Look here," she said, turning the cuff over so the underside was visible.

Serena leaned in until her face was inches away from the desk. She could see a shining silver bracelet embedded within the larger brass piece. "I see it. It's silver?"

"Actually, it's gold. Eighteen-carat white gold. Can you see the inscription? Do you need the M3 again?"

Serena did not answer the question. Not only could she see it, she could also feel it emanating a penetrating heat into her eyes. The word reached out to her, emblazoned in bold cursive strokes. She saw the word *Sun,* but what she felt and practically heard was a command.

"Paige, there's something under the inscription. You are going to have to open it," said Serena.

"What? W-what do you mean?"

"I mean there's something hidden inside the bracelet."

"You sure?" asked James.

Serena looked squarely at James. "Yes, James, I'm sure." She could tell from the warm confidence in his eyes that he was asking solely for the sake of Paige and her family heirloom, not because he had doubts about her accuracy.

"Faaaascinating," said Paige, her eyes widening with curiosity. She picked up one of her sharp, pointy tools and continued to pick apart the bracelet. She hunched over the desk with concentration, obscuring Serena and James' view.

It only took Paige a few more minutes before she sat back again and looked up at Serena in astonishment, her mouth half open. "I can't believe it. Serena, you are right. There's something inside."

Before Serena could say a word, Paige used a long, tweezer-like tool to remove a small rectangular piece of paper that was lodged within a compartment of the now-pried-open back of the bracelet. It could only have been about a half inch in size, and it was folded into fourths. She held it up in the air above her head for Serena and James to behold.

Serena and James each stepped towards the paper, impatient for a closer look. Paige put the paper down on the desk and gently unfolded it with the tweezers.

"It's a picture of a man," said Serena. "A very old black-and-white picture."

Serena and James positioned themselves on either side of Paige, and instinctively crouched down until their chins were level with the desk. The three of them sat silently with their heads in a row until James verbalized the thought that was hovering in each of their minds.

"Of course, I can't be sure, but this guy looks to be of Asian descent and dressed in a suit from the.... nineteen thirties. Maybe early forties."

Serena slowly reached one hand out towards

the picture.

"Careful, Serena," cautioned James.

"It's okay," Serena said as she used the fingernails of her index finger and thumb to take hold of one of the picture's edges.

The man in the picture was young, perhaps in his mid-twenties, dressed in a heavy tweed vest, a well-tailored matching jacket, and a white shirt with a contrasting dark striped tie. He had a serious look on his face and did not smile, but behind this stern demeanor Serena thought she could see a soft kindness in his eyes. She could tell from his posture and impeccable grooming that he had posed with pride. She turned the picture over, somehow knowing that the back had more to tell than the front. Serena read the teeny faded cursive writing aloud. "Sun Chanming, 1942."

She felt foggy and dazed by the picture's sheer inscrutability. "I wonder..." she said as she rose back up to standing and handed the picture over to James.

"Go ahead, Serena. You wonder what?" asked James, his eyes glued to the picture as he carefully inspected it.

"I wonder... I wonder why Gwendolyn did it. Why would she have taken all the trouble to hide a picture of this man—Sun Chanming—in her bracelet?"

"I think I can answer that," said Paige.

"You can?" asked Serena.

"Can you?" asked James.

"Yes. I know my Aunt Gwen," she said, forlorn affection seeping into her voice. Paige swiveled around in her chair so she could address Serena and James at the same time. "My Aunt was an absolute hopeless romantic. Notoriously so. Her hiding this picture in the bracelet means she was in love with him. I'm sure of it."

Serena's head swirled around at the thought of love having anything to do with the picture and the persistent signal that was being transmitting to her through it. James broke his concentration and looked up at Serena uncertainly, and she read the source of his confusion. His thoughts were questions that went back to the first time they had read about the Eye of Fire.

"But..." Serena said tentatively, afraid to offend. "Wasn't your Aunt... married? She was married to Douglas Whitmoor, right?"

"Yes, but here's the thing," said Paige. "She *despised* my Uncle Douglas. She was pretty much forced into marrying him by my grandfather, Grandaddy Boss, who was one of the most misogynistic and, more significantly in this case, most *racist* creeps that ever lived. Aunt Gwen always spoke bitterly about how he robbed her of her only chance to be with her one true love, but she never disclosed any details to me. And now I'm pretty damn sure that one true love was... Sun."

"Um... Serena? I think you should come

here," said James earnestly. "You're not going to believe this, but I think I know who this is. I think this is a picture of Charles Sun when he was a young man."

Serena positioned herself behind James, and leaned her head over his shoulder so she could see the picture from the same angle. "What do you mean?" Serena could think of only one Charles Sun, who was known to every human being on earth. "James—you don't mean Charles Sun of Sun Electronics?"

"I do. I mean *the* Charles Sun. Founder and CEO of the largest electronics corporation in the world." James tapped on the miniature picture to emphasize his point. "I read a piece in *The Economist* on him—I'd say three years ago now— and this picture is the spitting image of him when he was young and very poor, right after he immigrated to the United States from China. In fact, I'm almost sure I remember reading that he changed his birth name to Charles Sun when he decided to launch an American company."

"Shut the front door," said Paige, sinking back into the chair in astonishment.

Serena took hold of James' left arm and gently pulled him around so he turned to face her. She placed her hands on the tops of each of his shoulders and leaned forward, a smile dawning across her face as if he had just given her a car on her sixteenth birthday. "So if this really is *the*

Charles Sun... that would mean he's still alive."

"Better than that. That would mean that he's alive and living in L.A.," said James.

Paige sprang up from her chair to join Serena and James in their subterranean huddle. "I've got a far out idea," she said, snapping her fingers. Quick as a squirrel, she twirled around and gathered the picked-apart bracelet into her hands. She plucked the photo back from James and extended her hands out to Serena ceremoniously, as if she was giving her the greatest of offerings.

"You're going to need these," Paige said, her eyes tearing up ever so slightly.

Neither Paige nor Serena spoke or moved as each looked down at the vital pieces contained in Paige's delicate hands. Serena knew she would have to take the bracelet and the picture with her to Los Angeles, and she couldn't find the words to thank Paige for her sacrifice.

Finally, with a bow of respect, Serena just said, "Sun."

Paige nodded back, her eyes grateful and sincere, "Don't mention it, Zahra."

Chapter 17

James climbed the curved staircase to the second floor of the Spanish Palm Inn. Arriving at the top, he turned left and walked at a relaxed pace, glancing at the room numbers that were painted next to each wooden door that they passed.

"Two-eleven.... Two-thirteen... two-fifteen..." James counted off as they made their way toward the end of the long outdoor corridor. Right now, the evening was still colored in indigo twilight, but the night sky was descending quickly. Star-shaped sconces flickered on along the hallway in auto-response to the encroaching darkness. A cold, salty breeze was blowing from the not-so-far-off horizon to the west. She couldn't see it now, but Serena knew that if it were earlier in the day, she would have a striking view of the Pacific Ocean, whose shores were just a couple blocks away.

Serena deliberately followed a few feet behind James while he led the way through the arcade, as opposed to walking with him side-by-side. She wished she felt like this detour was no big deal, but the nervousness simmering in her gut seemed to indicate otherwise. She knew that the only practical choice was to stay put for a night. Ten a.m. the next morning was the only option Charles Sun's office gave her, and that was far better than she or James could have hoped for. *It's just one night... just twelve extra hours*, she reassured herself.

She looked down over the railing to her left and took in the details of the open-air courtyard that served as the lobby to the quaint Spanish Colonial hotel. Even though they were a mere twenty-minute drive from Rosethorn Manor, it was only now that she felt like she was in real Santa Barbara. The Spanish Palm Inn was a little oasis of arched doorways, colorful hand-painted tile fireplaces, and white stucco walls. Wrought ironwork graced everything around them from the entrance gate to the stair railings and chandeliers. The boutique hotel exuded Mediterranean charm from its terracotta-tiled patio all the way up to its rust-colored roof.

"Here we are—two-twenty-five," said James as he arrived in front of the room intended for Serena. Once she caught up to him, he handed her a one of the plastic key cards. "Open it up and make sure your room is okay. You never know what you'll end up getting when you use these last-minute travel apps."

Serena pushed the key card down into the

lock slot. Two green dots appeared along with a welcoming 'beep beep' sound. She opened the door and stepped halfway into the arched doorway. The compact room was a cozy blend of rustic and casual elegance for which the seaside town was so well known. It had a four-poster wooden bed with cream linens against one wall, a fireplace with two slipcovered armchairs positioned in front, and a little tiled terrace with wrought iron café-style chairs and a table. Festive pops of color accessorized the whole room in shades of orange, turquoise, and green. Serena felt the tension in her shoulders begin to release.

"It's lovely," she said to James, who was peeking inside from behind her. "I swear, you did a better job than I could have with two months to plan," said Serena, laughing.

"Glad you like it. You deserve a decent place to rest after such an exhausting day. And the pictures of this place reminded me of your house."

"Really?"

"Yes, really," said James.

"Don't let me forget to pay you back for however much I owe you," said Serena, turning all the way around to face him.

"That's the last thing I want you to worry about right now," he said.

Serena nodded, knowing exactly what he meant and grateful to him for saying it. She stepped out of the doorway and looked towards the end of the hall. "Is your room close?"

"Yes, just a few doors down at the end—number 233," said James, pointing down the hall. "Oh, when I checked in, the front desk said there are all sorts of toiletries in the bathroom, but they'll be happy to get you anything else you need."

"Thank you," said Serena. "After today, a shower sounds wonderful."

"Agreed," said James. "Dinner sounds good, too, don't you think?"

As if on command, Serena's stomach let out a plaintive growl. She folded her arms across her belly and hoped James hadn't heard it. But James's grin told her she had no such luck.

"I'll take that as a yes?" asked James.

"I guess I didn't realize I was so hungry," said Serena, rubbing her stomach in an effort to coax it to behave.

"Well, I'm not hungry," said James, "I'm starving. They also said they have a nice Mexican restaurant here. Want to join me for dinner?"

"Dinner?"

"Yeah, dinner," said James. "With me."

"Um, well, that would be... I mean..." Serena knew she should just say yes to what was a completely sensible idea, but couldn't manage to get her mouth to cooperate. Her body, however, had no patience for her indecisiveness. Her stomach gurgled again loudly in protest.

Mortified, Serena let out a laugh and said,

"Yes, dinner sounds great."

"Good decision," said James, holding back a chuckle. "How long do you need to get ready?"

"I think my stomach is telling me to eat first, shower later. So I should be ready in about fifteen minutes, just enough time to freshen up."

"Okay, then I'll pick you up, I mean... knock on your door in fifteen minutes." James took a couple steps toward his room, but halted and turned back around. He pointed to Serena's handbag, which hung securely from her shoulder. "You're going to..."

Serena was a step ahead of him. "Don't worry, I'm going to put Paige's bracelet in the room safe. Pronto." She hugged the leather bag in a little closer to her body.

James nodded with a smile and pulled his key card out of his jacket pocket. "Good thinking. See you in fifteen," he said with a wink.

Serena stepped back into her hotel room and shut the door. She opened the closet to her right, and right away spotted a room safe attached to the inside wall. She pulled out the small jewelry pouch from her bag and held it close to her chest while she considered what four-digit security code to use.

Serena's eyes brightened with clarity as she pressed the "CLEAR" button and then typed in a code that she knew she would not forget.

2-8-3-9

It was James' age, followed by hers.

Serena carefully placed the pouch in the safe, shut the door and pressed the "LOCK" button. She walked into the bathroom, flipped on the light, and looked at herself squarely in the mirror.

"Thirty-nine," she said with a sigh. It was the first time she had said her new age out loud.

"Can I bring you a drink while you look over your menus?" asked their waitress, a cheerful woman in her twenties with a sandy blond bob and slightly sunburnt cheeks. She smiled warmly at James and held her notepad expectantly.

"Any recommendations?" asked James, holding the cocktail menu and looking up to the waitress from his seat.

Serena could see that the waitress wasn't prepared for James' voice or his honeyed eyes. The waitress flushed, making her face even redder.

"Oh, umm... well," said the waitress, flustered. "The Terra Margarita is our signature drink and my personal favorite. It's made with one-hundred-percent agave tequila and our homemade lime mix, which is totally organic."

James gave Serena what she now identified as his 'rogue' look. "Sounds good to me. You up for a totally organic margarita?"

The waitress dragged her eyes off of James to Serena and smiled politely at her, waiting for her reply. By the keen look in her eye, she knew the waitress thought she would be insane to say no.

"Sounds good to me, too," said Serena, snapping her drink menu shut. "No salt, please."

"No salt for me, either," said James, handing the waitress his drink menu without taking his eyes off of Serena.

"Right on. Two Terra margies, no salt. You won't regret it," said the waitress with a nod of approval. "My name is Lacey—I'll be right back with your drinks and to get your order." Lacey flashed James another smile before heading for the bar.

"So..." said James, opening up his menu. "What are you in the mood for?"

Serena perused the extensive list of Mexican specialties, but she really wasn't in the mood to think. Their day at Rosethorn Manor had sapped all the analytical strength out of her and now her mind wanted a break. Something easy, predictable and delicious.

"Fajitas?" she blurted out as soon as she spotted them on the menu.

James grinned and shut his menu. "Perfect. Wanna share?"

"Sure," said Serena. "What kind of meat do you like?"

"How 'bout we do some chicken and steak?"

"Chicken and steak fajitas sound great. With extra guacamole," said Serena, licking her lips.

James chuckled and opened his mouth to respond when Lacey arrived at their table holding two margaritas. Serena's jaw dropped. The frosty glasses were filled to the brim and were the size of cantaloupes.

"Two Terra margaritas, no salt," stated the waitress proudly as she placed one glass in front of each of their placemats. "And I went ahead and brought you some chips and salsa to snack on."

"Wow... they're huge," said Serena.

"Right?" asked the waitress rhetorically. "So, have you decided on what you'd like to eat tonight?" The question was meant for both of them, but her eyes settled on James again with a smitten gaze.

"I think we'd like to have an order of the fajitas for two," said James. "Steak and chicken. Extra guacamole, please."

"Carne asada y pollo fajitas con extra guacamole... got it," said Lacey, scribbling on her pad. "Anything else?"

"I think that will do it for now," said James.

"Awesome," said Lacey, clicking the point back on her ballpoint pen. "Enjoy, you guys." With that, Lacey scooted off to a nearby table of four in need of menus.

James picked up his margarita with both hands. Serena giggled as she grabbed the ridiculously large bowl and did the same. "Should we toast?" he asked.

"Um... sure," said Serena. "To what?"

"Hmm. How about to dear old Professor Julius LeMott?"

Serena crinkled up her face and lowered her glass. "Ugh, don't joke. I feel bad enough for taking off on him. And now I'm going to be gone another whole quote 'sick' day. Lord knows what state he'll be in by the time I get back. I can just see him right now searching everywhere for his glasses. Hopefully he's finally letting his admin help him."

"I wasn't joking. I really mean it," said James. "If Dr. LeMott hadn't told you to consult with me about your fake research project, then I wouldn't have met you. And we wouldn't be here right now." James lifted his glass higher, inviting Serena to join him.

"Well... I guess you have a point," said Serena, bashfully conceding to James' logic. "Then to Professor LeMott." They clinked their glasses together, each splashing some of the margarita onto the white tablecloth.

"Oops," said Serena and took a healthy swig from her glass. Lacey was right, she thought. "Mmm. Yummy," said Serena, her eyes becoming bright as the tequila traveled though her body.

James laughed mid-sip, got some drink caught in his throat, and coughed.

"What?"

"Nothing, I couldn't have said it better myself," said James.

Serena looked around the intimate restaurant. "This place is great. It has so much warmth with all the wood, the brick, and the lanterns. It's like it's bathed in gold," she said, taking another sip.

"You're right. Love the ceilings, too. Let's hope the fajitas are on par with the ambiance." James pushed the chip basket a little closer to Serena. "Chip?"

Serena grabbed a chip, dipped it in the salsa and took a bite. James did the same, and both of them munched silently for a moment.

"Thinking about tomorrow?" asked James.

"Actually, I'm thinking about the kids. It feels strange to be away. I know it sounds lame, but I haven't taken a trip without Asher and Drew in a long time."

"That doesn't sound lame," said James. "You're a mother, after all, with two young boys." James paused. "Does it feel good strange or bad strange?"

Serena picked up a juicy slice of lime that was perched on the edge of her glass and squeezed it into her drink while she considered his question. "Good strange, I think," she said. "I miss them... but this is big... for me."

"Yes, it is." James leaned forward and lowered his voice. "And by the way, this is big for me, too."

"More than you bargained for," said Serena,

smiling.

Serena expected James to respond with something clever, but it was clear from his pensive expression that he was distracted by something else.

"What?" asked Serena.

"What—oh, nothing. I was just wondering... I mean... you don't worry about the kids when they are away, right? Tom—he's a good father?"

"Yeah, no... I mean, no I don't worry. He's good to Asher and Drew. They have a blast with him," said Serena, realizing that the margarita must be working its magic. Normally this line of questioning would make her stomach flip, but she felt unphased.

"Well, good. Nice that you don't have to worry about that," said James.

"Yeah, the kids weren't the problem," said Serena with a crooked smile. *Shut up, Serena*, she thought and took another sip.

James' posture stiffened slightly. He took a long draught from his glass. "Do you mind if I ask... what was the problem?"

Serena raked her hand through her hair. She could feel a buzz warming up her head. "It's hard to explain," she said, knowing full well that was not quite true.

"Can you try?" asked James.

"Okay," said Serena with a sigh. She stared down at the ice cubes melting in her lemon-lime-colored drink. "Sometimes I think it was my fault because I should have known. There were signs, but I just didn't see them for what they were. You know, the little signs that are actually the really big signs as to who a person really is and what's important to them."

"Yes, I think I know exactly what you mean," said James.

"But then," said Serena, tossing her hair back, "something happens that is such a huge sign that you have no choice but to stop being blind and face the truth." Serena stirred the ice around with her red cocktail straw.

"What—" said James. "Never mind. I mean, what *was* the truth?"

Serena looked up at James and let out a sharp and bitter laugh. She leaned forward and motioned with her index figure for him to come closer. James leaned in until his chin was just above the chips.

"The plain and simple truth was that I was not the most important thing to him."

James sat back, pondering Serena's statement. "I find that hard to believe."

Serena sat back, and looked James straight in the eye. "So did I."

After a few moments of heavy silence, he finally asked, "And Asher and Drew? Are they the most important thing to him?"

Serena nodded. "They are. At least I think

they are. Which is all that matters anymore."

A sizzling sound erupted from the other side of the restaurant. Out of the corner of her eye, Serena saw Lacey approaching with a massive tray of cast iron slabs steaming with meat. They were surrounded by a colorful assortment of fajita fixings.

Before Serena knew it, Lacey was at the table saying, "Steak and chicken fajitas for two!" She unloaded the dishes and introduced what was presented on each plate. "Be careful, this plate is reeeally hot," she said to Serena, pointing to the chicken that was still cooking.

"Anything else I can get you?" asked Lacey.

"Um... maybe some water?" asked Serena, trying to come up with an antidote to her tipsy confessional.

"Sure, two waters coming right up." Lacey lingered to smile an extra two seconds at James, and then zoomed away.

As soon as she was gone, James said, "Listen Serena... I want to say one more thing, and then we can drop the subject. Regardless of what's happened in your past, remember that you matter, too—you matter immensely. I mean—all you have to do is look at everything that's happening right now to have proof of that. Tomorrow we are going to meet Charles Sun, for God's sake."

"Yes, maybe you're right. Thank you, James."

"No need."

Serena picked up a tortilla, but James stopped her, taking a hold of her hand mid-air.

"And Serena?"

"Yes?"

"I was listening to what you said in the car back at Rosethorn. And—" James stopped short, as if he were unsure whether to say the rest.

"What?"

"Believe me when I say Tom is the one who's the deranged idiot."

Serena gave a meek smile and took another sip of her margarita.

"Let's eat," was all she could think to say.

BY THE time they walked back up to their room corridor, a chill had set in with the night air, and the temperature felt like it had dropped fifteen degrees. Serena held her arms crossed tightly in front of her body with the sleeves of her sweater pulled over her hands like mittens. The warm, boozy feeling from the restaurant was wearing off, and sheer fatigue was taking its place.

"Cold?" asked James.

"Yeah," said Serena, shivering at the sound of the word.

"Well, then a hot shower will feel great," said James. "You should get inside before you catch a cold."

Serena looked down at the jeans and plum-colored sweater she'd been wearing for the past eighteen hours and laughed. "A new outfit and some pajamas would also be nice. I wasn't exactly prepared to spend two days in this," she said, waving her hand up and down her frame.

"You wear pajamas?" asked James, smirking.

Serena felt the heat rise in her cheeks. She pursed her lips and took a staunch pose with her hands on her hips despite the cold, not wanting to let on that she was the least bit embarrassed.

"I'm the mother of two boys, remember?" she said. "Pajamas are standard issue."

"Right, right," said James. "By the way, I meant no disrespect. I very much like pajamas."

"You do? So you wear them, too?"

"Absolutely not."

Serena and James laughed freely, together and at each other.

"Must be nice to be at the point where you are in your life... no huge mistakes, no baggage, no *pajamas*," said Serena. "And if you play your cards right, *you'll* never have any."

"Oh, I don't know, I wouldn't mind wearing pajamas one day," said James.

"Yeah, sure," teased Serena. "You in a set of plaid flannel pajamas from the Land's End catalogue. That'll be the day."

"Don't you think I'd look good in them?"

Serena's heart pounded in her chest, but she

tried to keep her cool. "I'm sure you would," she said with as much nonchalance as she could muster.

"By the way, you know the best thing about pajamas?"

"What's that?"

"They come off," said James, taking a step closer. "That is, if you want them to."

Serena stood speechless in the semi-darkness, her body now pulsing with heat despite the cold.

James reached over and touched her hand. "And by the way, I *am* playing my cards right."

Her gaze darted away from him and she felt her cheeks burn even warmer. "Yeah, you were up until two days ago when I showed up," Serena said to the ground. "But hopefully this will all be over soon and you can get back to your real life." *Your young, golden, uncomplicated life,* she wanted to say.

James gently lifted her chin, forcing her to look at him directly.

"Is that what you really think?" he asked, staring at her earnestly.

The intensity of his amber eyes was more than she could bear. She took a slight step back and felt her back come into contact with the door of her room. The cold shock of it prompted her to fish out her key.

"James..." she said, nervously digging

through her purse. "My life is at a different stage than yours... it's messy and hard. There are things you just don't understand because you've never been through—"

"But I can understand," said James, stepping closer to her, his voice becoming ragged with emotion. "I want—"

"No," said Serena firmly, instinctively putting her hand on James' chest in order to keep him from coming closer. He was much warmer than she anticipated and she could feel his heart thumping within his chest even harder than her own. "James, it takes time to know what you really want," she said, her voice breaking roughly as she used every ounce of strength in her reserve not to burst into tears.

Serena turned abruptly and opened the door with her keycard. She stepped inside, leaving the door cracked open enough so they could say goodnight. "We should get to sleep considering what we have in store for tomorrow."

"I'll agree with you on that point only," he said, leaning into the cracked door.

"See you in the morning, James."

"Fine. But after we solve this and you're out of danger—"

"*No*, James," said Serena, her words sounding more like a growl than a response. "Even then I'll be too... complicated for you." It was cold enough that she could see her breath, which made her refusal feel that much more tangible, her cowardice that much more visible.

James looked down at his shoes and shook his head. When he looked back up at her, his wounded expression made her feel as if she'd slapped him without using her hand.

"James... I'm—"

"Sleep well, Serena," he said, and pulled her door closed before she had a chance to say another word.

Later that night, Serena found herself running through the rain wearing nothing but Paige's watch strapped securely around her wrist. She was chasing after a black car driving away into the distance. The rain intensified with every stride she took until it became a deluge that blinded her, the baseball-sized drops of water beating her down so fiercely that she could no longer move. Serena crouched onto the flooded ground to seek shelter from the storm that raged around her. The steely wings on the watch suddenly began to grow, becoming larger and larger until they covered her entire body, surrounding her in the form of a giant winged egg. She was trapped inside the metal egg with the water rising around her, the black car leaving her behind, never to return.

Serena woke up in the darkness to the sound of her own scream. She bolted upright in her bed, out of breath, her hair still wet from the shower. The hotel room was quiet as a grave.

Trembling, she laid back down, alone with her
freshly tilled fears. She pulled the covers back over
her naked body and curled up into a ball,
wondering whether the nightmare was about the
past, the present, or the future.

Chapter 18

Serena stood on the corner of South Grand Avenue and West Third Street in downtown Los Angeles, her neck craned back in an effort to see the top edge of the soaring skyscraper. She squinted against the late morning sun, straining to make out the edges of the gleaming chrome exterior that stood against the cloudless blue sky. Further down, the side of the building was a matrix of what looked like a thousand too-shiny windows that reflected everything around them while remaining guardedly opaque. Serena pulled the leather strap of her handbag up tighter around her shoulder, feeling even more protective of the heirloom that lay inside it. This building looked entirely too futuristic and cold for whatever lay in store for her precious cargo. Out of nowhere, the image of the yellow pathway that led up to Devania's cottage popped into her mind, and she was knew at once what this unreal-real place reminded her of: Oz.

"What are you thinking?" asked James, who was also looking up while finishing off the iced coffee that he had bought on the road to refresh him on their drive down from Santa Barbara.

"Oz," said Serena.

"Ah. Well, I can certainly see why, given the circumstances. Although I'm sure that thing is a hell of a lot taller than Oz was."

"And Charles Sun is probably a lot more great and powerful," said Serena, dropping her gaze from the building back down to James, who stood by her side facing the large entranceway of revolving doors that led into the main lobby of Sun Tower. It was getting warmer, now, and Serena was not surprised to find that among his many talents, James seemed to have a real knack for layering his clothes properly for every situation, a gift she felt she had never possessed. He had shed his sweater in the car and now was bare-armed, wearing a sea-blue t-shirt that made him look like he was freshly plucked out of southern California.

"Good point," said James. "But let's not forget that yesterday, the mighty Mr. Sun did miraculously request a meeting with you, so you've obviously got some great-and-powerful-ness of your very own going on."

"That's flattering, but I'm afraid that had nothing to do with me."

"Serena, let's get real. This has *everything* to do with you," said James, his eyes filled with conviction.

Serena was thankful that there seemed to be

no discord lodged between them this morning. She felt sensitive and edgy after her night of restless sleep, but James was collected and confident, with all his focus concentrated on the day ahead. It was a great relief to find that James was still her intrepid ally.

She looked warily back up at the building. The tingling current that she felt every time she touched Paige's bracelet seemed to be humming through her whole body now. She literally felt like a live wire. But she resisted the urge to mention it to James, for she knew it was only bound to alarm him.

"I wonder which window he's behind," she said instead.

"Only one way to find out," said James, his eyes steadied on Serena.

A loud buzzing ring brought Serena's attention from Sun Tower down to her hip, where she could feel the vibrations of her phone from inside her bag. Almost happy to have a distraction to delay their entrance, she retrieved the phone. She looked down at the caller ID on the screen and let out an "Uggh."

"Who is it?"

"It's Professor LeMott. I left a voicemail this morning to say I was still under the weather—I'm sure he's checking in to see how I'm feeling. He always does that when I'm out sick. He'll worry if he doesn't hear anything from me. Let me answer it." Serena cleared her throat, even though she knew she intended to try to sound sick, and pushed the answer key. "Hello?" she answered in fake-scratchy voice. James chuckled and gave her a small roll of the eyes.

"Oh, hi, Professor LeMott, so nice of you to call." Serena gave James a pleading "behave" look and put her index finger up to her lips signaling him to "shhh" as she listened to the other end.

"Yes, yes. Still have a little bit of a sore throat, but I expect to be back in the office by tomorrow," said Serena, giving a little cough. James raised a questioning eyebrow at her fib.

"What's that? Oh, yes. Yes, I will. Rest and soup," she said, turning away from James and Sun Tower as she spoke so she could concentrate on her acting. James was grinning from ear to ear. "Thanks again for your concern, Professor LeMott. I'll see you tomorrow."

Serena turned around and walked back to James, who had moved closer to the building and was now standing right outside one of the revolving doors. A group of smartly dressed men and women in trendy business suits came pushing through, each one so absorbed by their cell phone that Serena felt completely invisible to them.

"You sure about that?" asked James as soon as she reached him.

"Sure about what?"

"That you are going to be back in the office

by tomorrow," said James. "That might be another lie, ya know."

Serena looked through the glass doors into the imposing white marble lobby. A lump of apprehension grew in her throat. "I'm not sure about anything. What am I doing here, James? This can't be right. I'm..." *A thirty-nine-year-old divorced research assistant living the suburbs with two kids*, she thought, but felt too ashamed to say it. "It was only when I mentioned Gwendolyn Whitmoor's name that the receptionist decided to give me the time of day. I'm nobody."

"Stop," said James. "Now that's a lie I won't stand for. I know that's not what the bracelet is telling you."

Serena shook her head, "No, you're right. It's not." Serena smiled at him warmly, feeling an even sweeter regard and appreciation for him having faith in her, even if it felt unjustified.

"Okay, then, are you gonna get in?" she asked, waiting for James to step into one of the heavy glass V-shaped compartments which she just noticed you didn't have to actually push—they were turning automatically.

"I think we both already know I'm in," James said jokingly, although Serena could feel a raw, truthful energy behind his words. He stepped back and extended his arm towards the door like a bellman. "After you, Zahra."

Serena watched the doors sweep by with a

swish-swish brushing sound. They sent a rush of cool air towards her face every time one breezed around. She looked down at her legs and mentally tried to encourage them to move. Her feet could not have been more securely grounded, yet she felt like she was stepping off of a cliff.

"Let's go in together, at the same time," she finally said.

James' eyes lit up with surprise.

"Unless you don't want to, I mean... I guess it is pretty childish—"

"No, it's not," said James, taking her hand. "Together. Let's go."

Serena continued to look at James as the next "swoosh" went by, and she stepped into the oversized glass turnstile without taking her eyes off him. Once inside, the world went silent for a moment, as if they were underwater instead of under a million tons of concrete, metal, and glass. She heard only the sound of their footsteps and felt only the warmth of James' fingers gently pushing against hers as they moved forward in unison. Her mind blurred along with the perpetual motion of the doors. As they stepped through to the other side and into the enormous marble and steel lobby, a single clear thought arose in her mind like a lonely bubble traveling to the surface of a lake.

Fifty-fifth floor.

THE ELEVATOR doors slid open and Serena

and James found themselves face-to-face with a slight, young African-American man in thick-rimmed 'nerd' glasses, a navy blazer, skinny jeans, a crisp white shirt, and a hot-pink tie. He held an iPad in one hand and sported a sleek, hi-tech wireless headset on top of his short, impeccably groomed black hair. Serena spotted a shiny gold letter H in the center of his black leather belt. *H for Hermes* thought Serena, who suddenly felt decidedly car-crumpled and unstylish. He smiled at them warmly.

"Good morning, Ms. Rayborn, Dr. Riley. It's a pleasure to meet you. My name is Daniel McCort. I am Mr. Sun's senior assistant. It is my pleasure to welcome you to Sun Electronics." He politely stepped to the side to give them room to exit.

"Thank you," said Serena timidly, stepping out of the elevator first. "Thank you, Mr. McCort. It is our pleasure as well," said James, stepping out behind her.

"Please call me Daniel. So glad you were able to join us this morning," he said, leading them towards one end of the long, mahogany-paneled hallway into which they had exited. Richly patterned oriental carpets ran along the parquet floor and a series of large-scale modern oil paintings in soothing tones of blue and beige hung along the entire length of the corridor. Serena felt as if she had just walked into an opulent brownstone in Boston, not into the uppermost corporate stratosphere of a trillion-dollar electronics company.

Daniel stopped mid-stride. "May I offer you something to drink? Water, coffee, espresso, tea?" Daniel's quick, dark-brown eyes blinked behind his glasses with efficient hospitality.

"No, thank you, I'm fine," said Serena.

"Dr. Riley?"

"No, I'm good, too. Thanks."

"Then please allow me to escort you directly to Mr. Sun's office. He is expecting you presently." Daniel flashed a well-practiced professional smile and continued down the hallway with Serena and James trailing a few feet behind him.

Daniel arrived at a set of darkly tinted floor-to-ceiling glass doors. He placed the palm of his hand onto an electronic console that was set discreetly into the wall. The doors unlocked and the pathway opened up completely as each door slid horizontally and disappeared within the wall.

Daniel continued into a large vestibule, which led to another set of blacked-out glass doors. Two enormous, white porcelain vases adorned with an elaborate Eastern decorative pattern sat on the floor on either side of the doors. Recessed spotlights shone down on them from above, highlighting their impressive museum-quality intricacy.

Daniel stopped at the doors and turned to Serena. "Well, here we are, Ms. Rayborn. Please know that I am at your service for anything else either of you may need during your visit with us."

"Thank you, Daniel," said Serena, trying to sound more composed than she felt. She was was not sure if it was her nerves or the unsettling current that continued to jolt through her with increasing intensity, but something here felt very, very wrong. She could not put her finger on it, but she could *feel* it.

"I will, of course, be right here to escort you out after your meeting with Mr. Sun," assured Daniel, as if to ease her apparent trepidation. He nodded a confirmation to James. "Okay?"

"That would be great, Daniel," said James. "Thank you."

Daniel held up his hand and paused to give them a reassuring smile before placing it squarely on another electronic panel on the wall to his right. This time, a pleasant, melodic chiming sound could be heard before the doors were sucked away into the walls.

It took a moment for Serena's eyes to adjust to the sunlight that came flooding towards them once the doors were fully retracted. A stunning panoramic view of downtown Los Angeles suddenly took up every possible inch of optic frame. The spacious room seemed to float on a sparsely populated sea of high-rise buildings, the rest of Los Angeles sprawling out into the distant smoggy horizon. At the far right corner of this jaw-dropping picture stood an older yet more modern version of the man in the photograph sitting at the bottom of Serena's purse. *The* Charles Sun. Although the only name that sprang to Serena's mind as she looked upon him for the first time was Sun Chanming.

"Good afternoon, Ms. Rayborn, Dr. Riley. I am Charles Sun," he said, striding toward them. "Thank you so much for coming. Please, please come in and have a seat." He motioned toward two long taupe leather couches that sat in front of a sleek black desk.

Charles Sun gave a quick, deliberate nod to Daniel, who was waiting for instruction just outside the doors. "Thank you, Daniel." By the time Serena turned around, the glass doors had slid back into one solid panel and Daniel was gone.

Charles Sun was the most regal man Serena had ever seen. He had a full head of completely grey hair, but despite his age, the tone of his tannish-olive skin was unusually vibrant. She found it hard to believe this man had to be close to eighty years old. He was of medium build, but his countenance and commanding poise made him appear taller. He looked at them with piercing, attentive eyes. Serena had always wondered what a custom-made suit looked like in real life. Now she had her answer. Charles Sun's dark blue suit was so finely sewn that the silk practically glistened with craftsmanship.

"Thank you, Mr. Sun. It's such a pleasure to meet you," said Serena as she made her way to one of the couches. Charles Sun gave Serena an unhurried, gracious handshake.

James stepped over to Charles Sun and gave him a strong handshake before sitting down next to her. "Mr. Sun, it's an honor."

The leather couch was as soft as butter. Serena sank down into the cushy seat, placed her purse down next to her and looked briefly around the office. The room and the view went on and on into the space behind them, complete with a full-size black marble conference table surrounded by red space-age ergonomic chairs. Serena tried to fathom the kinds of heavy-hitter meetings that must take place inside this room. As she looked around the sun-filled office, there was no question that they had ascended to the top of the Mount Everest of the business world. Serena, however, could not shake the sinking feeling that they had also traveled to the bottom of something. The room was filled with light, but she felt a shadowy, dark presence that weighed down everything from the posh furniture to the very air she was breathing.

Charles Sun sat down across from them, maintaining the posture of a king as he descended down to the couch. He said nothing for a moment, but simply smiled at them with a welcoming familiarity, as if they were old friends who had not had a chance to get together in a very long time. He seemed to be politely sizing up Serena and James. Finally, his almost-black dark brown eyes settled on Serena.

"Thank you for coming on such short notice, Ms. Rayborn," he said, and then looked over to James. "Dr. Riley, I appreciate you making the trip down from Santa Barbara."

"Please call me Serena. And we are the ones who should be thanking you for being willing to see us so quickly. I know how busy you must be."

"One must make time for the things that are important to us in this life. And please, call me Sun. That is what my friends call me."

Serena was not sure how to respond. She resisted the temptation to look down at her bag. She felt like Paige's inscribed bracelet was burning a hole in her pocket.

"And please, call me James," James said, giving Serena a chance to recover.

"James, then," said Sun, giving him a slight bow. He looked back to Serena, a more solemn air coming over him. "I was quite intrigued to hear that you have... business on behalf of Gwendolyn Whitmoor?"

"Well, yes... sort of," Serena's voice halted as she searched for the right words to explain. "Actually, we were visiting her estate in Santa Barbara—Rosethorn Manor—and were able to meet her niece, Paige Quincy." Serena glanced over to James for help. She was not sure how say the next part. She had no idea how much Sun knew about Gwendolyn Whitmoor, but she did not want to be the one to break the news that she was no longer alive.

"Do you happen to remember a Gwendolyn Whitmoor?" asked James, picking up the ball in the conversation with perfect directness and timing.

"Very much so," said Sun, "and it saddened me greatly when I learned that she had passed out of this life." His eyes drifted into the space behind them with a distracted gaze. "I suppose that must be five years ago now." Serena saw a glimmer of the same expression she had seen on Sun's face as a young man in the picture—a sweetness beneath the rigid exterior.

"Yes, I believe that's right," said Serena.

"And what brought you two to Rosethorn Manor, if you don't mind my asking?"

Serena gulped. The phrase 'honesty is the best policy' sprang to her mind, but right now she didn't believe it for one second. "We were hoping to find out some information about what became of certain items in her estate... after she died."

"Ahhh, I see... Yes, she was quite the collector," said Sun, a knowing smile creeping onto his face. "And was your... mission successful?"

He definitely knows something, thought Serena. "Well, not exactly..." She glanced briefly at James, wondering what he would think about what she was about to do next. James gave her a perplexed look back.

Serena pulled her bag onto her lap and reached inside.

"Serena, wait—" said James, his voice filled with caution.

But she found the black silk jewelry sachet so quickly it felt like it was magnetized to her hand. She pulled the string that loosened the top, poured the contents into her left palm and extended it out to Sun. "We found this."

Sun took a pair of glasses from his suit jacket pocket and put them on, his eyes fixed on Serena's hand. He leaned forward. "What is it?"

"It's you, actually." Serena picked the photo out of her left hand, leaving the bracelet behind and held it up, picture-side facing out, in front of Sun's face. "We found it with Paige. It was hidden inside this very bracelet that Gwendolyn left to her in her will. And it's... you."

Sun stared at the photo and a look of understanding mixed with incredulity dawned across his face. Serena's arm felt electrified by the same reverberating flux that she had felt since her first contact with the bracelet at Rosethorn Manor. As she continued to hold the photo in the space between herself and Sun, the force felt greater than ever. "Your name—Sun—is also inscribed on the bracelet."

After what felt like a long time Sun reached out for the picture. "May I?" he asked, his voice barely audible, his arm paused in mid-air.

"Of course," said Serena, gently placing the photo into his hand.

Sun cupped both hands around the photo as if it were a delicate flower. He slowly rose from the couch, went over to his desk, and sat down in the black leather executive chair that sat behind it. He placed the picture down, pulled open one of the side drawers, and pulled out a small hand-held magnifying glass. Sun peered down at the front side of the picture through the magnifier for a solid minute before flipping it over to inspect the other side. He looked up at Serena and James, as if to ask whether they had also seen the name and date written on it.

"Sun Chanming, 1942," said James, in answer to his unspoken question.

Sun put the magnifying glass down next to the picture. He closed his eyes and took several long meditative breaths. When he finally did open his eyes, Sun leaned down and pulled open another, larger drawer on the bottom left side of his desk. He removed a stack of old, yellowed envelopes that were tied together in a bundle by a coarse, brown string. He held the stack in both hands and smiled softly at Serena and James from across the room. Only when Sun returned to the couch could Serena see that his eyes were moist with tears.

"Sun..." said Serena, "I'm sorry, I didn't mean to—"

"Please, there's no need to apologize, Serena," said Sun. "Funny, it's been so long and I've gotten so old, I'd almost forgotten my real name. Life forces us to give up so many things over the years, and then all we have are reminders of who we once were... and what we once had."

Sun looked down at the envelopes that he held on his lap, tracing the worn edges with one finger. On the top envelope, Serena could see a faded address written in old-style cursive. The thick black ink looked almost like calligraphy, the kind of writing produced at a time when people wrote with fountain pens.

"Are those... letters, Mr. Sun?" asked Serena.

"Indeed, they are."

"L-love letters?" asked James, the presumptuous question tumbling out of his mouth.

Sun looked from the bundle up to James. The sadness ebbed away from his face and he said with a teasing smile, "Ah. I see we have a romantic."

"Well, uh..." James said, a faint redness spreading across his cheeks. This time he looked over to Serena for help.

"Whatever did you mean by that, James?" asked Serena, trying to make the question sound as innocuous as possible.

"He means what I suspect both you and Dr. Riley have already guessed," said Sun. "That these are very, very old letters from my dearest Gwendolyn. Twenty-six, to be exact. Letters that ended abruptly when she was forced by her father to end her relationship with me and marry Douglas Whitmoor."

"Why... why would Mr. Quincy have done that?" asked Serena.

Sun narrowed his eyes at Serena, as if he expected more of her, even this early in their acquaintance.

"My birth name is Sun Chanming" said Sun, his voice cracking with sorrow. "I was a poor Chinese immigrant and a far cry from the socially acceptable Hamiltons, Vanderbilts, and Whitmoors he allowed to court Gwendolyn. Mr. Quincy did not consider me to be even remotely suitable for his daughter. The man was a living dinosaur of racism and classism. He hated me from the moment Gwendolyn told him she happened to meet me while I was studying English at the public library. The last time the man spoke to me, he called me an Oriental dog who wasn't good enough to shine his daughter's boots."

Serena and James turned towards each other, their eyes wide with astonishment. When Serena turned back to Sun, he was looking down at the stack of letters again, his mouth taut and brimming with anger.

"Sun... I can't tell you how sorry I am," said Serena. "It's terrible... what happened to both of you... so wrong and cruel." Sun continued to stare at the letters, smoldering in silence.

Serena wanted to say something, anything to console Sun, now that she had opened a Pandora's box of painful memories for him. "Paige told us... that you must have been Gwendolyn's one true love. This bracelet, the only thing she bestowed to her, was absolute proof in her eyes."

Sun looked up from the letters to Serena and then over to James, a look of thankful relief washing the bitterness from his face. "I always hoped, but never knew if she... It had been so many years... Thank you, Serena." Sun gave a deep sigh and fell silent again.

"How did you—what did you do... after she married Douglas Whitmoor?" asked James.

Sun let out a wounded laugh and looked around the commanding office. "Isn't it obvious? I built this instead," he said, making a sweeping motion around the room with one arm. "I devoted myself to Sun Electronics. I became Charles Sun and spawned a corporate empire instead of a life with the only woman who has ever owned my heart."

Serena felt the depth of Sun's heartache hit her like a wave. She leaned forward and carefully placed the bracelet on top of the letters. "You've given so much to the world, Sun," said Serena. "You are a technological visionary, truly."

Sun shook his head, a bemused smirk on his

face, and let out another injured chuckle. "Surely, Serena, you don't believe such things can ever make up for losing the love of one's life."

Serena swallowed hard and shook her head. "No. No, I know of course it doesn't." She kept her eyes intentionally averted from James.

Sun let out a sigh of sad acceptance. He gave the letters one last squeeze between his fingertips before extending the stack of envelopes with the bracelet balanced on top of it out to Serena. "Here you are, Serena. Please tell Ms. Quincy that I am more than happy to honor her request that her aunt's letters to me be returned to her. I cannot thank her enough for the avowal she has given me from Gwendolyn by sending you to share this with me." Sun kept his gaze centered on the bracelet that lay balanced on top of the letters.

Serena and James looked at each other in confusion, each equally baffled by Sun's request. As Serena stared down at Sun's hands, she suddenly realized, *Good Lord, he thinks we came here to get the letters back.*

"Oh, no, Sun. I'm afraid you misunderstand our intentions," said James, who had clearly come to the same conclusion.

Sun dropped the bundle back down onto his lap, securing the bracelet on the top with his fingertips. "No? You aren't here because you would like the letters back? I assumed that is why you went to Rosethorn—because Paige Quincy had enlisted your help, particularly your expertise, Dr. Riley, to find them."

"No, I'm afraid not," said Serena. "The bracelet just happened to lead us to you, but we didn't know anything about the letters. We were actually at Rosethorn in search of something... else."

"You didn't... that is to say, you did not come here because Miss Quincy found my secret letters to Gwendolyn?"

Serena and James both shook their heads in the negative.

Sun put the letters and bracelet down beside him on the couch, sat back and crossed his legs. He put one finger up to his lips while he considered this new information. "Fascinating. Well, then, please enlighten me, Serena."

"We were actually at Rosethorn to see if we could find out anything about what might have happened to a certain piece of jewelry—a necklace—that was auctioned off according to the terms of Gwendolyn's will. Coincidentally, according to Paige, the necklace was her Aunt's very favorite piece. She wore it every day until she passed away."

Sun raised an eyebrow. "I see... and was Ms. Quincy able to help you track it down?"

"Unfortunately, no..." Serena paused, trying to choose every word with care. "Paige told us that over the years, not even she has been able to uncover any clue as to its whereabouts."

"You see," interjected James, "as it would happen, this particular piece can't be easily located because it was auctioned off to a buyer that was—"

"Anonymous?" asked Sun.

Serena's heart started pounding. She couldn't believe her ears. "Did you just say—"

"Anonymous. Yes, I did," said Sun. He narrowed his eyes at Serena with a look of unwavering certainty.

Serena felt blinded by the flurry of questions that rose like a sudden tide within her. She stood up, feeling almost propelled by the weight of Sun's words. She caught sight of the bracelet which sat on the couch next to him and suddenly knew the reason it had been sending an unrelenting current through her from the first moment she touched it. She pointed to it, but said nothing, muted by the enormity of what this had to mean.

"Come over here with me, Serena," said Sun with a cunning smile, rising up from the couch. He walked over to the conference table and beckoned her to join him, waving her towards him like a kid with something top-secret to share.

James was the first to follow. "Come on Serena," he said, taking her hand. "I think we can trust him," he whispered, gently directing her towards the huge marble table.

"That's kind of you, Dr. Riley, but I think the real question is whether *I* can trust the two of *you*," said Sun, who now stood at the far end of the table.

Serena squeezed James' hand tightly and pulled him closer to the table. "Oh my God," she said, as she pushed herself in between two of the red rolling chairs. She leaned over and pressed the palm of her hand onto to the surface, as if she were trying to make an imprint. The black marble was cold to the touch, but to Serena, it felt like a river of heat had started to flow through her body. She gasped.

"What is it?" asked James.

"It's... here."

"What? What's here?" asked James. He looked around, his eyes wildly searching around the room.

Serena slowly lifted her hand and pointed to the very center of the table.

"*Can* I trust you, Serena?" asked Sun with a provocative smile, his hands clasped securely behind his back, as if he were standing in front of a throne.

Serena gave Sun a strong nod. "Without a doubt."

"Good," said Sun, with a nod of approval back.

Sun reached under the table and pushed up on something hidden from Serena's view. A low-pitched humming sound emanated from somewhere underneath the table. From the very center, which had appeared to be a single slab of unbroken marble, a square-foot section began to rise up like a black puzzle piece that had sprung to life and begun to levitate. As it rose higher, Serena heard something else—the soft sound of smoothly shifting gears. Within another few seconds, a shiny, clear material appeared beneath the piece of floating marble. Glass—a glass box was rising up. Serena gripped James' hand as she waited for what she was positive she would see next.

When Serena finally caught sight of the shimmering stone, hanging gloriously from a diamond necklace on a black velvet stand, the entire room seemed to recede into the background, her heart thumping so hard that her chest was reverberating like a drum. In one flashing moment, the Eye of Fire bore the light of its eternal power into her being and she remembered what she had done over five hundred years ago at the time of her death. The Eye of Fire had called her back to claim it, and now Serena knew why.

"Serena... you knew. You found it," said James, awestruck.

"The Eye of Fire," said Serena, giving him a smile of gratification. "But James, I'm pretty sure *we* found it." She gave James' hand one more squeeze before releasing it and walking over to stand in front of Sun. "It was you. You were the anonymous buyer."

She thought Sun would surely say something, but instead he only stepped to her side, reached under the table again, and pressed another concealed button. One side of the glass box slid down and disappeared into the table. Serena shivered at the sight of the Eye of Fire without any barrier between she and it. Sun leaned over the table and carefully lifted the necklace out of the case with both hands. He brought it over to Serena and held it up high in front of her.

"It's astoundingly beautiful, isn't it?"

"It certainly is," said Serena, her voice dropping to a whisper.

"But believe it or not, it's not as beautiful as Gwendolyn was. I knew she had worn it throughout her life, and therefore I wanted to have at least this part of her." Sun turned the necklace from side to side, allowing Serena to see the diamond from all angles. Serena's breathing went shallow at the sight of the stone's stunning radiance up close. She had seen it a thousand times on its altar, sparkling like the ocean shining in the brightest sunlight and glowing like fire burning in the darkest night.

"Would you like to hold it?" asked Sun.

"No," said Serena, stiffening and stepping back.

"But... you've done so much work and come so far to find this historical piece. I would assume that you would want to—"

"Sun, let me explain at last. I am not a jewelry historian or an ancient gems admirer," said Serena. "I am—well, I mean to say I was protector and guardian of the Eye of Fire. Five hundred years ago. In ancient India, that is."

"You aren't ser—"

"Serious? Yes, Sun, I'm afraid I am. It was my sworn duty in my kingdom's temple to protect the Eye of Fire on its sacred altar, but... I failed. The temple was raided, and in the process of trying to defend it from being stolen, I was... killed. But before I died, I kind of... um... cursed it."

"You *cursed* it?" asked James, stepping in front of Serena and standing next to Sun. He cocked his head to the side and put his hands on his hips. "Serena, you never told me you *cursed* it."

Serena bit her lip guiltily. "Sorry, James, I didn't fully remember until being in its presence again. But... yes, I did."

"Wait a minute," said Sun, turning to James, "*Doctor* Riley, do you also believe that Ms. Rayborn—Serena—was who she says she was?"

Serena could see by the look on James' face that her claim—she had cursed the Eye of Fire—was still sinking into his brain. She wondered if this last revelation would be the straw that broke the camel's back, finally causing James' belief in her to falter.

"Dr. Riley?" prompted Sun again.

James jumped to answer, but Serena threw her hand up and motioned for him to not speak.

"Sun, please believe that I would never dishonor you or your past. I am Zahra, Devadasi of

Golconda, High Priestess and Guardian of the Eye of Fire," she said, throwing her shoulders back and locking her eyes with him.

James smiled with approval. "It's the truth," he said.

Sun stared down at the Eye of Fire, which lay draped on the palms of his hands, as if he were trying to unravel the hidden history that had until that moment been indiscernible. He looked back up to James and then to Serena with a look of distress crinkled across his forehead.

"Serena, how did you come to realize all this?" asked Sun.

She stepped towards him, as sudden urgency springing into her body. "Sun, I'd love to tell you one day, but right now we don't have time."

"Why?" asked Sun, looking back and forth between them, a puzzled look on his face.

"Yeah, why? What are you talking about, Serena?" asked James.

"When I say I cursed the Eye of Fire, that means I placed a powerful hex on it to ensure that not a single other person would ever benefit from possessing it. Right now, it will bring only hardship, misery, and ultimately destruction to whomever retains it."

Sun and James gave each other looks of chagrin. Sun looked down once again to the huge diamond that sat in the center of his hands. From the expression on his face, Serena could tell he found it hard to grasp that something so magnificent could be anything but a blessed treasure.

Serena stepped over to Sun and gently placed her hand on his shoulder. "Sun, you remember Gwendolyn wore the Eye of Fire every day until the end of her life. Do you happen to know what became of her?"

Sun's eyes met hers with a spark of insight. "She... I have heard it said that she went... mad." He winced that as he said the last word.

"Are you saying..." said James, "that was *the curse*?" He stepped towards Sun, but then stopped short as if getting too close to the Eye of Fire would expose him to some kind of deadly radiation. "What kind of curse causes a person to go... *mad*?"

"A doozy of a curse, that's what kind," said Serena. "Every second that you keep it, Sun, puts you in further danger."

"Then..." said James, shaking his head in despair. A look of realization swept over his face and his shoulders dropped as if they were suddenly carrying a heavy burden. "Good God, Serena, that explains why each and every person that has possessed The Eye of Fire has had tragedy befall them in one way or another. What on earth do we do next?"

Serena closed her eyes and took at deep breath to settle her resolve. When she opened her eyes, James and Sun were looking at her intently, wide-eyed with anticipation.

"When the Eye of Fire is returned to its altar, the curse will be broken." Serena gulped hard. "I need to take it back."

"Are you actually suggesting that I just *give* you the *Eye of Fire*?" asked Sun. "My last remaining connection to Gwendolyn? Not to mention one of the world's most valued treasures?"

"I'm not suggesting, Sun. I'm insisting," said Serena. "I'm sorry, but it's the only way. And we need to act quickly, before the power of the curse brings more harm."

"Wait a minute," said James, putting his hands up to pause the debate. "Serena, okay, assuming that the curse will be broken when returned to its altar—it's impossible. Even if you were to travel the eight thousand miles to India, Golconda's temple was destroyed. The altar no longer exists."

"I know," said Serena. "But I have an idea. I think there's a way."

"What way could there possibly be—" said Sun. Then he froze, his mouth wide-open in mid-sentence, as if his vocal cords had suddenly been ripped out from his throat.

Serena had heard it. The whole sound was completely unfamiliar, and yet she recognized aspects of it. A tinging sound—the breaking of glass—and a tight, airy, zipping sound—like an arrow traveling at high-speed through the air.

Before Serena could put all the pieces together, Sun slumped forward, the Eye of Fire slipping from his grasp and his body following as if he were diving after it. He collapsed and came crashing down like a marionette whose strings had been savagely cut.

"Sun!" screamed Serena.

James and Serena jumped forward to break Sun's fall. James pulled back on Sun's shoulders from behind to soften his descent and Serena caught his head before it hit the ground. Sun folded forward into a ball in his expensive suit, with only the back of his head visible, his face completely out of sight. Both Serena and James instinctively pushed him over to his side in order to lay him down on his back. At first the only thing Serena saw was Sun's pinched face, his eyes tightly shut as he writhed in pain.

"Serena—oh no," said James, panicked. He jumped forward, threw open Sun's jacket and pressed down on the left side of his chest with both hands.

Then she saw the pool of blood.

Serena let out a shrill scream and looked frantically around the room. Something caught her attention as her eyes flew past the panoramic window behind them. There was a little crack. No, a little hole.

"A bullet, Serena. It was a bullet," said James. "I think it went all the way through him from back to front." He continued to apply pressure to Sun's chest in a determined effort to stop the bleeding. Serena's breath caught in her throat as she saw the fresh red stain on Sun's white shirt grow wider and wider beneath James' hands. "We need to call 911. Now," said James.

Serena sprang up from the floor and flew to the sliding glass doors where they had entered the office.

"Help!" she cried and raised both fists to start pounding on the doors. Serena's arms were still in mid-air above her head when the doors swept open and Daniel appeared before her. His face flipped from composed to alarmed as soon he saw Serena's unhinged demeanor.

"Ms. Rayborn? What is it?"

"Daniel, call 911. Sun is hurt—badly."

Daniel wasted no time with questions. With a touch to his headset at his left temple, he was connected to an emergency number. "911. Immediately," he said, trying to see around Serena towards whatever the commotion was on the other side of the room.

"Come here," she said, dragging Daniel by the coat sleeve over to where James was hunched over Sun on the floor. Sun was still conscious, but his eyes were squeezed shut, his face beaded over with sweat and twisted into a tortured frown. His breathing was labored and shallow. Daniel shuddered, looking at Serena in horror and disbelief. "Daniel, tell them it's a gunshot wound and that we need an ambulance immediately," said James, only looking briefly up at Daniel to make sure he understood the gravity of the situation.

Daniel nodded. "We need an ambulance," he said loudly into the headset. "Immediately. It's Mr. Sun. He's been shot. Please hurry." Daniel's face was stone serious as he listened to the person on the other end of the line. "They should be here in under five minutes." He knelt down helplessly beside James, who was caked in blood up to his wrists.

"You shot... you *shot* Mr. Sun?" asked Daniel, turning to Serena with complete dismay written all over his face.

"No! Oh, Daniel... I realize how this must look, but we would never—"

"Then who did this?" he asked, covering his mouth with his hands as if he were about to be violently ill.

"We don't know," said Serena, getting down on her knees to join them. "But there's a hole," she said and pointed to the glass wall behind them. "I think... I think the shot must have come from another building."

"But... *why*?" asked Daniel, looking desperately back and forth from James to Serena. Before either of them had a chance to answer, Daniel's eyes flickered up to the open glass display case that sat empty on top of the conference table.

"He... he actually *opened* the case for the

two of you?" asked Daniel.

"I... did," whispered Sun.

The three of them, stunned to hear his strained voice, leaned in closer to Sun's face. His eyes were still closed and he took quick, forced breaths from his mouth, which was still open from the monumental effort of speaking.

"Sun, you are going to be okay," said James. "The bleeding has slowed down a bit and the ambulance will be here any minute."

Sun let out a moan and his face crinkled up in pain as if something sharp had just been thrust into his back. He struggled to move his arms at his sides and arched his back. His eyes fluttered open briefly and he made eye contact with Serena. "T—t-take it," he choked out on a garbled exhale.

"Stay still, Sun," said James, keeping his hands steadily pressed into his upper chest. He looked warily at Serena and Daniel. "I think he's trying to get up."

Serena crawled forward so she could get as close as possible to Sun's head. She turned her head to the side and held her hair up over her ear and hovered directly over Sun's face.

"What's wrong, Sun? What do you mean 'take it'?"

"Take... it... back. Do it... *now*."

"What's he talking about? Take what back?" asked Daniel.

Serena sat back on her heels. *He's right...*

it's time, she thought. She reached below James' taut outstretched arms and slipped her hand underneath Sun's back. Her middle and index fingers felt something hard and she pulled, scraping her nails on the rug along the way. The Eye of Fire emerged from beneath Sun's coat, hanging from the diamond necklace hooked on Serena's trembling fingertips.

"My word..." said Daniel.

"Daniel... take her to the plane... *now,*" gasped Sun.

"Sir?"

"Zahra," Sun coughed out.

Daniel shook his head in confusion. "Who's Zahra?"

"I am," said Serena. "I don't have time to explain."

Daniel nodded. "Understood." He leaned over Sun and said, "Right away, Sir. Don't worry, I'll take care of it."

Sun's eyes fluttered closed again.

Daniel hit the side of his headset, pushed his glasses up to the bridge of his nose and stood up. "I need the car and the plane right away." He looked down at Serena, who was still crouched next to James on the floor. "Where to, Ms. Rayborn?"

James looked at Serena, his brow sweaty from the effort of pushing down on Sun. His worried expression told her he was wondering the same thing.

"San Francisco," said Serena.

"San Francisco," echoed Daniel into the headset, springing into action and taking quick strides towards the opposite end of the room. "Okay... good," he said in response to whoever was speaking rapidly on the other end. "Dr. Riley, the paramedics and the police are on their way up. Ready when you are, Ms. Rayborn," said Daniel, with one foot already out of the door.

"For Gwendolyn... go *now*..." exhaled Sun. He clenched his teeth in pain as his head dropped to the right towards the floor.

"He's right, Serena," said James. "Remember, whoever did this is still out there. You need to go. *Run*." James continued to lean above Sun, his body strong and stationary, his arms firmly planted on top of him as he spoke. "I'll take care of Sun," he assured her, his voice sounding even huskier than usual.

Serena tried to will her body to leave, but her legs felt like they were cemented to the floor. "James..." she said, her voice trembling.

She did not know why, but she suddenly needed something desperately from him before she left. She closed her eyes, keeping both hands clutched around the Eye of Fire. As she leaned in closer to James, the only thing she could feel was her body moving forward into his space and the radiating heat of the stone. Her lips crushed against his sooner than she anticipated, and she felt something burst inside her like a dam breaking. A single hot tear rolled down her face and in between their mouths.

Serena opened her eyes. "I have to go."

"Serena..." James said, the edges of his voice softening. "Be careful."

"I will."

Serena tightened her grip around the Eye of Fire and jumped up from the floor. She ran by the couch, looping her arm through the strap of her purse as she headed towards the door.

"Let's go, Daniel," she said and sprinted into the hallway toward the elevators.

Chapter 19

Serena could hardly believe they were already in the air. According to Daniel, they would be descending into a private airport just south of San Francisco in only twenty minutes. Serena looked down at the Pacific coastline and remembered that it had taken her and James a total of seven hours to make the drive down to Los Angeles. It seemed impossible to her that was only yesterday. Even more inconceivable was the fact that she had the actual Eye of Fire in her hands and would be attempting to return it to its destroyed shrine in less than an hour. Daniel had asked Serena if she would rather not carry the stone once they boarded the plane. She told him no, and he looked not one bit surprised. Without her ever having to explain exactly why, Daniel seemed to understand that Serena was now the one and only custodian of the diamond, and that the responsibility was hers alone.

Daniel sat at the front of the plane speaking into an actual hand-held telephone. Even perfectly-pressed Daniel was starting to look pretty worn around the edges. He still wore his hot pink tie, but he had loosened it and now the knot hung lower, towards the middle of his shirt. His white sleeves were rolled up to just below his elbows, showing his sinewy, dark brown forearms. Even though she couldn't hear what he was saying, Serena knew he was making car arrangements for after they landed. A few minutes before, he had asked Serena for the address of their destination. Serena handed him the now-tattered blue card that Kirsten had given her for her Journey Magnification session. Daniel raised a curious eyebrow briefly before heading to the front of the plane to make the call, as smooth and discreet as a CIA agent who knew better than to ask questions about a classified mission.

Daniel hung up the phone, walked to the back of the plane where Serena was seated, and perched in the first-class-sized caramel leather seat positioned across from her. "We're all set, Ms. Rayborn."

"We? You mean... you are coming with me?"

"Of course," said Daniel, picking up a bottled water and taking a sip. "Mr. Sun seemed to be quite adamant that I make sure that you... and the necklace get safely to where ever it is that you need to go."

"But Daniel," said Serena, "you aren't going to be able to go with me the whole way. It's...

complicated." *And probably dangerous,* she thought.

Daniel gave her a rueful smile as if he were mildly insulted. "Then I will take you as far as you will allow me." He focused on Serena's hands, which held the Eye of Fire cradled in her palms and the attached necklace interlaced between her fingers. "I think you'll agree that Mr. Sun would have wanted me stay with you as long as possible."

"Yes," said Serena, nodding her head in agreement. Her thoughts shifted back to Sun and the last request he made of them as he lay on the floor in agony. "I know he would have," she said, the image twisting up her insides.

Daniel's smile fell away as though he could see what she was thinking. "I hope... Mr. Sun..."

"James will make sure he's okay," said Serena. "He will."

Daniel nodded with a sigh of cautious optimism.

Serena peeked out of the window again at the Central Coast, the several-hundred-mile area that provided a picturesque and diplomatic link between The Beach Boys' southern and Steinbeck's northern California. Even though she was twenty thousand feet up in the air, she could almost sense that the sandy beaches were giving way to leafy grape vineyards as they inched their way closer to their endpoint. "When do we land?"

"In about ten minutes."

"Gosh, that was fast," said Serena.

"Yes, private jets end up being much faster than commercial ones. No waiting in long air traffic control lines on a congested runway."

"One of many nice perks," said Serena, looking around the luxuriously appointed ten-seat cabin and taking a sip from the glass of the cranberry juice that Daniel had served her when they boarded. He had also given her a small plate of chocolate chip cookies. Serena picked one up and took a small bite. She couldn't begin to guess how they were so freshly baked. "Um... Daniel?"

"Yes, Ms. Rayborn?"

"Do you think it would be possible for me to make a phone call, too?"

"Why of course, Ms. Rayborn," said Daniel, standing up. "Let me set you up with an outside line." With the necklace held close to her chest, Serena followed Daniel up to one of the seats at the front of the plane. A black phone console sat on a small retractable desk next to a chair behind the cockpit.

"Go ahead. You just pick up and dial."

"Like a normal phone?"

"Ha—yes, like a normal phone," said Daniel with a warm smile and turned around to leave her with some privacy.

"And Daniel?" called Serena as she brought the headset to her ear.

"Yes?" asked Daniel, looking back over his

shoulder.

"You can call me Serena, you know."

Daniel chuckled, his eyes dropping down to the Eye of Fire gripped to her heart. "Thank you, but I don't think so, Ms. Rayborn," he said. "Now go ahead and make your call. We'll be landing soon," he said, and headed to the back of the plane.

Serena smiled and dialed Mallory's cellphone, one of the few numbers she knew by heart. It only took one ring before she answered.

"Hello?"

"Hi, Mal."

"Thank goodness. I almost didn't answer 'cause I didn't recognize the number. Where are you calling from?"

"From a plane."

"A plane? Why the hell are you on a plane? Wait, first, where have you been for God's sake? Your text message only said that you had to take an unexpected trip down south with that professor dude. I've been really worried, Serena. I thought maybe Doc Hotness kidnapped you to Tijuana or something."

"It's Dr. *Riley*. We drove down to Santa Barbara and then to L.A."

"Okaaay. Then why are you on a plane?"

"I needed to come back fast. Mal, I have to go back and see Devania."

"What? The last time you saw that sorceress of the suburbs she totally freaked you out by telling you that your life was in danger. Why on earth would you want to go back there?"

"Because she was right—my life *is* in danger," said Serena, lowering her voice. She glanced up at Daniel. "I just saw Charles Sun get shot right in front of me."

"Who's Ch—you mean Charles Sun, like the *billionaire* Charles Sun?"

"Yes, *the* Charles Sun. But I can't get into that right now. I need to go back to Devania so she can hopefully help me undo what I did in India. And I just wanted you to know because I'm not... I'm not sure exactly what's going to happen when I get there."

"Holy crap, Serena. I have no idea what you are talking about, but I can meet you there."

"No, Mal—"

"And Serena, there's something else..."

"What?"

"Well, when I was trying to figure out exactly where you were yesterday morning, I called your office... and I kind of spoke to your... boss."

"Professor LeMott? Oh shit, Mal. What did you say?"

"Well, I um... told him that you said that you had to take an unexpected trip and that I was trying to find out where. But he seemed to think you were..."

"Sick."

"Yeah, he said you called in sick. Sorry.

Seriously, my bad."

Serena let out a heavy, exasperated sigh. "Great. Not only do I have to figure out a way to return the Eye of Fire back to its shrine in another realm, now I'm going to get fired in this one."

"*What?*"

Serena felt a subtle shift in the plane's altitude and small pop in her ear from an increase in air pressure. "Nevermind. I gotta go. We are beginning to land."

"So I'll meet you at Devania's?" asked Mallory.

"No."

"But—"

"No buts," said Serena. "I need to go alone this time. I'll call you after."

"Swear?"

"Swear."

"Okay, Serena... I hope you're right about this," said Mallory. "Then I'll see you at the end of the yellow brick road."

Serena couldn't help but be comforted by Mallory's inside joke. She cracked a smile. "Okay, I'll see you there, Mal."

She felt a stab of apprehension as she glanced down at the Eye of Fire. She could only hope she was telling Mallory the truth.

COME ON Devania. Answer, damnit.

Answer.

Serena pressed down hard on the doorbell for a third time. She glanced back warily towards the darkly tinted town car where Daniel was impatiently waiting for her to return. She knew that his confidence in this whole expedition had been shaken as soon as they pulled up to 17 Bramblewood Lane. He rolled down the window when they came to a stop in front of the house, as if he were hoping that the dark grey glass had somehow created an optical illusion. After a few moments, he realized that this was indeed their destination, sank back into the seat next to her, and shook his head skeptically as if to say, *This can't be the place.*

The car windows were too dark to actually see Daniel, but Serena shot a fake confident smile toward the back seat of the town car anyway, since she knew he was surely watching her every move. She searched her brain for what to do next.

Suddenly, she remembered a trick her father had taught her that she'd not thought of since she was a teenager. *Standard spring-lock door knob*, she thought, examining it more closely. She discreetly pulled her wallet out of her purse, and took out a credit card.

Making sure to obscure Daniel's view of her right arm with the rest of her body, she wedged the card into the gap between the door and the frame, bent it away from the knob, and pushed the door hard. The door swung open into the foyer.

"Thanks, Dad," she said to herself, and then stepped through and waved a cheery goodbye to Daniel as if someone inside had just greeted her and everything was going according to plan.

"Devania?" yelled Serena, quickly closing the door behind her. "It's Serena. Are you here?"

Serena stood still for a moment and looked around the dimly lit, circular, orange room, waiting for an answer. Silence. The house was eerily quiet. She laid her hands on her chest and patted the top of her cotton sweater. She felt the hard edges of the Eye of Fire protruding from beneath the soft fabric of her v-neck. Now that she was inside, Serena was glad that Daniel had insisted that she put it on before exiting the car. The necklace felt weighty and warm against her skin, but there was also something more happening. Serena felt as if she were being pulled forward by the neck—as if there were something tugging on the stone. She relaxed her body and let the sensation draw her forward. Before she knew it, she was walking through the green door at the far side of the room.

Serena fought the urge to call out for Devania again as she slipped silently through the outdoor passageway that led to the gold door of the Meta House. She opened the door in one smooth motion and closed it behind her as fast as she could. Once inside, she closed her eyes and relaxed the back of her body against the door with a small sigh of relief. She had made it at least this far with the Eye of Fire still in her possession. A barrage of warm, exotic scents filled her nostrils, bringing back the memory of the first time she was in the Meta House. The familiar smell added a small comfort to quell her edginess. She could practically feel Devania's presence still lingering in the air.

Not a bad dressing room, is it? Devania's words came echoing back to her ears as clear as day.

She looked around the room. "Devania?" she called out in a hushed tone, even though Serena knew for certain she was not there. She walked over to the large velvet settee that sat in the middle of the room, and put her purse down on top of it to free up both of her hands. She pulled the Eye of Fire out from underneath her sweater and laid both of her hands across it, one on top of the other. Its warmth penetrated her from her hands to her feet and she was filled with an electric force that propelled her body forward. Serena kept her hands pressed into the stone, closed her eyes, and took slow, deliberate steps as it pulled her towards the far side of the room. Unlike her first venture through the Meta House, she was not startled when she heard the duet of voices beckon her to reach out and take hold. As Serena stretched out her arms to make her wardrobe selection, she knew she would not be wearing her sweater for long.

Serena suddenly felt the rug underneath her

bare feet and strands of metal beads pouring over her over her body from her neck down to her toes. She opened her eyes and immediately went over to the large wooden mirror that stood a few feet away. Her breath caught in her throat and she realized, exhilarated, that she was wearing the very same gown and crown that she had worn the day of her Journey Magnification.

When Serena saw, however, that the necklace had disappeared from around her neck, a jolt of panic went through her. Then she looked further down and saw that she was holding the Eye of Fire in her very hands. It had been stripped away from the diamond necklace. The majestic stone sat in her palms, naked and glimmering like a ball of white fire. She hoped this was a good sign. A sign that her plan would work.

"Hello, Zahra," she said softly to her reflection with a little smile.

"Zahra, you say? And all this time I thought it was Miss Rayborn."

Serena recognized the voice behind her immediately, but she could hardly believe her ears. She spun around towards the now-open gold door of the Meta House. When she saw him, she stumbled back, almost losing her balance.

"*Professor LeMott?*"

Professor LeMott was disheveled as usual, in one of his worn navy-blue tweed suits, but he looked nothing like his normal, jovial self. His round face was splotched red and he was breathing erratically in short, angry bursts. Beads of sweat collected on his forehead, and his thin grey hair was matted down on his head. Serena had never seen Dr. LeMott look at her with anything but affection, but now he glared at her through his glasses with a look of unbridled contempt.

"Wh-what on earth are you doing here?" asked Serena, trying to hide her dismay at his wretched appearance.

"That's quite an amusing question," said Professor LeMott, strolling towards her with his hands jammed into his jacket pockets. "Surely, I should be the one asking what *you* are doing here, Miss Rayborn, my sweet, dedicated, terribly ill assistant."

"I—I am..." said Serena, struggling to find a starting place for her explanation, "I'm so sorry, Professor LeMott. I can't imagine how this must look. But I assure you, I can explain what's going on...."

"I take it you are not sick, then?" asked Professor LeMott caustically. He eyed Serena's attire from her crown to her feet. "I'd say you look anything but sick to me. That's quite an impressive outfit for someone suffering with the flu." He moved towards her with a twisted, ugly smile. His tongue flicked out nervously and wet his lips.

Serena's stomach turned in disgust. At that moment, Professor LeMott reminded her of a slimy, repugnant snake. She closed her fingers tightly around the Eye of Fire and pulled it up closer to her chest. She drew her shoulders back, and coolly raised her chin. She felt elevated with the crown on her head. "I'm sorry I lied to you, Dr. LeMott, but I am in the middle of an... emergency. Lives are at stake."

"Oh, and I suppose one of those lives just happens to be the dashing and oh-so-esteemed Professor Riley?" hissed Dr. LeMott, the color rising in his chubby cheeks.

The accusation caught Serena completely off guard. Knowing about her lie about being sick and going out of town was one thing. Mallory had told him that. But knowing about James? She wracked her mind and tried to make sense of it.

"Did you really think that you and Dr. Riley could go behind my back and conduct your little 'research project' without me finding out about it? I dare say you think me a fool. You both left quite a trail on your computers at the university. Nothing is secret in a digital world, my dear," he said with a venomous sneer.

Serena felt her own cheeks warm with indignation as she felt herself go from contrite to offended. Whatever her transgression for hiding what was really going on, Professor LeMott had been an indecent little rodent for spying on her and James.

"Professor LeMott," said Serena with a little

more severity and taking a firm step towards him, "I'm sorry, but I have to go. There's something urgent I need to attend to."

"You, my dear Miss Rayborn, need to attend *to me.*"

"As I said before, I do sincerely apologize for not being honest with you, but what has happened has happened and I assure you, I had good reason..."

"Bullshit," scoffed LeMott. "Spare me your pathetic apologies."

"How did you even find me?" Serena met LeMott's hostile gaze, her face stern and unyielding.

"That is a *university-issued* cell phone you have, my dear, thanks to my generosity. Equipped with GPS in case of loss of theft. Or in this case, in case of losing the scheming, disloyal, ungrateful little witch under my employ," said LeMott, practically spitting out his words.

Serena felt like she'd been slapped in the face. She looked over to her purse sitting on the settee in the middle of the room, her phone safely tucked inside.

"*You tracked my phone?*"

"Obviously. Thank you for suggesting that I make better use of my dutiful assistant Morgan. As you said, she does have absolutely superb technical skills. And she, unlike some other assistants, has been very willing to help me advance *my* future," said LeMott smugly, his eyes filled with vicious bitterness.

"Now—what did you call yourself in the mirror? Oh yes, Zaaahra. Come here, Zahra, and hand over that little gem."

LeMott took his hands out of his pockets and rubbed his sweaty palms together as he crept a step closer. Serena followed his malicious gaze down to the stone firmly clasped at her chest, her hands wrapped so tightly around it that no part of its shining surface could be seen.

"You... want the Eye of Fire?" she asked. "But... *why?*"

LeMott snorted and then let out a pig-like laugh. "*Why?* Why, she asks?" he said, spraying saliva as he spoke. "Oh, yes, I'm sure like everyone else, you think that all the great treasures of this world should go to the likes of the fortunate and charismatic Dr. Riley. Well, my dear, my time—*my pay day*—has finally come. The perpetually hard-working and unrecognized Professor Julius LeMott is finally going to get what he deserves and retire in style. To hell with academia. After thirty years of being ignored and under-appreciated, it's finally *my* lucky day. The Eye of Fire is going to make me richer than I ever dreamed."

"Then this is all for greed? You mean to *sell* it? Like on the black market?"

"Don't be so naïve," sneered LeMott. "The world *is* a black market. And, as I've found out over the years, the only real way to get ahead."

"But it belongs to—Charles Sun." Serena spied the staircase leading downstairs on the other side of the room. She started slowly walking away from LeMott and making her way around the settee in that direction.

"*Belonged* to Charles Sun. Not any more. My buyers made sure of that," said LeMott with a nasty snicker. "But of course, I don't need to tell you that. You were there. In fact, I believe you still have some blood on your cheek."

Serena's breath halted. She stopped in her tracks, suddenly feeling sick to her stomach. "That was you? *You* shot Mr. Sun?"

"Well, I can't take credit for pulling the trigger. But yes, my clients are quite resourceful and determined to get what they want. And since they've promised me the other half of their already considerable payment for my services once they get the Eye of Fire, I am quite committed to getting what they want as well. But unfortunately, you took it, my dear. And just as you seemed to have no problem taking it from Sun.... why should I mind taking it from you?" LeMott stalked her around the room, following her step by step.

"Sun... he gave it to me."

"How convenient. Yes, I'm sure he gives away hundred-million-dollar ancient diamonds every day. No matter," LeMott said, his face turning dark. "Now *you* are going to give it to *me*."

Serena felt the gravitational command of

the Eye of Fire drawing her down into the room below the staircase.

"Now, Miss Rayborn."

"Zahra, if you don't mind."

"If my buyers were willing to take such good care of Sun when he stood in their way, just what do you think they'll do to you, Zahra?" asked LeMott with a sinister smirk. "I promise you, giving the stone to me is the only way you'll make it out of this house alive."

"We'll just see about that," said Serena and broke into a run toward the staircase leading down to the Elemental Chamber.

In a snap, LeMott lunged at her like an unleashed rabid dog, jumping across the settee. Serena was shocked by how nimble LeMott was, given how awkwardly he usually moved. He knocked her purse to the ground as he scurried across, and attempted to grab her with both arms. Luckily, his arms were a hair too short and she was able to jump out of his reach, falling backwards into the row of gowns hanging on the wall behind her.

She held the Eye of Fire in her right hand as she bolted towards the sunken staircase. She rounded the banister, gripping the brass railing with her other hand. LeMott hurtled forward at her again with all of his might, letting out a loud trollish growl with the effort. He took a swipe at the arm holding the Eye of Fire, but he tripped on the edge of the settee, fell forward and landed on his belly on the floor at Serena's feet with a loud thump. To her dismay, he didn't miss a beat, and clawed frantically at her ankles to stop her descent down the stairs. He caught a handful of the long beaded metal strands of Serena's dress in his grip and immediately let out a ragged, guttural scream.

When Serena looked back, she saw that Professor LeMott had definitely been hurt. He held his hands together, licked them feverishly, and howled in pain. Fresh, red burn marks appeared across his hands and forearms. Serena looked down at the bottom of her dress, which was glowing neon green where LeMott had touched it. Her metallic dress had seared him like acid.

"You burned me, you poisonous bitch! I will see you in hell before I let you get away with your betrayal. You work for *me* and Eye of Fire is *mine!*" he screamed with rage as he thrashed forward towards her like a fish wrangling on land, still holding the wounds on his hands and arms. Serena jumped back against the wall and out of the way of his injured tantrum. LeMott was beet red with fury.

"Professor LeMott—I quit. So I'll see you in hell," said Serena as she bounded down the staircase. As she approached the bottom, the Eye of Fire sent a pulsation throughout her body like a supernova about to explode. She heard LeMott's heavy footsteps moving at the top of the staircase as she reached the bottom of the chamber.

The Elemental Chamber was even colder

than she remembered it. A shiver rippled up her spine as a strong, cold wind blew against her face and body, throwing her hair and the long beads of her dress back behind her. It was dark as night, but she kept moving forward, holding one arm out as her eyes adjusted to the pitch black of the room. Serena recalled that Devania had lit the torches on the walls, but there was no time for that. Besides, the darker the better, with LeMott tracking right behind her like a mad bounty hunter. She squinted into the darkness and searched the ceiling of the cavernous stone room. It didn't take her long before she recognized what she was looking for, not too far in the distance. She breathed out a sigh of solace. The Alchemic Orb still hung in the center of room, glowing in a ghostly sphere of purple vapors.

LeMott's pounding footfalls became louder and louder with each lumbering step down the staircase. Serena could tell that he was moving a little slower since she burned him, but nevertheless it would not be long before he caught up to her in his rampage. She had no time to waste. She pushed all thought of hesitation out of her mind and ran over to the grey stone steps leading up to the grass-covered platform beneath the Orb. Clutching the Eye of Fire to her chest with her right hand, she used her left hand to steady herself as she climbed up to the top. Once she got there, she held her crown securely on her head and laid down on the soft flat knoll. She closed both hands tightly around the Eye of Fire and pulled it against the base of her throat, fiercely gripping it with all of her strength.

"Eye of Fire, I'm taking you home," she said, concentrating hard on the Alchemic Orb. The swirling nebula turned suddenly from purple to midnight black. The wind died down to a whisper and a fiery white light started to glow like a star from within her hands. Serena knew why the Eye of Fire was glowing. It was the sign of its return to the source and power of its people. Serena wanted to look at her hands, but she didn't dare. She kept her gaze focused on the growing black cloud of the Orb.

"You are not taking anything home. Or anything *from me.*" Serena heard a raspy, seething voice.

Then without warning, something clamped down viciously around Serena's neck like a vise. Her windpipe collapsed under the weight of Julius LeMott's dense, compact body. She wanted to keep her eyes open to the Orb, but she was forced to shut them tightly as she struggled for every breath. His meaty hands contracted harder and harder around her neck and hands. The Eye of Fire pressed into her trachea, its pointed base stabbing through her throat like a knife. When she finally summoned the strength to open her eyes again, the Alchemic Orb was gone.

The room was no longer bathed in darkness.

Firelight flickered around the edges of her view of a masked man looming above her head, choking her with huge, muscled arms of steel. He wore a black scarf tied around his face, leaving only his dark eyes and hard-edged mouth visible. His dark, oiled hair was drawn to the back of his head in a long braid.

His grip bore down mercilessly from above and prevented her from moving her head in any direction but straight ahead. Serena, however, did not need to see the rest of him, for she had recognized him at once. She knew that the man also wore a dark brown leather vest laced up the front and embroidered with the insignia of a neighboring enemy. She also knew with certainty that he had a dagger attached to his waistbelt. Even after all this time, she could never forget the man who had stolen the Eye of Fire from its altar and murdered her.

"LeMott," she choked out.

In a moment of unexpected recognition, her killer loosened his grip slightly and raised his eyebrows at the name. It *was* LeMott, though embodied in a completely different human form. She did not know what his name had been five hundred years ago, but it was he. The confused assassin paused in the midst of his slaughter, allowing Serena to catch a small breath.

"Serena," her assailant finally said, comprehension flooding over his face. His mouth lingered open with the revelation of her identity.

"Zahra..." he said, as he looked around the room, bewildered by the complete transformation.

Zahra knew this was finally her chance. She heaved the Eye of Fire away from her throat and bashed the pointed end of the stone into the killer's head, hitting him right above his eyebrow. He fell over to the side, crippled with pain. A red stream of blood gushed from the large gash on his brow and splashed onto her chest. Before her assailant had a chance to recover, Serena sent a mighty kick heel-first into his exposed abdomen.

"GRRRUGGH," he cried out as he lurched forward, clutching his belly.

As soon as she was freed from her enemy's grip, Zahra's lungs filled with a surge. She rolled over onto her side and gulped in waves of air. She crawled forward on the ground, knowing that she must not stop moving, regardless of how disoriented she was from the lack of oxygen. She took a second to look up at the room to get her bearings. The majestic red-tiled vaulted ceilings told her that she was in the heart of the temple, on the east side of The Shrine Room. The altar of the Eye of Fire would be only a few hundred feet away, a massive stone edifice that sat in front of the ever-flowing Waterfall of Light.

Pushing herself onto her bare feet, Zahra stumbled away from the thief, who still held a hand to his head and was wiping the blood away as it poured into his eyes, blinding him. He could not have been more physically different than LeMott. This man was well over six feet tall, had almond-brown skin, and looked as strong and muscular as a bull. He would not be nearly as easy to escape in a fight as LeMott would have been. She did not want to find out what he would do to her if he were able to get his hands on her again.

Zahra heard the sound of rushing water coming from her right. She twirled around unsteadily towards that side of the room. The altar stood in front of her, magnificent and unbroken. The Waterfall of Light gushed out from somewhere high above the stone wall behind it. A narrow, rocky staircase stood in front of the altar and ascended about sixty feet up to a small, square plateau: The Seat of Abundance. In front of the Seat of Abundance, a triangular shaped hole had been carved deep into the rock. It sat empty, waiting for her to return the Eye of Fire to its rightful place.

Zahra made a dash over to the altar and started climbing the stairs. She moved as swiftly as she could, but not only was the staircase no more than a foot wide, it had also been purposefully constructed so that each step was steeper than the one before. If she moved too quickly, she would trip, or worse, lose her balance and fall completely off the side to the ground. Even though she was only a third of the way to the top, she was already quite high, at least twenty feet. If she fell off, she would most likely break her neck.

She cupped her hands more firmly around the Eye of Fire, steadied her feet and looked behind her. Her pursuer was already at the base of the altar. He was looking up at her, his dark eyes peering at her from behind his mask with the focus of a trained hunter. His golden brown forearms were smeared with the dark red blood from his wounded brow. For the first time, she could see his gleaming white teeth. Zahra saw from his sinister grin that he was sure he would win. He knew that he would get the stone, and, as he had before, kill her.

Zahra turned back to the stairs and continued her precarious climb. Her pace slowed down as each step became more difficult to reach than the last. She gripped the stone with one hand, using the other to help pull herself up to the next level. She could hear the footsteps behind her moving at a faster pace than her own, but she did not look back. Only a few more steep steps and she would be at the Seat of Abundance. She dug her fingernails into the crevices of the stone as she clawed her way up. Her hands were slipping from the sweat of her labor.

How will I escape him when I get there? she thought anxiously. She looked imploringly at the Eye of Fire, which was cutting into her hand from her death grip.

"*Please. Tell me what I need to do,*" she

whispered to the stone as she heaved herself up the final step. Her foot slipped on some loose stones and she fell forward, sliding on her stomach across the Seat of Abundance. She scraped her elbows as her arms came crashing down, splayed out and fully extended. Her chin smacked down hard against the rough rock.

"AAAAAAGGGHH!" Zahra screamed, tears springing into her eyes from the painful impact.

She bit down on her lip and dragged herself up to standing. Just behind the altar, the Waterfall of Light poured down the entire wall of the room in a massive torrent. The only sound she could hear was the thunderous splash of falling water. A bright stream of sunlight shone down on her from a huge skylight far above in the domed ceiling. She opened her hand, desperately hoping that she had not dropped the stone. The Eye of Fire dazzled in rainbow of light so bright it practically blinded her. At that moment, she knew what to do.

Zahra stepped forward and reached her arm out as if she were going to place the stone into the niche that had been carved out to shelter the Eye of Fire. Pretending to lose her footing, she fell forward onto her knees at the Seat of Abundance. She sat down as if crestfallen, and turned around to face him. She started trembling with fear.

Her masked predator had just reached the final step. He stepped up to the stone plateau and loomed over her like a ravenous bear. He said nothing, but smiled with certain victory. He offered out one hand to her while he slowly pulled out the dagger on his belt with the other. Time for her to give up the stone to him. His blade glimmered in the light. Time for her to die.

It was not hard for Zahra to look drained with defeat. She was still out of breath from the climb and her body was throbbing with scrapes and bruises. She felt the warm wetness of blood trickling down her chin and onto her neck. She extended the Eye of Fire out to him, her hand shaking as she yielded to losing the battle.

"It's yours," she said.

The killer leaned over to take the Eye of Fire. Zahra tried to wait until he was at the perfect angle, one from which she knew his balance could not recover. Quick as lightning, she kicked out her legs with all of her strength and knocked both of the bandit's feet out from under him. A look of panic washed over his face as his feet, followed by his body, went plummeting off the side of the altar.

"NOOOOOOOO!" he screamed.

He swung the dagger up over his head and brought it down in one final stroke as he vanished over the edge of the staircase. The blade came straight down into Zahra's leather-clad belly, cutting clean through her side like an arrow. The blade pulled out of her side as quickly as it had entered, disappearing along with the thief's trailing arms. A stream of warm blood gushed down her side and onto the cold rock of the Seat of Abundance. She felt herself start to weaken as the puddle of red grew larger and larger beneath her.

"Please, I beg of you... no... for Asher and Drew..." she breathed out raggedly as she pressed down on the wound with one hand to try to slow the bleeding. Ripping pain racked her body as she forced herself to stand up.

Zahra stumbled forward, her head becoming lighter and lighter with each step. *Mokam,* she thought, summoning her power. *Release.* She inserted the Eye of Fire into the triangular hollow of its sacred altar.

"James... I did it," she said faintly, before collapsing to the ground.

She had wanted to hear his name out loud, but all she could hear was the roar of the waterfall before a flash of white, sparkling light filled all of her senses.

Chapter 20

The water had slowed. She no longer heard the boom of it rushing across stone. It had subdued to a gentle trickle that was soothing to her eardrums. The sound coaxed her eyes open. A blurry, white room was filled with a greyish light that concealed whether it was day or night. She tried to focus her eyes. The room was modern and filled with equipment. *Medical equipment*, she thought as she caught sight of various electronic monitors beeping in colors of red and green. She searched the room for the source of the trickling water. There was a guy in a blue t-shirt standing in front of a silver sink at the wall to her right. The sound was coming from a faucet. He held a clear plastic cup beneath the running water, filling it up as quietly as possible. Her heart jumped back to life. James.

"James," she said, but nothing came out. Her throat and mouth were as dry as sandpaper. She tried again. "James," she whispered.

James' head whipped around. He put down the cup of water and was next to her so fast it seemed like he had taken no steps at all. That's when she realized that her mind was groggy. They had given her something. The gears of her brain felt drugged and slow moving.

"Serena," said James softly, leaning over her with a tired smile. "You're back."

Serena tried to move an arm toward him, but it felt weighed down and stiff. A piercing pain shot through her side. She winced with a moan. She looked down and saw a plastic tube secured by tape coming out of her wrist, leading to a clear bag of liquid hanging on a metal apparatus nearby.

"Shhhhh," said James, laying his hand on top of hers. "Don't try to move. You've got an I.V. Not to mention some pretty nasty injuries. So try to stay still." James hovered over her, waiting for a sign that she understood.

"Okay," Serena croaked out of her dry mouth.

"How about some water? You technically are hydrated, but your mouth must feel parched," he said.

Serena tried to nod. *Ouch,* she thought, wincing again.

James strode back to the sink and picked up the cup of water. He came back, brought the cup to her lips, and slowly tilted it until she could take small sips of water. Serena looked more closely at James while he concentrated on getting the fluid inside her. His hair was tousled and his shirt was wrinkled. A thin layer of stubble covered his jaw. It was obvious that he hadn't had much sleep. Still, she noticed the lack of sleep did nothing to diminish his looks. He was just as handsome, only a bit more rough and frayed around the edges. Even in her haze, she found James' infallible attractiveness endearing. He stopped to give her a break and she smiled to herself.

"A little better?" he asked.

"Yes," she said, her voice sounding a bit more like her own.

She looked around the hospital room, keeping in mind that she should move only her eyes and not her head. The lights were off, but dim daylight spilled in from a window on one side of the room. The room was small but well appointed with new-looking medical machines. Her body was neatly folded into an extra-long twin bed with white linens and an ivory blanket. She was inclined at slight angle, propped up on firm pillows.

"Where am I?"

"Bennett University Hospital," said James.

Serena looked down at the white hospital I.D. bracelet on her wrist. She registered that the university logo was on it, a small "B" in thick, block-lettered navy blue. She gazed back up at James. It took some effort to get his face back into focus. "How long have I been here?" she asked, her voice trailing off hoarsely at the end.

"Since last night. It's seven a.m.," he

replied, the stress of every passed hour pressed across his brow. "You gave us quite a scare. Don't think I'm not going to get you back for that." He patted her hand with a look of sweet admonishment.

"They gave me pain killers?"

James gave a strong nod. "You can say that again."

Questions started to swirl in Serena's head, but she couldn't seem to tease them out and articulate them. Finally she just asked, "Who's "us"?"

"Me, Daniel, Mallory, Devania..."

The last name snapped Serena's attention into focus. "Devania?" she said, her voice gravelly. "She was *here*?" Her body started to sit up involuntarily. She regretted it immediately. A sharp pain rocketed through the left side of her body all the way up to her head. "Ugggh," she said, sinking back into the bed.

"Remember, no moving," said James. "Otherwise, I'm going to have to stop talking to you until you are fully recovered." He smiled at her and asked, "Deal?"

"Deal," she agreed.

"Okay, then."

James reached behind him and pulled up a beige chair that was sitting in the corner next to the window. Even in her clouded state, it looked like the most uncomfortable chair Serena had ever seen.

She hoped that was not where he had slept. He sat down and leaned over as close as he could to make sure she did not have to move her head to see him.

"Yes, Devania was here. She found you at her house and had you brought here by ambulance. And thankfully, once she got you here, the University called me. I was the last contact logged into your cell phone."

Serena tried to recall the last time she remembered seeing her phone. As she tried to scroll back, her head started to hurt. A picture of her purse sitting on the settee in the middle of the Meta House popped into her mind.

"Hey, don't think too hard," said James, gently patting her on the arm. "Devania was here when I arrived. So was Daniel—he followed the ambulance. Boy, was he ever worried about you. Devania said that she found you completely knocked out at the bottom of some stairs in her home. The paramedics said that you must have taken a terrible fall. You had some internal bleeding, especially on the left side of your abdomen. But it stopped... thank God." His voice cracked and he paused to compose himself. She saw for the first time that James' golden-brown eyes were rimmed in red from the long night.

"I..." said Serena. She wanted to say *I'm sorry I couldn't escape LeMott's dagger*, but she didn't dare yet. "I'm sorry," she simply said.

"Shhhh," hushed James. "Don't be silly.

I'm the one who's sorry... I should have never let you go alone. If Sun hadn't been shot..."

Serena felt her heart sink upon hearing Sun's name and the recollection of what had happened to him just before she fled with Daniel.

"What... what happened... to Sun?" she asked, her question barely audible above the beep-beep-beep sounds of the monitors surrounding her. She closed her eyes to brace herself for the answer.

"Hey, it's okay, Serena," James said, patting her hand again. "He's going to be fine. He's still in the hospital, but luckily the bullet didn't hit any vital organs—went straight through his pectoral. I flew back up as soon as I knew he was stable."

Serena felt relief wash over her. She opened her eyes and smiled broadly at James. Smiling made her realize that there was also a dull ache coming from the bottom part of her face. She used her non-I.V. hand and felt around the sore area. Her chin was bandaged up.

"My chin?" she asked, still feeling the gauze and tape.

"Yeah," said James. "Seems you bumped that pretty hard on the way down, too."

Serena rolled her eyes and breathed out a sigh of embarrassment. *Fantastic*, she thought. She wasn't so loopy that she didn't know what having a huge bandage on her chin meant. *I must look like Frankenstein*, she thought. She stroked around her jaw a little more and felt papery strips of bandage tape stretching up the sides of her face. She suddenly remembered tumbling forward and smacking her chin onto the cold stone of the Seat of Abundance. Serena cringed.

"Y'okay? Does it hurt?" asked James, his body rising up with concern.

"No... it's not that... it's..." said Serena, not sure where she should begin. "Nevermind. It's okay, my side is just sore," she fibbed.

James narrowed his eyes at her, unconvinced. He held the cup of water up in front of her again. "Want a little more?" he asked.

"Yes, thank you," said Serena. She fought the urge to move her head towards the cup and instead waited for James to bring it her.

James glanced up nervously at the front wall of the room. There was a plain white round wall clock hanging on it, the no-nonsense kind that Serena remembered from elementary school. He gingerly pressed the cup up to her mouth.

"Serena, I know you are still in a lot of pain right now and things are probably pretty fuzzy..." James paused in between sips and gave her a wary look. "But before everybody else gets here—"

"Everybody else?" she asked, pausing mid-swallow.

"Uh huh... I texted Mallory for you and she stopped by late last night to see you while you were still out. She said she would be back sometime this morning. And I expect Asher and Drew will be coming with their Dad any time now," said James calmly.

Serena struggled to understand how James knew all the things he was relaying to her. She blinked and replayed what he had just said to her in slow motion in her head. *Asher and Drew will be coming with their Dad any time now.* She opened her mouth to ask, but again, the right question eluded her.

James spoke up quickly to keep her confusion in check. "I saw that Asher was calling your phone last night, and the third time he tried you, I answered. I thought that you'd want the kids to at least know where you were." James put the cup down on a small table next to the bed. "I hope that was okay," he said, his eyes unsure.

Serena tried to imagine how a conversation between Asher and James would have gone. Her head was already foggy. Now it was foggy and spinning.

"What—what did you tell him?" she finally asked.

"That you'd had a fainting spell, fell, and injured your side. Asher was pretty upset— understandably—so he put Tom on the phone. I told him that the hospital was keeping you overnight for observation but that the doctors said you would be fine, which was fortunately true by that point. Told him that it might be best for them to come see you this morning after you'd had a good night's sleep." James gently smoothed back some of her hair that was lying across her forehead. "Sorry for bending the truth a little. I didn't want to lie, but I didn't think you'd want the kids to be completely freaked out. I was really hoping that you would wake up before they got here."

Serena tried to sift through the information, her mind straining to push itself into a higher gear to grasp James' account of all that had happened. It seemed to her that the intersection of the pieces of her life had shifted so quickly, as if it had been a year, not merely a day. One intersection struck her as strangest of all.

"You talked to *Tom*?" Serena asked.

"Yup, I did." James kept his expression cool, but she saw a glint of something not quite neutral in his eye.

"Thank you, James... for handling all that for me," said Serena. "Especially for Asher and Drew's sake."

"Of course. Hopefully I did okay."

"You did better than okay." Serena reached out and found James' hand, which was just beyond the edge of the bed. She gave it a small squeeze of thanks, which was surprisingly difficult to do without moving the rest of her body. After she squeezed, her hand felt too tired to let go.

"My part was easy," said James. He scooted forward on his chair and glanced down the hospital bed at her injured body. "But you, on the other hand, clearly did *not* have it so easy," he said, distress seeping into his voice. He took a deep breath and encircled her hand in both of his. "Serena, what happened to you? What happened to the..." James stopped and searched her face for permission to ask.

Serene gave him a warm smile. "I took The Eye of Fire back, James."

"You took it... *back*?"

"Yes, I did."

James gave her a perplexed look. "What do you mean? Back to..."

"Back to the Mahakali Temple in India. That's why I had to go back to Devania's. James, the curse is broken. No one else will get hurt," said Serena happily. She was speaking quickly and she was getting a little lightheaded from the exertion. She stopped for a moment and took a breath. The breath helped clear her head, but sent a sharp pain through her side. She wrinkled her face.

James recoiled slightly at the sight of her discomfort. "Serena, stop. I shouldn't have asked you in your condition. You don't need to tell me all this now—"

"No, James," she said, shaking her head in spite of the pain. "I do... there's something else I need to tell you." Serena could hear the beep-beep-beeping from the heart-rate monitor increase in frequency as she spoke more rapidly.

"I know—I know who shot Sun. It was

Professor LeMott. I mean—he was responsible. He was there, James... at Devania's. He was after the Eye of Fire. He tracked us through my phone and he had black market buyers who shot Sun for it. And then..." Serena pushed out the words even though her bottom lip had begun to tremble. "He tried to kill me for it. I know it must sound crazy... I couldn't believe it, either... but I swear, it's true." Serena blinked hard and felt fat tears roll out of the corners of her eyes and down into the mesh gauze that covered her chin.

"Shhhh sh shhh, Serena. Slow down," said James. "Professor LeMott tried to *kill* you at Devania's?" he asked, horror rising in his voice.

"He did, James. He tried to... in the Elemental Chamber..." said Serena, and then added cautiously, "but then also... at the temple in India. Only after we traveled back did I realize it."

"Realize what?"

"That LeMott was the one who originally stole the Eye of Fire from its shrine and murdered me long ago," said Serena. "And yesterday... he almost succeeded again." Serena smiled at him even though it hurt her chin. "But James, he didn't this time. I returned the Eye of Fire to its rightful place in the sacred altar. I won," she said proudly.

A grim look came over James' face as he considered what she was telling him. His gaze dropped down to his hands, which were still wrapped protectively around the fingers of her left hand. "Serena, I need to tell you something," he said finally.

Serena felt her throat constrict with disappointment. *He doesn't believe me.* Serena pulled her hand away and kept her eyes averted from James. She blinked back the tears and kept her eyes focused on the tubing coming out of her arm. "Never mind. I don't expect you to be able to understand. You... you weren't there."

"No," he said. "That's not it at all. Don't worry, I *believe* you. And not just because I trust you, but also because—" James put a hand on her shoulder. "Serena, look at me."

Serena looked back up at James. There was no doubt in his eyes, only trepidation. He was afraid to tell her something.

"What is it, James?"

"Professor LeMott," he said softly. "He's dead."

"*What*? Professor LeMott is... *dead?*"

"Yes. They found him at Devania's, too... on the floor, just a few feet away from you. Devania told the police she didn't have the first clue as to why he was there." James paused and then added thoughtfully, "But now, I guess the reason is clear."

"But... but... *how?*"

"Heart attack."

Serena felt as if she'd just been dropped down the steepest run of a rollercoaster. She was appalled and astonished at the same time. She shifted her feet, which lay safely sheltered within the warm blankets of the hospital bed. She had used those same feet to kick LeMott's legs out from beneath him, his former body from the ancient world falling to his demise far at the bottom of the altar.

She had thought the moment she had avenged the Eye of Fire was glorious, but the magnitude of power behind her triumph now frightened her. She tried to picture her boss, Professor Julius LeMott, expired on the floor of the Elemental Chamber. *Heart attack.*

She needed to tell James everything. "James..." she started, but was interrupted by the sound of a high-pitched voice coming from outside her hospital room door. The voice was small and big at the same time, bursting and bouncing with energy as it echoed down the hallway towards her room. Every cell in Serena's body woke up with the recognition of her precious flesh and blood. It was the untamable voice of her darling Drew.

"Aaaaaasssher!" he called to his brother. "Mommy's in room two-five-six AAAAAA, not BEEEEEEE!" Serena could hear Drew's light footsteps running erratically towards her room door like a baby bull in a china shop.

"SSSSSHHHH," responded the more mature voice of Asher. "Are you trying to wake up the whole hospital? People are sick here. Be quiet and stop running. This isn't Disneyland, Drew."

Asher sounded like he had gotten older in just the last few days.

James gently released her hand and stood up. "Asher and Drew?" he asked with a knowing smile. He pulled on his shirt to smooth it and ran a hand through his hair.

"Yes," said Serena, her hand feeling strangely cold without James' warm fingers surround it. "Do I look okay?"

"Beautiful," said James bluntly, as if stating an irrefutable fact.

Before Serena had time to be embarrassed, the door of her hospital room swung open. Drew was panting from his run down the hall. He paused in the doorway as he scanned the room.

"Mom!" he exclaimed when he caught sight of her. His chubby-cheeked, flushed face lit up with a smile.

Asher appeared behind his little brother just seconds later. "Hi, Mom," he said shyly from the doorway. "Go on in, Drew," he said, giving him a little shove into the room. "Walk. Don't run," he warned.

Drew took small, exaggeratedly slow steps towards Serena in his orange rubber Crocs. He was wearing his favorite black and yellow Batman t-shirt and clover-green shorts that didn't match in slightest. It wasn't until he was at her side that he seemed to notice that James was standing next to the bed.

"Hello," he said brightly to James. "I'm Drew."

James leaned down a little to shake Drew's hand. "Very nice to meet you, Drew. I'm James. I work at Bennett University with your mom."

"Very nice to meet you," said Drew shaking James' hand vigorously with the enthusiasm of a puppy.

"And you must be Asher. Nice to meet you, too," said James, straightening and offering a slightly more adult handshake to Drew's big brother.

"Nice to meet you, too," said Asher. He gave Serena a worried sideways glance and added, "Thanks a lot for answering my Mom's phone."

"No problem whatsoever," said James.

"Mom, are you *okaaaaay*?" asked Drew dramatically. James stepped back and walked around to the other side of the bed to make room for Drew and Asher. Drew snuggled in close by Serena's left ear and lay his head down on the pillow next to hers. His big green eyes looked warily up and down the hospital bed. "Did you break any *bones*?" he asked, half-scared, half-excited at the idea.

"I'm fine, bug. No broken bones. Just a bump on my chin and a bruise on my side," she lied. She flashed a quick glare at James. He shot her a quick, conspiratorial look back that agreed not to say anything more about her injuries.

"Good!" shouted Drew, as if all his worries had instantly been wiped clean.

Asher was not so easily convinced. "Really, Mom? Are you *really* okay?" he asked, his eyes roving uneasily from her I.V. to the monitors. Finally, his concerned glance settled on her face. "You look super tired."

"Really, Ash. Sure, I'm a little tired, but I'm going to be fine. I'm so sorry to have worried you guys," said Serena. Her heart swelled as she took in the faces of each of her sons. She was more happy to see them than she could have imagined was possible just a week ago. She wanted so badly to stroke Drew's little cheek, but she kept her arms still. She knew if she moved, the pain would give her away.

As she looked at them, she considered for a moment that the boys seemed to be visiting her in the hospital without any adult supervision.

"Where's your father?" she asked, truly curious.

"Dad should be here in a minute," said Asher. "He was on a conference call and the nurse wouldn't let him down the hall while he was talking on his phone."

Business as usual, thought Serena. But instead she said, "It's so good to see you guys. How was Yosemite? Did you guys have fun?"

Instead of answering her question, Drew sat up and looked back at his brother with a haughty smirk. "See, Asher, I told you that Mommy was going to be okay after the fight. She won." Drew crossed his arms and gave Asher a defiant look that said *I told ya so*.

"How many times do I have to tell you, that wasn't Mom, silly," Asher argued back.

Serena and James looked at each other, each wondering the same thing.

"Drew-bug, what are you talking about? What do you mean, 'Mommy won'?" asked Serena, gently.

"I saw you defeat the evil guy and return the treasure," said Drew, turning back around to Serena. "You won, Mommy."

Serena tried to keep calm as she listened to what was Drew telling her. *It can't be*, she thought.

Asher stepped up behind Drew to better explain. "He thinks he saw you in the GXG video game that we showed you, Mom. Remember? *The Rings of Prophesy*. Drew was the one who made me call you over and over again to make sure you were okay. He's convinced that it was you he saw win at the end of the game. I've tried to tell him it's just a game, but he just won't listen," said Asher, shaking his head at his brother's dumb little-kid notions.

"I saw her. Just because you didn't see it, doesn't mean I didn't," insisted Drew. "She won."

"Well, Dad agrees with *me*," said Asher. "Remember what he said, it's *just a game*. It's impossible that you saw Mom."

Drew bit down on his lip, scowling with frustration. "Well, Dad didn't see it, either. And Mommy always says *nothing* is impossible," he said, stamping an indignant foot on the floor.

As if on cue, Tom knocked on the open door, announcing his presence. His cell phone was still in his hand, as if he were expecting another call at any moment.

"I see you guys found your mom," said Tom, taking in the scene for a moment from the doorway before strolling over to the bed. As she would have expected, he seemed calm, collected, and completely unphased that they were unexpectedly gathered in a hospital.

"Hey, Dad! We found Mom!" yelled Drew.

"I can see that. No need to shout, bug." Tom strolled over to Drew and mussed up his already shaggy hair. He took a step in James' direction and extended his hand out for yet another handshake.

"Hi, I'm Tom, Asher and Drew's Dad."

"James Riley. Very nice to meet you," said James, giving Tom the stiffest handshake Serena had ever seen him give anyone. Serena felt a self-conscious twinge. Something about having both James and Tom in the same room as she lay disabled in a hospital bed made her feel... nervous. But she was too tired and achy to use her mental energy to dig beneath surface of her anxiety.

"James... I mean Dr. Riley is a professor at Bennett," said Serena, hoping that would suffice for an introduction.

"Is that right?" asked Tom, shoving a hand in the back pocket of his beige chinos. "What do you teach, Dr. Riley?"

"I head up the Relics and Ancient Antiquities Department."

"Cool," interjected Asher, who had been standing quietly on the left side of the bed behind Drew. Serena noticed that something lit up in Asher's face.

"Mom, what's rel-llics?" asked Drew.

"'Relics' mean something very valuable that is ancient," explained Asher, relieving Serena from the effort of answering the question. "From long ago, in the past."

Drew's eyes widened with understanding. He skipped around to the other side of the bed and looked up at James. "You mean like something like *The Sword in the Stone*?" he asked him. He bounced on the balls of his feet, hoping he was right.

James smiled and crouched down to Drew's level. "Something exactly like that, Drew," he said. He looked over Drew's shoulder at Serena. *Something like the Eye of Fire*, his eyes said to her.

Drew turned back to face her on his heel like a spinning top. "Get it, Mom? Isn't that cool?"

"Yes," said Serena with a nod. *Ouch.* She

could feel herself getting more worn out by the minute. The fatigue caused by all the blood she lost was catching up with her. The pain in her left side felt stronger now. She wondered if the drugs were wearing off.

Tom's face revealed a trace of concern. "You really got banged up from that fall, huh?"

"Yeah, you could say that," said Serena, "but the doctors say I'll be up and running again in no time." She smiled cheerily at Drew and Asher to deflect the question, even though her chin was screaming in pain. She spotted a dark gap among Drew's top teeth as he smiled back at her, giving her the perfect opportunity to change the subject.

"Drew-bug, did you lose another tooth?"

"I sure did!" exclaimed Drew, pointing with pride to the hole where his upper left incisor used to be. "I can put a straw through it and drink with my mouth shut!"

Asher rolled his eyes. "It's gross."

"No, it's not," said Drew, his feelings hurt. "It's... it's..."

"Gross," repeated Asher, with a dismissive roll of the eyes that Serena knew Asher knew would push Drew's buttons.

"NO. IT'S. NOT!" yelled Drew. He ran back over to Asher and gave him a shove in Tom's direction.

"Hey, hey, hey boys. Cut it out. You are here to help your Mom feel better, not to show her how badly behaved you can be." Tom gave them a reprimanding glare.

"Sorry, Mom," said Drew.

"Me, too," said Asher, looking apologetic for purposefully irritating his brother.

"Com'ere, Drew," said Serena. "Let me take a closer look."

Drew walked back up to the side of Serena's head and gave her another huge grin.

"Well, I'd love to see you drink through that with a straw. Sounds like quite a trick."

"You would?" asked Drew, thrilled at his mother's encouraging challenge. "Dad, can we go to the café downstairs and get a lemonade for Mom? Then I can show her my straw trick before my new tooth grows in too much."

"You just want an excuse to get something to eat," said Asher.

"Nuh uh, Mom loves lemonade and she said she wanted to see my trick," said Drew. "And *she* won't think it's gross."

Tom walked between Asher and Drew and put a disciplining hand on each of his sons' shoulders. "Okay, boys. How about we ask Mom." Tom looked over to Serena. "How does a lemonade sound?"

Serena could tell by the sympathetic look on Tom's face that he intended to use this little excursion as a way to give her some time to rest.

"Lemonade sounds delicious," said Serena.

"Okay, then," said Tom, clapping his hands together, which was always his way of saying 'let's get the show on the road.'

"Yay! Let's go!" exclaimed Drew. He gave Serena a kiss on the cheek before skipping gleefully towards the door.

"We'll be back, Mom," said Asher. He started to hug her and then halted, afraid to hurt her chin. Instead, Asher decided to follow his brother's example and gave her a peck on the cheek, a sign of affection that was rare for him these days. It warmed her heart.

"Thanks, Ash," she said, trying not to get teary-eyed.

Tom leaned over the bed and extended his hand out to where James stood on the other side. "If we don't see you when we get back, Dr. Riley, it was a pleasure meeting you."

"Likewise," said James, giving him a more generous handshake the second time around.

Tom hesitated for a moment, looking back and forth respectively between James and Serena, as if he were pondering something. "Relics and Ancient History," he said, pointing from James to Serena. "Those fields sound pretty close. Your studies must have a lot in common." It was a statement, but the way Tom said it, Serena knew he meant it more as a question that he wanted answered.

James smiled coolly. "Yes, you could say

there's a lot of overlap. I'm lucky to have Serena as a colleague. She's... brilliant."

Tom's eyes narrowed just a hair's breath. He gave James a silent nod in agreement, but to what, Serena couldn't quite be sure. Perhaps it was because her head was so damned foggy, but they seemed to be speaking in code.

"Dad, you coming?" Asher was leaning in through the cracked door.

"Yeah, I'm coming, Ash," said Tom. He put his hand on Serena's shoulder and gave it a little squeeze. "Rest up. We'll take our time getting that lemonade," he said with a smile, before turning and then heading towards the door. Tom's cell phone started ringing as the door shut behind him. "Tom Phillips, here," he quipped into the phone as he stepped into the hallway.

Serena and James took a collective exhale after Tom and the boys were gone. James walked around the bed and sat back down in the chair, his face alight with renewed excitement. She knew that he was as blown away by what just happened as she was.

"Serena... Drew... *he saw you*," said James.

"I know," said Serena, barely believing it herself. "In the very same place where I first saw myself in the beginning of this. I'm so..." Serena stopped, unsure of how to express her feelings.

"You're what?" asked James softly, leaning over her.

"I'm... I'm just so grateful that he could... that he *saw* me," said Serena. "James, Drew could really see me as Zahra... and he was *proud* of me."

"He's not the only one, you know."

Serena kept her tired eyes centered on his. "No?"

"No. I see you, too."

Serena felt her cheeks warm beneath her bandages. "Yeah, sure you do," she jested nervously. "You see a woman bandaged up like a mummy from her chin to her feet. Lovely."

"Don't worry," said James, leaning in a little closer. "The doctor said the chin, along with everything else, will heal. And more importantly, your lips still seem to be perfectly intact."

Serena felt her face burn so hotly that she knew she must have been crimson red, even through the bandages. James had not forgotten what she did right before she fled from L.A. with the stone. And he had no intention of letting her forget it either.

"But you're wrong," James continued, "That's not what I see at all."

Serena's breath caught in her throat. "What do you see?"

James slowly stood up. He leaned down until his cheek was pressed against hers, his lips brushing up against her ear, burrowed deep in the tangle of her hair.

"I see fire, Goddess," he whispered.

The first rays of morning sun splashed through her hospital window, filling the room with warm yellow light. The new day had officially begun, and she knew James was right. For the first time, Serena saw the fire in herself, too.

ACKNOWLEDGEMENTS

I am so grateful for the friends and family who have been on this long journey with me as I've worked step by step, year by year, to bring *Eye of Fire* into the world. It's been a process that goes so far beyond the writing of the book. Those who are close to me know it's been a process of deep personal evolution and becoming. It's been a road, so often rocky and uncertain, that's challenged me to embrace my purpose and true spirit. The support, love and faith I have received from every person who has cheered me on has been a gift that I'm so honored to have received.

Special heartfelt appreciation for my original writing group: Zahie, Lou and Ida. Your talented and voraciously creative minds continue to inspire me every day. I will always aspire to make you happy with and proud of the words I write. Lou, my dear writing partner, editor and darling friend...the love and commitment you have given to me and to my writing have brought new meaning to the saying, "It's not the destination. It's the journey." You have made this journey so meaningful and held my hand without fail every step of the way.

Thank you to my Mom, Dad and my brother Rodney for always, always having so much faith in me. As far back as I can remember, you have wholeheartedly supported everything I've always wanted to accomplish. Your love and faith in me have been a fuel I've survived on when I've been lost for what seemed like years in the Forests of Doubt.

So much gratitude for my mother and father in-law, Andi and Jeff, and my brother-in-law, Dillon. Your enthusiasm has been such a gift and I feel I have joined a family of fierce, loving tigers that would do anything for me in any fight I have chosen to face.

Everlasting love and thankfulness for my son Kieran and my husband Nat. Kier, being your mother has made me better, stronger, and more courageous than I ever could have been without you. Nat—our love is at the very core of everything I do. Thank you for always believing in me and encouraging me to follow my heart. Luckily for me, my heart lies with you.

And thank you to every single one of my readers, present and future, for joining me on this wild and wonderful journey. I hope you enjoy the ride and will stick around for, in the words of Rick to Louis at the end of *Casablanca*, "the beginning of a beautiful friendship."

ABOUT THE AUTHOR

N. M. Chambers was born in Philadelphia and spent much of her childhood and early adulthood practicing the flute, writing poetry, playing video games with her brother, watching adventure movies, and listening to music while reading books and song lyrics.

She holds a bachelor's degree in social anthropology from Harvard University and a law degree from Harvard Law School. After becoming a certified yoga instructor in 2005, she eventually traveled to India and studied writing at Stanford University's Continuing Studies program, where the seeds of her debut novel, *Eye of Fire,* were sewn. She lives in the heart of Silicon Valley in California.